1

Lunar Effects

A Fanciful Romance

by

Stephen Faulkner

This one is to my wife Joyce, with love

Chapter 1 – Tremblings

In retrospect it seems to be a rather minor thing but, at the time the discovery was made, it was viewed as one of the most monumental findings to have been made in modern times. When all of the data that had been garnered and gathered from numerous sources had been collated, codified, tabulated and put into a reasonably logical order so that the facts would be plain to see, the only viable emotion that was available to those who understood the ramifications of the results was simply one of awe and disbelief. Something quite impossible had happened. Astronomy had observed. Physics and Mathematics had supplied the necessary calculations, Geology had corroborated the findings though with understandable regret, and Plate Tectonics, in its boisterous infancy, could only shake its swollen head and shrug in disgust.

It was impossible.

Shock waves, however, were already being felt at the great distance of almost 239,000 miles. Tides were becoming erratic, weather patterns were shifting at a delirious rate from the normal North-South, South-North loops to broad East-West configurations. The Gulf Stream was bending and bellying out further and further into the Mid-Atlantic while the Japan Current's warm sweep of air drove inland across the steppes and vales of China and Russia. Tokyo was experiencing its first late spring frost with cherry blossoms spiraling off of trees in sudden unwarned death throes.

It was an unthinkable, laughable notion to anyone who knew anything about the nature of rock and gravitation and the forces that hold worlds together. The negatives were all there and always had been but this fact did nothing to lessen the brunt of the truth: there had occurred a five minute long quake in the first quadrant of the visible portion of the moon at full phase.

The fact of Luna being at full when the quake was discovered was what would later concern those of a more vulgar or common bent who did not know the true meaning of this unusual occurrence. Fable and myth were rife with stories of men and women and nature being altered and perverted by the unseen gravitational activities being foisted on the earth by the moon in full phase, especially on the personalities of the more susceptible members of the race of beings that called themselves human. The word lunacy is derived from the Latin appellation for the Earth's satellite. The phases – full, new, half, quarter, waxing, waning – were all seen to have specific effects on the emotions and deeds of men and women; the full moon has been predominantly blamed for such effects. What, then, would such an aberration of the ancient pattern as the shaking of the causative entity – the moon – produce in the minds of the uneducated?

Such considerations seemed, for the moment, to be absent from the purview of the numerous families of the scientific community in their quest for reason and cause. Each of these families were working their damnedest to come up with something – theory or solution – that would be viable, easily digestible that would not cause any lasting psychic heartburn on the unsuspecting public.

In a dark quarter, Astronomy had once coupled with the wizened old Master of Navigation to produce the offspring come to be known as Astronautics and it was through the use of her parents' old toys that floated along the upper periphery of Earth's pull that she first became aware of something amiss. Conferences with Old Man Mathematics and his mistress, Physics (whose love child, Quantum Mechanics, busied himself in another room with the previously unasked questions about the make-up of reality) supplied a goodly sum of equations to uphold Astronomy's contentions about the nature of the observe phenomenon in the vicinity of the night sky inhabited by the lumbering hulk of crated rock called Luna. The calculations were checked and rechecked with the help of Old Man Math's grandson (fathered by Electronics with Physics' conniving daughter, Calculus) named Computer Science. Computer-Whiz, as he was affectionately known, with his square brain and chattering, binomial voice, blinked his raft of diode eyes and fed out his agreement to the already posed theories on a toilet paper profusion of green bar paper. It did happen, was the contention, as long as the equations which had been fed into his entry points were all correct. Luna in the sky with her halo of stars had indeed hiccoughed and belched and gave off an uncustomary shudder.

This confirmation was all that was needed before the results could be given the acid test. There was, then, a new door to approach, a new view to be shared on the subject. The reaction was almost as violent as the alleged quake itself. "No," said

Geology as he quickly sifted through the data that had been handed to him, "This load of crap doesn't mean twiddly-beans. The Compu-Kid's whoosamawatsis of fiddle-de-glick must be off kilter somewhere in his wiring. These computations seem to be in order but something must have gone wrong somewhere. What you're telling me is that nothing is as it should be, that something that, under any circumstances simply cannot happen now has happened. Have you all checked this with Quantum Mechanics yet? He'll tell you the same, I'm sure of it."

"We did," said Physics as she eyed her bedmate Old Man Math as he diddled nervously with his slide rule. "Q.M just made a face after reading the evidence and called us liars. But it all is true, Sir. Observations and calculations all confirm each other."

"Well..." said Geology, hedging.

"What we really came for," Astronomy broke in. "Was to talk to P.T. It's his considered opinion which we seek."

P.T. (Plate Tectonics) was a child about whose birth revolved many unverifiable tales, the most popular of which was that he had sprung whole from the fecund mind of Geology himself. It is also said, though, that such stories of his sudden appearance on the landscape had come about as a result of gall bladder trouble on the part of the father through the use of mega-doses of powerful laxatives. Most assumed, however – and most likely correct – that the child had been there in the home of Geology all along; dormant until that time when, with a sprinkling of water and words over the inert form at the critical time of his special cognitive powers, he came to life spouting paroxysmal theories, tearing down long-held beliefs, creating havoc and making a general, all-round pest of himself, as children often do.

P.T. appeared briefly in the room, conferred with the Computer Boy, shook his raggedy head and sighed. "Maybe I was wrong," he said. "I was sure that a planetoid with the paltry gross mass as that of the moon would surely be devoid of any Vulcan activity. None had been found before this, so why now all of a sudden? This calls for a complete reworking of even the most basic theoretical assumptions on which we have for so long based our purest, most fundamental tenets. Is Q.M. available for consultation in this matter?"

"I think so," said Physics, the mother of Quantum Mechanics, cocking her furry head quizzically to one side. "Is his input really necessary?" The fact of the matter was, that even though she was immensely proud of her progeny and stimulated by her discussions with him, she did find him to be rather scary.

"All input is necessary in a matter of this magnitude," P.T said sternly. "We're all in this together, remember. We must all have a hand in deciphering the meaning of this strange occurrence if we don't want to end up looking like fools."

"We can call a general conference," offered the boy's father, Geology, now coming to a full realization of the enormity of their concerns. "All the Physical Sciences in a closed door meeting."

Everyone agreed to the notion whole heartedly. It would be a stimulating diversion even if nothing came of it.

"Be sure that the door is locked, too," cautioned Old Man Math as the necessary calls were placed (the newly invented contraption called the telephone being a product of his incestuous dalliance with fidgety Electronic Engineering). "If it gets out that we've all made a blunder of this magnitude, we'll all be laughed right out of Academia and back to the drawing board – forever. I mean, after such a gargantuan faux pas as this, who would listen to anything we had to say anymore, hm?"

"Certainly not I," said crass Creationism who had surreptitiously entered the room while the conversation was rising to its conclusion. A snide, supercilious smirk was the only expression he wore on his oft beleaguered countenance.

Chapter 2

The moonquake itself lasted only one minute and eighteen seconds. Subsequent minor aftershocks continued what were assumed to be thunderous rumblings with a total elapsed time of three minutes for three tremors. The entire event, from initial quake to final aftershock, happened over a period of little more than thirty-five minutes. The cross-discipline undertakings of the scientific community did take place almost directly following the discovery of the "lunar event," as it was officially called, though not in the ludicrous manner posited in the first chapter of this book. A full symposium on the subject was not convened until more than a month after the fact. The initial gross results of the lunar upheaval – largely tidal and weather pattern changes – had already righted themselves by the time the academic leaders in the physical sciences met behind closed – though not locked – doors in a conference hall at the Jet Propulsion Laboratories in Pasadena, California. Papers which had been prepared by esteemed members of the departments of Geology, Astronomy, Physics, Mathematics and related disciplines of several of the larger universities on the theoretical causes for the lunar quake and the possible long and short term effects that might be the end results of such an unprecedented, once-in-a-lifetime (in eternity?) occurrence were read, applauded, coded for classification, then summarily filed away and forgotten. Very little was really accomplished despite the fervor and concern with which the whole affair had been initiated.

It had been begun not, of course, with Mother Astronomy perusing the heavens in her undying fortitude and noticing a visible tremor on the face of the smiling Man in the Moon but through a real though incredibly lucky fluke. An amateur stargazer with a 50 power telescope in a Philadelphia suburb, blessed with an unusually cloudless spring night sky, happened to be peering at the face of the largest and, therefore, the most easily viewable body in the night sky. Because of the Apollo landings and later research work in the area of lunar studies, the moon had ceased to be of any real interest to serious astronomers; all that could be known about that piece of celestial real estate was, it was assumed, now all down on paper with absolute certainty. It was time to look elsewhere for green cheese monsters and other exciting discoveries about the universe. But to the amateur, the looking would always be fun and the locating of the Seas

(Tranquility, Serenity, Rains, Crises, Clouds, Fertility, Nectar) and the larger of the innumerable crater depressions (Posidonius, Copernicus, Tycho, Archimedes, Ptolomaeus, Plato) would forever continue to be an adventure for the observant neophyte.

This fellow in his Pennsylvania backyard, however, had a keener eye than most and, consulting his map of the surface of the moon, placed his eye again to the lens and was soon a bit puzzled to find the crater Posidonius to be somewhat larger than depicted on his map. The depression seemed to edge itself more pronouncedly into the Sea of Serenity, to push its lower border a bit closer to the Taurus Mountains than it should. He made a sketch of what he saw – freehand, but still quite accurate – and found by comparing map to drawing, that the difference was of about a quarter of a degree or less. Nothing to be concerned about, surely, but at such a distance, he knew, that fraction of a degree could translate into many miles. A week later he was back to the telescope and astutely made another quick sketch of what he saw. More comparisons were made against the map and he found that the level of the degree of change had broadened even more. Back to the telescope to confirm his findings, he peered at the object of his interest in disbelief. The evidence was clear; the crater was expanding.

A call to a friend whose interest in stargazing was also quite sharp brought corroboration of the event. Luckily, the friend had connections, however tenuous, to the observatory at Penn State. The university observatory had its major instruments presently trained on the Horsehead Nebula but the friend's connection – a former professor of Astronomy whose introductory course in that field that the friend had taken some years back – agreed to turn one of the observatory's optical telescopes to the described quadrant of the moon. That started the ball rolling, clearing up some of the mystery surrounding the sudden readings of X-rays which were being recorded by the satellite born radio equipment maintained by the observatories at Palomar and Leck as well as by satellites in synchronous orbit between the earth and its natural satellite. Vulcanism. A volcano on the moon, situated in the northeast quadrant of the Sea of Serenity. The heat of the rising magma was throwing off X and gamma ray particles which were causing a mild shock of static interference in radio, television and other wireless reception on Earth. The answer to these particular minor problems had been found and the source located. Anyone with even a modicum of knowledge about the physical make-up of the moon, however, would tell you that such an occurrence as volcanic activity on the moon was quite impossible.

Notes were compared, calculations gone over again and again and run through the computers of Penn State, Columbia, Harvard, M.I.T., Princeton, Yale, Cal-Tech, Rutgers, Notre Dame and Georgia Tech in the United States alone as well as the gargantuan battery of electronic wizardry at J.P.L. countless times. Figures don't lie, especially when regurgitated from the belly of a series 5000multi-sequential equations masher. Everything checked out, much to the consternation of all involved.

J.P.L. put out the call to all the Astronomy, Geology, Physics departments of all the above schools as well as those of universities in Europe, India, South America, Japan, Australia, Canada, Mexico, Central America and Asia for their resident authorities in those and other fields to attend the conference mentioned earlier which was to be convened in the main auditorium at the Jet Propulsion Laboratories. Plans had to be changed, however, since the call came at the inopportune time of final exams and the need for grading papers and exams and for the working up of syllabi and curricula for the coming summer and fall semesters. Some of those invited to attend simply could not be reached, others bowed out on the grounds of transportation at such short notice was much too expensive, laborious, inconvenient or, simply, that other plans had already been made and could not be broken or put off. All tendered their regrets, though, at not being able to be present at so seminal a meeting of the minds of their own and other associated fields of inquiry into such a unique and exceptional phenomenon.

Those that did appear came eloquently prepared and the papers read during the three day conference were, as one attending physicist put it, "Right on target." The reason was most likely due to the fact that, by the time the conference was announced, information germane to the occurrence in question had been available to the academic community in some form or other for more than three months. All the works submitted prior to the scheduled conference expressed awe at the fact that much of the knowledge which had been gathered about our satellite over the centuries, a goodly portion of it in the United States, had been so blatantly false. This phenomenon so recently discovered forced all facets of science to completely re-evaluate their long-held assumptions regarding the true nature of the lunar interior. It had been assumed to be cold and inert, incapable of any volcanic activity or tectonic shift. Now, something new had been discovered, and so....

After some weeks and months of intensive study the finest available minds in the fields of Physics, Geology, Plate Tectonics, Astronomy and Volcanology could only conclude that more study was necessary.

"At least this has one enlightening aspect to it," one of the experts in Drift was heard to say. "It has taught us how much we still don't know about the subject at hand and will stop us from taking our precious 'truths' for granted."

"The search for truth is never ending," said another, this one a physicist. "Once you think that you've got a handle on something so you can comfortably turn your attention somewhere else, old Mom Nature finds a sneaky way to slip you a chunky piece of humble pie like this." The scientist, a stout man in his late thirties with a boyish face, shook his head good humoredly. "Just what we need," he sighed wearily before ambling off to attend to undefined obligations in another area of the campus.

Chapter 3

The most unusual of the small slew of papers, theses, monographs and studies which were allowed to be presented at the conference was one by a member of the teaching staff of Odell College's Department of Psychology and Psychiatry. It was entitled "Considerations for the Individual Psychological and Gross Sociological Consequences of the Lunar Occurrence." Its author, Doctor Raena San Gregorio, a prim, attractive woman of solid build in her early forties , had appended the twenty page monograph with a four page bibliography which, among the more staidly academic publications also included Bram Stoker's *Dracula*, Mary Shelley's *Frankenstein*, C.G. Jung's *Undiscovered Self*, Fritz Perls' *In and Out of the Garbage Pail*, Hitler's *Mein Kampf,* synopses of several Hollywood "B" movies devoted primarily to monsters of various descriptions, Sylvia Plath's *The Bell Jar*, Saint Exupery's *The Little Prince,* Hermann Hesse' *Der Steppenwolf,* Alvarez's *The Savage God*, Theodore Reik's *Myth and Guilt*, de Sade's *Justine* and the film script *for I Was a Teenage Werewolf.*

In the last few paragraphs of the text of the work the author made sure to allow herself a way out, her own way of saying, as had the others at the conference, that the facts were not yet all accounted for and that more time and resources were needed in which to study the resultant situation more closely.

"This author is aware that the views stated in this paper are, for all intents and purposes, mere theory and speculation based on very scanty evidence culled from the social service records available within a short period of time following the appearance of volcanic activity on the lunar surface. In order to obtain a more comprehensive appraisal of the situation arising as a result of this occurrence, a concerted effort on the part of all the social and welfare service agencies should be made to glean all possible pertinent data so that a full theoretical basis can be fully established.

The theories and speculations which Ms. San Gregorio postulated in her paper dealt with the increased number of instances of lycanthropy, apparent neurotic symptoms, delusions, suicides (successes and failures), aural and visual hallucinations and sexual deviancy within the limited confines of the small college town in which the author lived and worked. Hence the appearance of the works of popular fashion dealing with monsters, madness and suicide (not to mention the werewolf movie synopses and scripts) which appeared in her lengthy bibliography along with the more professionally stolid of psychological works – though some exception might be taken to include Doctor Perls' whimsically serious work among the ranks of "staid" psychological literature, esteemed as his name might be as the prime mover behind the development of the Gestalt method of therapy.

Professor San Gregorio's arguments were well taken, even those regarding lycanthropy, that area of study regarding werewolves and the means by which an individual affects such an uncanny transformation. What, she asks, is the operative factor here, as well as in regard to instances of neurotic transparencies, full-fledged madness, suicidal behavior, falling hair, improper healing of lesions, extended menstrual flow and the loosening of social restrictions in the temperaments of those persons given to more accepted forms of expression? The Full Moon. And what would be the outcome should the moon, when at the zenith of its waxing phase, suddenly commence to shake, to wobble and vibrate? Answers, though sketchy for the most part, were suggested in her monograph: the same as on any full moon night but increased considerably. From the professor's research and observations in the Odell vicinity the increase in the instance of gross behavioral changes had more than doubled on that night in comparison to a "normal" full moon night. It happened there, she rashly speculated, then certainly such increases in the behavioral exhibitions of the population must have been noticed nationwide, even throughout the entire world. Cross-referencing files with institutions, social service agencies, suicide hotlines, police and sheriff departments, clinics and hospitals for the days in question would surely support the Professor's conclusions. The undertaking, she realized, would be a monumental one and most likely would not be carried out, at least not to any comprehensive degree.

In her address to the conference Ms. San Gregorio made one more supposition, one which she had not seen fit to commit to paper but which she felt obliged to share with her peers in the several fields of the physical sciences.

"These are the fringe dwellers we are talking about here, really," she said. "The nutty, neurotic, crazy-mad, suicidal and animalistic fringe of society. A full moon may be all the impetus a man or woman of such a description needs to drive him or her over the line to commit acts that he or she normally would not otherwise carry out. We do not fully understand the effects of the gravitational pull of other forces which the moon exacts on the human mind and personality to bring about such often drastic change, but, in many cases, it does exist and does occur. Now, this.... An earthquake on the moon; a moonquake, if you will-- It's preposterous, unthinkable, impossible, the stuff of science fiction. But it has happened, and the instances of nuttiness, madness, paranoiac fear and sheer terror have increased among the fringe element of the human species precipitously as a direct result. But, as I've said, this is only the fringe element that we're talking about. An inherent weakness in these people has made them unusually susceptible to the pull of the moon's gravitational field, and thus, to the aberration of that field caused by the moonquake and thereby renders them – some, though not all – to the ranks of what is euphemistically called 'certifiable,' "

Professor San Gregorio paused here to lean against the podium; apparently attempting what she assumed was a dramatic pose. She only succeeded in causing the microphone to sing a shrill song of complaint which quickly levelled off to a loud buzz of feedback once she removed her thick forearms from the speaker's stand. The loudspeakers settled themselves and Raena San Gregorio continued the extemporized portion of her presentation in a low, bemused voice. "I propose, then, ladies and gentlemen, that we all have been affected by this unprecedented event, and not only on the professional level. Oh yes; it is certainly a puzzle and it poses a serious threat not only to the accepted view of the formation of the interior of the moon and its true nature but also to the credibility of science as a whole. It poses problems which must be solved if we are to be able to hold our heads high in pride for being an astronomer, a physicist, a geologist, a mathematician, or a practitioner in of any of the related fields of study and knowledge. The major problem will be that of ourselves. To be able to look in the mirror in the morning and honestly say to your reflection, 'I don't know who or what you are anymore.' To understand that we have all been affected in some subtle or profound way, just as the man who yesterday was a sedate Wall Street executive and today, after these last few months of contemplation on the enormity of what has happened in our night sky, now cries uncontrollably in public for himself.... and cries for the world."

She remained silent after that as she surveyed her audience with a wide arc sweep of her vision from right to left and back again that took in the entire auditorium from front to back and up to the balcony and back down to the notes on the podium in front of her. She then smiled and said, "Thank you for your time and patience, ladies and gentlemen. I will be glad to answer any questions you may have now."

Chapter 4 – Sleeping Time

"Listen," said Charlie, leaning across the rickety table so that his face was closer to that of his listener. "This is the way it goes."

Charlie Calderone's jaws worked themselves almost out of his conscious control. He had become an avid gum chewer since coming to the ward and even without a wad on his tongue or tucked into the back hollow of his cheek his mouth still worked a semi-masticating mime to the time of some jazzy beat he seemed to keep playing in his head. His eyes were dull but lively as he craned forward across the card table in an effort to be better understood by Nurse Constance Hawkins as he explained the complexities of his being there, four months now, in the open ward of the State run institution. The commitment papers had been signed by his sister with a proviso allowed to be added through some wheedling by her attorney husband that Charlie not be put in a locked ward. Only fair, he told the nurse who listened with grave interest. After all, he wasn't violent or truly crazy, just a bit self-destructive, but that was really just a passing phase.

"One that you're still dealing with, though," Constance noted sagaciously. "If you weren't here, under strict supervision, you'd probably be out there somewhere with your nose in a paper bag lined with rubber cement or airplane glue or something equally dangerous, wouldn't you?"

Charlie worked his jaw to one side in what he assumed to be a thoughtful expression but which only succeeded in making him appear unfathomably moronic. "That," he admitted. "Or else I'd be blowing some really dynamite weed."

"So, then," said Constance, spreading her thin arms in warm appeal. "Isn't it better to be here where there aren't any of those temptations? What would you gain, anyway, wasting your mind like that?"

"Got any gum?" he asked, not meaning to change the subject but just feeling the urgent need. "I used up the last of what I had. Grace's coming tomorrow but I sure could use...."

"You know the staff isn't allowed to give favors, Charlie. You buy or bring your own. You'll just have to wait until your sister gets here tomorrow. You know the rules."

"Yeah," he said, sitting back, darting his eyes around the dayroom. Only a few knots of people here and there and they were slowly dispersing. Most of the others were already in their rooms, reading, talking, sleeping, spacing out. "Rules. I guess that was the first reason. Waste my mind, you say. Escape the rules was how I saw it then. With a full tube of Ducco in the bag, man, my head'd be just spinning off my neck and I could almost feel the brains crash out like a trap door had opened up right about... here." He turned his close-cropped head so that she could see where he was pointing, just above the nape of the neck to where the skull meets the spine. "My eyes'd fog up some and I'd get so dizzy I could hardly see or stand or sit or walk and I'd feel like I was floating ten feet off the ground, bobbin' along slow and simple, gawking dopy at who or whatever was there. Women looked like big soft balls of dough in dresses, jeans and tops walking down the street and I just wanted to lay into one of them like they was a bed that could feed me and suck me dry and I wouldn't even notice or care.... 'Cause that's love, Babe, pure and no-lie-love, to be held like that. Or is that a grass high I'm tellin' you about? What was it that I was saying? Was I talking about sniffing or smoking?"

"Sniffing," Constance prompted softly, lulled by his excited descriptions. "It seems like an awfully nebulous way to be, doesn't it? I mean with everything so distorted."

"Maybe," he agreed, trying to be amenable. "But better, nicer, softer and happier. And no rules, no worries, no cares. I once came down off a high right in the middle of the street. And I mean the street, right in the middle, tip-toeing the yellow line like it was a tight rope and I was Philippe Petite without a balance bar. It was like Boom! I never crashed so hard in all my life. I was just joy-joy-joy walking along with the traffic, letting the cars pass me by, some coming at me and swooping on behind me and others going along with me the way I was headed but just faster, slipping by me with a toot or a raaaah! of their horns as they skimmed by me and went on ahead. Heh! Tight rope walking that yellow line free and sweet and happy as a bird and just then, WUMP! I was all of a sudden as jumpy and scared as I've ever been like I was falling off the top of some tall building like I'd never been before. Just two seconds ago I was fine and free and beautiful and then, there it was. Reality. Rules say you shouldn't walk in the middle of a busy street like that, you could get yourself killed. But dope opens up the possibilities to you, you see? You see with new eyes, feel with new skin, work out of yourself like a butterfly coming out of its cocoon. Know what I'm saying?"

"I know exactly what you mean," she said with a surreptitious glance at her watch. "And you said it yourself: escape. And, speaking of...." She got up quickly, murmuring something about bed check.

"Mine'll be empty, Connie."

"Nurse Hawkins is my name," she corrected him sternly, turning a warning eye. "You know that."

He shrugged as he rose to his feet, scraping the chair away from the little table. "Rules say Nurse Hawkins. But can't a friend call you Connie?"

She thought about this for a moment and then smiled slyly. "A friend would be in his room when I came to check. Yours is down at the far end of the hall so I won't get there for a while yet."

"And what about those two," he asked, indicating the two men huddled in a far corner of the dayroom. The last hangers-on, the last stragglers in the room, each bent forward toward his companion, foreheads touching as they traded their respective views and secrets in coded chunks of inanities

"Traumer and Harblin have bed watch tonight. They'll take those two back to their rooms before they finish their run. Now am I going to have to put you down on my report as 'Absent from Room'?"

"On my way," Charlie promised, turning toward the greenly lit hallway but, before he had gone three steps in that direction he turned and raised his voice plaintively: "Connie?"

"Yes?"

He smiled, his turn to be sly. "Just checking, Friend. See you tomorrow when you come in."

Connie laughed at Charlie's childish manipulation. Friend, she thought, shaking her head. Well, he was one, really. The two of them shared a closer relationship than just about any other two people on the ward despite the forced stricture of the patient-nurse proprieties. There were others that were stronger, but theirs, as a patient-to-nurse, nurse-to-patient thing, was quite unique. He had, over the months, opened up to her, become comfortable enough in her presence to tell her his secrets of getting high on glue sniffing and grass smoking, to confess his fears and desires. Though she did not fully reciprocate with much in the way of her own bursts of candor and confidence, there was a sharing that they had worked out between them that, in its own way, held in it the possibilities of a true friendship. Caring and sharing, she thought, rolling the words around, mixing them together into c-sharing and sh-caring. She didn't like the sound of that last one, though, sounding, as it did, of something like fright.

She looked over the day room lazily, watched the two nodders in the corner bent to their insular burblings as if collaborating on a work of genius.

"Come on, guys," she said loudly as she strode over to them. Neither head turned, the two men were so busily enmeshed in the web of their own words. "Bedtime in fifteen minutes," she said, hovering near.

The older of the two men glanced her way and waved dismissively. "Gaha," he said and turned back to his companion's staring serenity.

"This is not really the way, you know," he went on, continuing their conversation. "We've been here before but it's not really, really all right I think just 'cause it happened then like that. I mean then like that, you know...."

"It happened," cut in the younger one with a wide stare. "Always does when the plates move and makes your head grow. That's where you are. Growing head and withered brain with the plates in your crany-yum shifting out of gew-gaw. Wick! Too fast, too fast as it always does just comes about too quick to catch it in time. Like fish in the sea, all swimming the pool swirls down there in the B'Hammies. There's something to all that. Blue light, red light, whorehouse, home to sex and the mad mongering salesman on the running road with track shoes still in their sample cases, all over the place. Your arms pump, your feet kick but that's how it is when you can't get back, can't get back and you know it like gospel and there you go, just running and crying like a drooling babe on its tottery feet trying to find its way back into the cribby cradle it calls home. And there's you spitting luck like broken teeth but that's only the head plates loosening their hold. You'll see. You'll see. They move, yes, they move. They move here...." With a pointing finger to his left temple. "...to here...." Temple to chin. "...and over to here." Chin up to the lower lip then across the lips to the septum. He scratched his left nostril and began to poke an inquisitive finger inside. "And if you dig deep enough you can feel them there, right through to the eyeball."

"I know, and then your sight changes and the world is new and ugly and barren and broken and black as charcoal bits in your porridge. Bear shit and weasel jism all over the place and nothing you can do about it. Gads, what a state of affairs."

"They move too fast, that's all. Wick! All out of gew-gaw. But it's only me. Only me. I'll be all right as long as I can push them back into place, back where they all belong."

"Won't help. Your feet kick against the ground and you're running but it's just there. You can't get away. Nope. Can't get away. But then I say why the hell not try anyway? Eh? Why not just tempt fate and give it the old college go and do it?"

Neither of the men looked up from their disjointed discussion when a new clatter of footsteps entered the large room. The nurse had told them that the boys would be coming to take them back to their rooms. That much had registered through to their consciousness, their impaired cognitive abilities. As Nurse Hawkins turned to leave, the older man made a half-hearted goosing swipe at her behind but missed. It was a try anyway, he surmised. Nothing did much good nowadays, not even the effort when it was made. He enjoyed the tickling of the fellow's breath on his neck, though, and the strong feel of the arms about his chest as he was hauled to his feet, guided out of the dayroom to the hall and then to his room and his bed where the fires always raged in his head. More to come, he thought crankily. More to come and to talk about inside the head when the blankets were pulled over his face, only his eyes showing. And what had that other voice been talking about? Where had all that come from, all that crap about plates and spitting out your luck? Just talk, he figured, just the blabbering word masturbation of the back quarters of his head where the sludge pile of thoughts and ideas and memories of a life forgotten lay buried. As usual.

But, well, he thought, deriving some pleasure from the act of thinking. I sure am an imaginative old duffer to come up with a gargle of ideas like that. Plates, hmph! Didn't even know I had that in me; didn't even know it was there.

Chapter 5

Vardis Harblin and Gordon Traumer shared a room together as did all of the patients on the ward. The two of them had arrived on the ward the same day and were immediately assigned the same room. They had become fast friends in the time that it took for each to realize that the other possessed an outlook and temperament extremely complementary to his own. The fact that both of them had entered the institution under his own volition – *voluntary commitment* was the official phrase used – helped to make things easier at the outset of their relationship. There was no stigma attached for being one who had been abruptly cast into this den of crazies and neurotics. Each had come to the decision without coercion, had come to the hospital by his own choice. Each man respected the other for the uneasy options that the other had to choose from in order to bring him to this place.

When the time was right secrets were shared, confidences respected in equal portions on both their parts. The fact that they shared the same space for sleeping may have been a factor in their individual growth-- since neither of them ever had any real friends, either growing up nor as adults—and in the deepening of their understanding of one another. Just perhaps. The fact that they shared the same room was definitely a deciding factor for their being on Bed Watch together for that week. Ward rules were clear on this point: "The occupants of each room are to take on Bed Watch duties for one full week in rotating succession. The only exceptions to be made are for non-ambulatory patients and those who are prone to periods of violence. The occupants of each room are to act as a team during the length of their watch period which will extend from a half hour prior to Lights Out until a half hour past."

"All that this Bed Watch shit means is that we're supposed to babysit for the ones who are either too stupid or totally whacked out to know when Lights Out are," crabbed Vardis as he and Gordon steered the older man to his room.

As they passed the Director's office and nurse's station in the glass box that started the hallway to the patients' rooms, they heard the sound of a news report coming from the radio that one of the nurses kept on through the day.

"What are they talking about?" asked Vardis as they made their way to the finish of their rounds. "Something about the moon? What happened on the moon?"

"Maybe some hotshot with a telescope found a new mountain or something," Gordon said, offering a remote possibility. "And I say so what? It doesn't matter to us, does it?"

"Yeh," Varis said with a quick shrug. "Guess not. But hey, what's Terry yelling about in his room? He should be in bed by now. Wasn't Nurse Hawkins supposed to have given him a shot by now to get him to sleep?"

"I think so. Hey, Terry, my man, what's all this about, podner? Whatchoo doin' outta bed, hey?""

"Ngagh!" yelled the older man, popping out into the hall for the third time as if something in the room disgusted him. "There be wrongness in there," he said. "I can feel it. The air burps like an old woman with diapers and she'll be coming, she'll be, coming after me with her tits a-swingin' like razory sharp axe blades all ready to cut off me man parts with a swing swish here and a dip dap there and there I'll be, be bleeding out me life from me crotch with my dorbles and peck laying dormancy like on the floor just callin' to go back home. Oh, I beg you, boy-os, don't let her love me, just don't let'er lub me the way she wanna do. My privates're too valu'ble a commodity to lose like that. Please!" he finally screamed as he began to cry uncontrollably. "Just please don't let'er. Please don't. Ngagh! Please, I'm beggin' ya, please!"

"Back in you go, Terry," Gordon sweet talked as he gently ushered the old man back into his room with an easy shove. Terry's young bunkmate was already drowsing fitfully under his blanket, looking like a ball of human shaped debris under the sweep of wrinkled cloth. "Go ahead in now. There's a good fella. And don't you worry your head none; we'll be sure to keep her away from you. There you go. There you go. Sleep tight now Terry."

"Damned gerah you will," Terry shouted, nodding harshly before pulling the lockless door to his room shut behind him with a solid, padded thud.

"Gerah!" Vardis aped the old man's voice with glee. "What a strange old fart. Hey, Gordy, Whadaya think of that, eh? Scared some old lady's gonna come along with her boobs hangin' like meat in the butcher's window and she's gonna love'em to death. Jeez! Just weird, man."

Gordon sighed tiredly. "Seeing how bad he is makes me wonder what the hell we're doing here," he said seriously. "I mean no one put us here. We signed the papers ourselves, you and me. So why don't we just walk right on out? Leave, say bye-bye to this hatch before we end up like old Terry there, convinced that there's nothing right in the world and who knows what horror is coming to get us. Remind me again, Vard, why are we here?"

"Your reasons are your own," said Vardis. "But mine...?" They strode leisurely back to their room, peering into the rooms along the way as they went at the dozing, tossing, sleeping figures since the last real detail of Bed Watch had now been completed.

The ward was shaped like the capital letter H with the day room and the dining hall comprising the sides, the hall toward which all the patient's rooms faced being the crossbar. There were twelve rooms along this hallway, six on either side, nine of them for the eighteen patients, two bathrooms with toilets, shower stalls, sinks and a small vestibule with lockers where the patients could change their clothes. The men's bathroom was much larger than the women's since it also doubled as a janitor's closet. The last room, near the day room, was the glass walled office used by the nurses and director as a lounge as well as where the endless stream of paperwork that filled the files of the individual patients was completed and filed in the memory banks of the computer which networked the six workstations that were arrayed at equal distances from one another around the periphery about the room.

There were rumors being circulated from patient to patient to patient that each room was going to have another bed added to it, making each one a triple-- thereby raising the ward's population capacity to twenty- seven. It was all just an unsubstantiated rumor, and no one knew who had started it. Just the mad ramblings of unstable minds, someone said, and so it shouldn't be trusted.

There was also a small anteroom beyond the dayroom through which visitors, doctors, janitors, nurses and social workers came and went and through which new patients came and the occasional released patient confidently met the outside world for another go-round. This was the easy ward, they all knew, the assignment to which all the workers on the hospitals psychiatric payroll vied for. There were no locks on any of the doors within the ward and the door to the outside, located at the far end of the tiny ante-room, had only simplest of latch locks on it, meant more to keep undesirables out than to keep patients in. All this gave the ward more a feeling of a sleep-away camp than that of a ward for the mentally unsound. The small populace, for the most part, was docile, quiet and easily controllable.

"My reasons for being here all started out from my having periods that were truly unreal," said Vardis, using what had come to be a favorite word in his vocabulary for describing his spasms of darkness, the details of which were often sparse, ill-recalled and hazy even at their best. "As if I'm not where I'm supposed to be, like my mind has been drained out of me and injected into – and this is really going to sound like pure insanity – like I've become something else altogether. Listen, I've seen the bottom of a lake through a fish's eyes, a mountain top from the perspective of a hawk flying over, a forest like a bear would see it as is crashes through the brush and sapling trees, and I've slinked through alley fence holes on cat feet and pulled the rest of my body behind me on through to escape the dogs that were chasing me. Not just seeing, Gordy, but actually being whatever body I'm put into. God doesn't think too much of me, I know it. Not the way he's thrown me from furry body to a furless one, from place to place and fucked up situation to the next like some damned shape-shifting ball of some kind of magic sludge or other. I don't know."

Their shared silence lasted only a few moments. Vardis looked to his friend for a reaction; a comment, either a suggestion or something derogatory, maybe even laughter. It wasn't laughter that Gordon offered but Gordon knew that his friend was expecting something from him, so he said softly, "Just dreams, that's all." He stopped there as he realized that this didn't sound right, even to himself, so he tried again. "Have you talked to anybody who could tell you what you or your body looked like when you – um – weren't all there?"

"Yes," Vardis said and clammed up, nothing more to say.

"And...?"

"It was a cousin of mine, a girl about my age. She once saw me a few years ago when these things first started. She said that I looked like I had seen something that had turned me to stone. My eyes were open wide, my mouth hanging open like I'd seen a ghost and hadn't gotten over the shock yet. I stayed like that, she said, for over two hours."

"Did she try to wake you?" Gordon asked, again not sure if he was using the right word.

"When she first saw me like that, she didn't have time to do anything because she was going to the movies with some friends and they were waiting for her. When she got back, there I was, the same as when she had left me. Then, when she tried to shake me out of it, I automatically grabbed for her. Her scream was what finally brought me around."

"What do you mean, you 'grabbed for her'?"

"I was sitting in a chair and she was standing in front of me," Vardis explained further and sounding embarrassed as he did so. "She was wearing a sweater and a skirt. When she leaned over me and shook me, I stuck my mitt right under her skirt, right up to her panties."

"No wonder she screamed," Gordon muttered. "Probably thought you were trying some sort of trick just to sneak a feel. Did you get a chance to explain?"

"Not just then. She ran right into the bathroom and wouldn't come out until I left. I tried to talk to her through the door, but she yelled for me to get the hell out of there whenever she heard my voice."

"What were you that time? I mean what had you been before she shook you?"

"All I remember is it being hellishly hot and I was desperately looking for some shade," said Vardis calmly, as if this were the real story, the important part that he had meant to tell all the while. "Trying to find an overhanging rock that would shield me from the sun. It was terribly, roasting hot. So maybe I was in the desert somewhere. There was gritty sand and pebbles all over. Cactus and shrubby looking plants. I had just eaten a mouse whole and I had to digest. The sun burned like hellfire and I just had to get some shade to help cool me off--a breeze, some water, just something cooling. I was parched and frantic. The mouse I'd eaten was still kicking inside my gut, evidently not quite dead yet in the juices there and I needed to rest. Sliding around, looking for a napping spot, nice and cool. Just to rest, please. And then the earth shook or just maybe I shook and suddenly I had arms. Imagine: arms! Human arms and hands again. Human again – you just don't know what that's like, to be real again with your own hands and skin and I reached out to find what or who it was that was shaking me. Cloth – I felt cloth. And skin, smooth and dry and warm, then cloth again but this was dry cloth and thin, framed in girlish, chubby skin with a warm softness beneath that filmy cotton. Then, a scream like a siren, the cloth pulled away from my hand and there she was, yelling at me, calling me a pervert, a creep and a filthy minded sneak and she ran from the room into the hall and then into the bathroom and she locked herself in."

He sighed and bent forward to hold his head in his hands. Something had been let out of him like helium squeaking out of the pinched open end of a party balloon. Vardis watched his friend's face with a concerned expression, as if he wasn't quite sure that all he had divulged was a smart thing to have told Gordon, but there it was and it was done.

"A couple of weeks later I called to apologize, to explain to her, to tell her I thought that I might being going stark raving bonkers; off my gourd and way out on a crazy limb of the sanity tree... or something like that. She took it very well and told me that there was nothing for me to apologize for, said that she shouldn't have tried to wake me up or to have overreacted like she did. When she asked me what I had been dreaming when she shook me, I let her know all about it. When I was done telling her about all the animals I had been over the past maybe six or more months, that was when she told me what I looked like to her when I was a snake trying to find shelter from the deadly hot sun."

Chapter 6

EVERY PARTING IS A POTENTIAL FAREWELL. The words arranged themselves in thick, block capital letters over the dispersing dream like a banner on the wall over a birthday cake as Gordon woke to the sounds of shouting, shrill singing, and door slamming. "Beginning!" he said in response to the words on the wall, not knowing why he felt so sad. Morning always had been a happy time for him, so imbued with the promise augured by the light of a new day. Why should he be sad?

He looked out the window at the darkness, the iridescent balloon of the moon in the sky like a sailor's beacon. Still night, morning yet to come. Thoughts formed slowly in his sleep-fuzzy mind. And what was that godawful racket? He looked over at Vardis' bed, oddly unconcerned to find his friend gone, the pillow and blankets warmly rumpled as if only recently vacated. Gordon rose and went out into the brightly lit hallway.

Old Terry, whom he and Vardis had earlier seen to his room, was beating on the corridor wall between the door to his room and the bathroom next door, with bare fists. This was unusual behavior for a man whose amiable pattering delusions were seldom broken by anything more violent than an occasional animal yelp. His knuckles were skinned raw and bleeding from the pummeling he was inflicting on the lime green wall which he had opened up with the strength of his blows he had meted out on it, straight through decades of paint right down to the original cracked plaster.

"Garuh! Hah!" he yelled with each thrusting blow. "G'damn not right! Can't get back! Not from here, not now, not anymore! Garah!" He pelted at the wall then danced and trotted, ran the length of the hall and back, ranting his anger all the while only to come back and batter the same blood smudged patch of the wall. It was a ritual of some sort, thought Gordon, never having seen the old guy act this way. He had always been a little further off the beam than most of the rest of the residents on the ward, but still a mellow mannered nut. What the hell had set him off like that?

"Garah!" Terry yelled, as if that were an answer to anything.

The scene in the dayroom might supply the answer. There seemed to be something going on in there. Gordon edged out of the range of Terry's back-swinging elbow and loped away toward the dayroom. As he was just about to pass by the squarely lighted, glassed-in office that housed the administrative office and the nurse's station he caught sight of Charlie Calderone's heartthrob, Nurse Hawkins. She was seated behind the Director's desk with a look on her face that reminded Gordon of Vardis' description of himself, his face in the mirror when his mind was literally elsewhere. Hers was the same as that, almost catatonic in its vapid, slack-jawed stare into space.

"Miss Hawkins?" he called excitely as he sped into the room, the soles of his bare feet stinging with the friction of his slide to a sudden halt. "I think you'd better come. There seems to be some sort of commotion in the dayroom and it's well past Lights Out."

Her head was limp on her shoulders as she rolled it with great effort to its upright position so her eyes could meet his worried gaze. "Don't let it bother your britches, Brown Nose," she said thickly. "Just fun and games is all it is, just fun and games. It'll run its course soon as by the by."

"But...."

"Oh shit," she moaned, yawning. "Don't bother me. Just let me be like I be where I be...." She giggled giddily for a moment at the sound of that. "It's a wonder how I got this way, really. It just happened all o' sudden. Just a sweet, silly, sly salty wonder it what it is, this way I right now this moment in time but I just can't say...."

"Can't say what?" he asked, now very concerned. He crouched before her where she sat sagging in the office chair, peered deeply into her dilated pupils, studied her blank and pretty face. "Are you all right?"

"Perfect," she said and then, thinking about it, "Just different. All o' sudden it come on being just different than it had be – been? – before. Different, that's all. Different... but just perfect, too."

"Can you tell me what kind of different? Can you describe it?"

"It? Unreal's what it is, friend. Like nothing.... Oh Lordy-my, and just like everything you've ever seen, heard, smelled, tasted and felt and yet different in so so so so so so many little bitsy subtle ways. Everything," she finished her description groggily. "And different, too."

Like my eyes see, that's all is what she was thinking in the back shadows behind the talk and yatter. *My eyes see, my eyes see the shine through and true lovingly with*

lost labor lilting lightly lashed to the tumbrels of timeless yes, oh my body. Oh yes, my
eyes. Oh yes my serene pleasure pressing pulsating pleasantly petering away my
pleasure, my pleasure, yes. Just let it stay with me. Mine is the sight and succor of true
content. Let me be. There is nothing more than here here here. Just let me lay lustily
lolling in its lonely legerdemain making me disappear into the nothing, this thing that is
me me me me, nothing more, no, nothing more just allow, let, enjoy and be and sleep the
sleep of souls subversively slurping solid sustenance strained seeming so silly , so
shapelessly, so sharing, so solipsistic, so ssssssshhhhhhh.....

It was dark in the dayroom, but the sounds were bright. Tingly clatters of
silverware brought from the dining hall and scattered across the floor were danced
upon with excited improvisatory polkas and renditions of The Charleston and
fandangos and waltzes. Doors slamming, rushing figures elbowing past Gordon to join
in the fun. Chairs toppled so that their legs angled up like bulls' horns in most
unnatural chair positions. The ceiling fixtures flickered and flashed in impromptu light
shows to delighted applause. A puppet show using only naked hands so that the
watcher had to imagine the faces, the postures, pretend that the manipulator was
hidden, that it wasn't his mouth that was moving to squeak and bark and laugh and
yack the individual voices of his hastily contrived creations-- Gunch and Pooty he called
them. Terry's young roommate squatted naked in a corner, surveying the scattering of
toys and games, books and tables with the imperious, lackadaisical smile on his face of
a bored sovereign.

Game pieces soon were littering the floor from window to door, wall to wall to the
hallway entry, lost under tables and into far corners so that their identities as aspect of
different games were soon lost for each one: marbles, checkers, tiny green wooden
houses, larger red-barn shaped objects, king, queen, rook, pawn, bishop, knight,
tiddlywinks, Colonel Mustard, Atlantic Avenue, Water Works, Old Maid, plastic coil of
rope, tiny lead dagger, plastic gingerbread children, bean bags, ten of hearts, Jack of
clubs, dice, dominoes, pick-up sticks, suction cup darts, jacks, rubber balls, soft balls,
hollow plastic balls, whiffle balls, ping-pong balls, knock-hockey pucks, Frisbees and
assorted pegs, buttons, tokens and chips, all strewn across the floor in the shapes of
galaxies and the radar picture of a hurricane heading for shore, all laid out like the
detritus from a toy store implosion.

And the grown up children played, frolicked, gamboled, fought, laughed, cavorted, shouted, "Free! Free today!" as they smeared and spattered the walls with urine, finger paints, feces, pencil and crayon and chalk marks and water and ashes from the trays on the little tables out in the anteroom where people waited for their turn to see their son, daughter, mother, father, sister or friend for a few hours of chat or play or just silently consideration of one another because there were no words to say from their embarrassed centers about this person who used to be a part of their lives.

But now, "Free!" was the catchword, the password, the high sign of the night. Free, free, free to do what one pleased. Tonight, while the cats are away all dopy and deliriously sated in the office from whence all the happy residents' shenanigans could be seen, and from which came no reprimand or harsh word of rules and regulations. That was their newly found freedom: to do, to be without care or cringe. And not one of them took notice that the door to the ward, their prison lay wide open to the main hall to the main part of the hospital, to the world beyond this little haven of fun and freedom.

They all delighted Gordon with their carefree nonsensicalities and at the same time disgusted him. "We chose to stay here, remember?" said Vardis, surprising him for coming up behind him so stealthily, so suddenly. "We can leave anytime that we want."

"But is it what we want?"

"There is no 'we' involved here, Gordy," said his friend with a shrug. "Individual choice is all. I brought you a change of clothes in case you like the idea."

It was only then, at the mention of clothing, seeing the proffered bundle, that Gordon realized that Vardis was fully dressed in jeans, shirt and sneakers. "Chilly outside in these," he said, plucking at the thin fabric of Gordon's flimsy pajamas. "Catch your death in no time."

"But the question still is: 'do we want to?' "

"Maybe we do and maybe we don't. Doesn't hurt to be prepared, one way or the other. Like that one, there."

"That one" was Charlie Calderone, also fully clothed, who was weaving through the toss and tumble of the dayroom, skipping over wrestling bodies, sprung jack-in-the-boxes, kicking at a plastic bowling pin and sliding past a couple that was sensuously, passionately kissing while standing up, their hands down and up and under each other's clothes as they searched hurriedly for erogenous zones and regions and quadrants before the rules and orders came back into play. Charlie made his way slowly and carefully to the door to the anteroom and nonchalantly through to the other side.

"He's not like us, you know," Vardis observed thoughtfully. "He's been committed, could get his ass into a whole lotta trouble once all this stuff settles down."

Gordon eyed his friend suspiciously. "I don't really know you all that well,'" he said. "Maybe you and Charlie set this whole thing up so that I'd go after him with you. You do seem to want to get out of here a lot more than I do. This could be some kind of trick."

"Could be," Vardis admitted. "Just like I tricked my cousin into sitting close to me so I could sneak my hand under her skirt. Which doesn't change the fact that Charlie's outside now, getting his ass more and more deeply soaked in hot water. You coming?"

"All right," Gordon sighed. He took the bundle of clothes his friend held out to him. "Let's go after him."

So this is how I'll tell it, he thought as they went through the door into the wide main hall and down the stairs. This is how I'll say it happened. Changing into outdoor clothes in the men's room, leaving my pjs in the sink. Caught up with him outside on the hospital grounds, finally, after a winding run through the trees. Charlie was laughing when we got to him, yelling crazily that he had done it, he had done it. It wasn't his fault, he told us. The time was just right to do it. No drugs or voodoo mojo like he might have planned it for himself but why be choosy? Do it when the doing's right and it was and so he did it. The moon's for howling at, the air's for whistling through your teeth, the trees are for pissing on to make them grow. We did it, he kept yelling as if daring someone to come and find him, to pat him on the back, congratulate him for his clear-headed finesse. Over and over he yelled, "We did it. We did it. We did it. Weeeeedi-i-i-i-i-i-d i-i-i-i-i-i-it!!"

But that was all the scream crazy joy that was left in him. We hadn't been gone from the ward for more than a half hour and he wanted to go back. He had had his fun but now home was calling. Connie would expect to find him when she came back tomorrow for her afternoon shift so they could have their daily chat and she might even let him help her with the cleaning up and then his sister Grace was going to be here tomorrow and bring him chewing gum and a new batch of sci-fi's for him to pour over. He was so anxious and hyped that neither Vard or I had the heart to tell him that Connie never left for the night, that she even looked as bad as he probably did after his worst glue sniffing binges. Letting things get so out of hand she would probably lose her job. And after the rough and tumble like this one, all visitor privileges would surely be suspended at least for a few weeks, maybe a month.

"And what about us?" Vardis asked, as if the final decision in the matter of what the two of them would do lay solely with him.

"Dunno," Gordon said. "Been away from the real world long enough now that I'm not sure I'd feel comfortable there anymore. I mean maybe it's right that we should go on back. But.... I just dunno."

"I could go back right now," Vardis proclaimed in all certainty. Then his bravado ran out of him and he looked kind of deflated. "But to what...?" He made a farting noise with his mouth as if to say that that was the best he could think of. In his mind he found himself looking at a blank slate. Surely there was something to go back to but for the life of him he couldn't think what it might be. The desire to find it – whatever "it" might be – he saw, was greater than the knowledge of what it was that he sought. Maybe Gordy's answer summed it up the best. It's right, that's all, just the right thing at the right time. That brouhaha in the dayroom and Charlie's saunter out the door back to the real world so they felt they had to go after him was really a kind of celestial sign, just the push they needed to get their rears in gear and get going. "Anyway," Vardis said. "As long as we've come this far...."

Charlie was already going back, heading toward the lights and caged windows, the toys and friendships that neither Vardis nor Gordon had found there. They clapped their hands together – Gordy's left to Vard's right – and held them aloft as they hooted their good-byes to their inmate friend. "Every parting," said Gordon as they turned to find the gate that would lead out onto the street. "Is a potential."

Vardis nodded and smiled at this. "I like that. Something like, "For every closed door another one opens up." You read that somewhere?"

"Nah. Just dreamed it."

"Oh yeah," said Vardis, clapping an affectionate hand onto his friend's muscled back. "Now they're surely the best things to get you wondering: dreams."

Chapter 7 – Home

"This is my room, Willie!" Thanielle shouted at the figure hastily retreating from her bedroom. The boy's slamming of the door behind him left it shaking in its jamb for several seconds after his swift exit from the room. Thanielle ran out into the upstairs hallway after him. "And you'll knock before you come in or not at all! You hear me?"

"The Corrianos can hear you down on the next block" their mother called up from the kitchen. Her next breath brought a lilting singsong to her raised voice. "Will-lee? Have you been bothering your sister again?"

"I just wanted to borrow her radio," Willie's voice lamented petulantly from his room.

"You could have just asked!" his sister shouted, though volume wasn't necessary. She was standing right in front of the closed door to his bedroom. He opened the door wide enough so that he could thrust his head through and grin idiotically in her face. "May ah pliz borry yo' rah-dee-oh, sistah dahlin'?"

"Go to hell," she said quietly then returned his dopy faced smile before stalking back to her room. She closed the door and made sure to lock it this time.

Haven, she thought, using her private name for the tiny, cubicle shaped room. *The place to be. Away from the caterwauling insanity of this place called home. Ig! This is home? I wish I was somewhere else, like the Seychelles, Honduras or Alaska, maybe Tahiti, Fiji, Java, Sri Lanka, Crete, Athens, Paris, Barcelona, Bora-Bora, Hong Kong or even Beijing where everyone is the same as everyone else and there are no shouting matches between mother and daughter over the length of her time away from home and uneasy silences between father and his little girl. Would that I had been the second rather than the first child born. For Daddy, the first born should have been a boy and he would have had Grandpa Petar's name: Nathaniel. But it was a girl so he had to make the best of it. The name he gave was similar except to chop off a little at the front and then add something to the end and voila! Thanielle. Still, though, she's only a girl. Pretty like a truck stop barmaid, all meat, muscle and small of breast. Still and all, the face of a model; a model who forgot to diet and succumbed to too many good, hearty meals. Not fat, though. Big boned is what they call it. Big boned Thanny Petar with the big, boyishly pretty face. Clothes hang on her – me – like sacks and wrappings. Plain, that's what it all is. No use complaining, though. It's what I've got, this body, this face. It's what I look like, what I am.*

Haven looked dusky in the waning light of the evening. The light on her dresser cast a warm half circle of light. The ceiling light made her think of the fixtures in the hallways at school, so like the fluorescent rods that hung from the ceilings in public places so that, skeeved out at the idea, she never turned it on. Better to stumble like a blind person to the globe-headed oddity on the dresser or the goose-neck wall model that arched over the headboard of her bed to fumble for a switch to light up a small swath of floor or bedsheet than to light up her room like the waiting room at a train station.

She closed the blinds and curtains, changed quickly out of her baggy jeans, pullover top and the customary "foundation" items, as her mother referred to her underwear and into her friendly, thin and ratty bathrobe before hopping onto the bed. Naked but for this, she thought, flapping the loosely belted front of the robe, airing her tanned skin and white breasts. Without thinking about it she took off the robe and tossed it onto the floor so she really was lying naked on the top of the elaborate floral pattern of the bedspread. *Rebellion in my own little way. Or at least as much as I can have in this house, this room, my Haven.*

She reached up and snapped on the gooseneck lamp and angled the light away from the desk and into her lap. Her notebook was within easy reach on the desk; the pages made a shuffling sound as she opened the cowhide patterned cover and turned to a clean sheet. She looked down past her small, well-formed breasts that one girl in the showers at school called "just perfect," and down to the sparse tuft of hair guarding her virginity to the book propped on her angled legs. Daddy would have a sheer fit if he saw me like this, sitting here bare-assed like some incestuous invitation for him." she thought, and liked the idea. *Look good to you, Daddy? Like a taste, Willie? Little girl has a hairy twat and tits and everything the book of how-to says a woman should have. Vagina and breasts, she corrected herself in her mind. Mustn't be vulgar now.*

Smiling at a foolish thought, she began to write.

"Every action I take for the benefit of another extends my being that much further, makes me that much better a person. Every selfish action I take whose only purpose is to somehow benefit myself only serves to pull me farther into myself, shrinking my being smaller and smaller, making me less of a person for each selfish action and more of just a thing. I had been taught all this – the words are different though the spirit is the same – and have believed it and lived by it all my life."

She reread the paragraph as she angled the lamplight above her closer to the page. She crossed out the word extends in the first sentence, drawing a scribbly line through it. Instead.... She tapped the pen point onto the paper and groaned, finding herself unable to think of an appropriate substitution. Having rewritten the word "extends" over where she had crossed it out, she continued her thought-journal.

"So why is it that it's the good-natured boob that gets all walked on? I should know; I've been on the receiving end of someone else's selfishness and I certainly can't be to blame for the treatment I've gotten. Though I really can't call Gerald's way of doing things selfish. He warned me ahead of time that ours wouldn't be a permanent thing, that it would definitely end someday. I told him that I understood, but I couldn't help crying when he broke the news that he had this trip planned and that he didn't know when he would be back, if ever. 'Maybe, maybe not,' he said. 'But the probabilities are closer to 'not' so don't get your hopes up too high for too long, Sweetie.' That was two months ago. He said that he was going to London but the postcard I got two weeks later was from Berlin. A real Grand Tour, he wrote, making it so I won't know where to think of him being until he gets back. If ever."

The writing was depressing her, so she stopped. Why concentrate on things that you know are going to make you miserable? The past is gone and there's no way to change it. No way to change the charming, sexy, warm and happy ways of Gerald Twickham, either.

Twick-ham, she thought, breaking the name into its syllabic components and she smiled. She fished the pen out from where she had let it drop on the sheet between her bare legs, felt the coolness of the skin of her hand as she brought it up to the paper and wrote: "All the boyfriends I've had, now that I think about it, have had silly, funny sounding last names. Twickham, Bloris, Hyslop, Gardless, Rabinour...."

A series of lewd thoughts came to her and she scribbled them down, telling herself that this was one sheet of paper that she would be sure to throw away. But, for now....

"Joe Bloris of the wide mouth, cold fingers, dirty talk.; Perry Hyslop of the hairy chest, sloppy kisses, hand on my tit (over the blouse); Ben Gardless of the warm grip, tongue in my ear, blouse unbuttoner, nipple hungry mouth and indecent suggestion (I slapped his face); Adam Rabinour of the groping paw, vise-tight hugs, hand in my pants so fast I couldn't stop him (and didn't want to), the expert pressuring touch, right where I needed and wanted it to be.

"And Gerald Twickham of the happy face, the gentle way, the caressing voice, slim body, massaging touch on my thighs and breasts (he hated the word tits), the seducing words, slick hot sliding tongue, indecent suggestions (all of them ultra-willingly accepted, the physical logistics tried and improved on after a number of attempts for each of them. I could go on and on about him and what we did and what I felt – but I'll do that in a separate notebook and be as hornily detailed as I can be when I get it all down on paper. Just watch out!)"

Thanielle rose to pick up and put on her bathrobe so she would be covered for the few moments she would be out in the hall to get to the bathroom. The writing was depressing her again. She had thought that this – the writing, her thought journal as she called it – would help her to forget or, at least, to come to terms with Gerald, she and Gerald, she alone in this house with this family that was inescapably her own. A different course of action, she decided, wiping herself and flushing the toilet. As she passed her brother's room she heard the buzzing twang of the stereo that he had gotten three years ago for his birthday, cranked up to near maximum volume.

"Find her, blind her," sang the nasal voiced tenor through the door. "See who designed her/Act like a dummy/'Til you finally grind her."

He can play that thing all hours at the highest volume and the folks don't care or say a word about it, she thought angrily. "Can't you lower that damned thing?" she asked loudly with a pound on the thin wood of the door.

"Bug off!" he called back and, with a snicker that, though hidden beneath a fog of wailing lyrics and screaming guitars, was still quite clear. "This is my room!"

She slammed the door to Haven and leapt onto her bed, twisting in the air like an Olympic diver so that she landed heavily onto her back. This caused her robe to flap open, the pen and notebook that lay next to her on the mattress to jump as if startled. Caught up in her anger at her little brother, she wrestled herself out of her robe, nearly ripping it at the seams to be rid of it. She hadn't bothered to lock the door. Sitting naked on the bed with her back propped against a pillow against the backboard, the notebook poised on her bare knees, knowing as she did so that she would probably not be able to read her own scrawling penmanship even by tomorrow.

"If Gerald had asked me to go with him to London, Paris, Berlin, Rome, Munich, Prague or wherever, I would have jumped at the chance without any hesitation. To be with him, yes, but more to be away from here, this house, this family of mine that makes me wonder how I have come to be a part of it and to loath it so much. If I were to construct a family with myself as the selfish center, it would be nothing like this one. Mother (me), Father (whoever), children... (maybe). I would be the head, the brains, the one giving all the care. No one would do or say or even be without my express permission...."

The pen slipped from her loose grasp as she scribbled viciously over the last sentence. She retrieved it and tried again.

"If I were to construct a family, starting with myself, I would try to make sure that it would be devoid of all selfishness, abrasiveness and any kind of rancor. I realize that this is just a fantasy, since I wouldn't know how to go about avoiding or being rid of these things. But if I were to start it would be with the right choice for a husband." She shook her head at such a bland, benign and obvious conclusion. "Gerald, a husband?" she wrote and sighed. "The probabilities, as he would say, point to the conclusion that it most likely would not come to pass. And for that I am glad."

She got up and laid the notebook and pen on the little desk. The clock said eleven-ten. The calendar showed the following night to be the one in which the moon would be full. Neither mote of information held any special meaning for her. She picked up the book she had been reading on and off for the past few weeks and, positioning herself back on the bed under the angled desk light, she turned to where a folded blue tissue marked her place.

Several riveting pages later, she looked up to the sound coming from over by the door. "It's late, Thanny," came her father's voice. "You going to bed soon?"

And without warning, giving her no time to find something with which to cover herself, the door to Haven, her inviolate, private sanctuary, had once more that night been breached and entered without invitation and without any recognition given to the word "PRIVATE" that was printed in capital letters, 24 point bold face type and pasted at eye level to Haven's door.

Chapter 8

Thanielle woke the next morning aching. The bruise on her left buttock, inflicted by the buckle whistling at her through the air on the end of the narrow-tooled strip of leather was sore to the touch. Bare skin, she thought, wincing. If I had some covering there when it came, it wouldn't hurt so much now. The mark on her shoulder that had only been red from the knuckling hits of last night now showed a finger-width blister at its center. There was only one mirror in the room, the full length inside the closet door and she dressed without looking at it the whole time. She preferred to feel the severity of her various humiliations than to study them in any detailed degree.

Her right knee ached where her frenzied flight ended from the improvised whip and its stinging buckle. She recalled herself laughing hysterically when she fell, hearing the jaded roar of her father's voice as he swung his arm high to gain the furious force of the blow against her bare haunch, hearing the hateful words he yelled at her as if her ears were underwater, sounds muted and strange. "Slut" sounded like shlush and "tramp" became tarap and "whore," behind the whizzing buzz of the flying, biting buckle became a pleading, simple "who."

Who, she had heard, knowing then that this was the man who did not, could not understand this girl, this young woman, his daughter whom he was now mercilessly beating. He wanted to know, her mind frantically conjured, *who?* Who are you? Tell me, I want to know. But his questions were asked with belt straps across the bare skin of her back and buttock, fists pounding against arms, shoulders and neck, slaps across her stunned and frightened face. Cheeks as pink as posies, red as blood, tears glistening in long streaks down to her chin; she sobbed and blubbered for him to stop, to give her a chance to explain, but even if he had stopped, she knew, she would not be able to tell him, would even loath the idea of explaining something to him that was so close to her, so dear and simple to her. That was it, she thought the morning after. That was what she hated about him, her father: that he had never taken the time in all these years – her entire life – to listen to her about what it was like for her being his daughter, about her goals, her ideas, her loves, likes, hates and dreams, about the mundane and important things that made her who she was. He understood nothing.

Now, today, even if he would drop everything and stop right then to give her his full and undivided attention for anything and everything she might have to say to him, she would tell him nothing. The beating she had taken the night before at his hands made it much too late for any kind of peace to be made between them.
She hated him now and that was all there was to it.

"The final line," she wrote in her thought journal, her strokes broad and childlike across the page. "Has now been crossed and now the way is fully open and freedom looms. I have my reasons now, but I always did, really. They were there but I chose not to use or even see them. Now the choice has been narrowed. It's not an "if" anymore, but a "when". And I shall be ready when the time comes. And it will be soon, I'm sure of it."

And so she made her plans, eyed the clothes in her dresser drawers and her closet, made lists of what to take with her to make traveling light and efficient. She made sure that the cinch straps on her backpack were tight against the square aluminum frame, the laces not frayed. She tugged at the shoulder straps that held the major weight of the pack close to the hips so that her shoulders would not fatigue too quickly. She tested it against her body, made sure that the bruises she had sustained the night before would not interfere with the carrying of such a heavy load. A small duffel with a canvas handle would serve well for any overflow.

Food would have to be of the non-perishable variety, clothing consistently reusable, toiletries at a minimum, money at safe and easy reach, Travel light, travel far, far away. I hate this house, she thought, also thinking that hate was too lame a word, that it didn't hold the poisonous punch that she felt deep within her for this place, this dead Haven.

She spent her afternoon in town, laying in a small but ample supply of boxed, canned and paper goods, light springtime clothes, as well as foul weather attire. Forget the binding underthings; bras and girdles were for her mother's generation, she who was always worrying about her sagging, failing figure. My hips are wide but firm, my tits small and easily contained in a t-shirt or even a tank top. Movement from place to place will keep me trim, light sleep and small meals help to shed the excess pounds, what little there are.

Her savings soon drained down to near empty from the small private account set up in her name by her father, "to teach her the meaning of the value of a dollar." She made her way back home quickly, snuck in the back door to hide her surreptitious cache behind the hanging dresses in her closet along with the useless pants suits and bagged formal wear that she would never get a chance to use, thank God.

Willie returned home from school, passed her silently on his way to his room to study. The stereo was immediately turned on, and then turned loud. Sister baiting; tell me to turn it down and you know I'll be a bastard about it.

"...hear'em whip the women just around midnight..." reprimanded the scratching, squawking voice. Her complaints shouted through the wall for him to turn it down were heeded, though, if only out of pity. He called to ask her to come into his room and told her to shut the door when she did so out of curiosity. He lowered the volume on the stereo to just above the level of audibility. He apologized for his behavior the night before, called himself a silly jerk, called himself stupid and immature. She thanked him, beginning to regret her hasty plans in light of her brother's good graces.

"I met Benny Gardless on my way home from school," he said, getting to the point he had intended to make when he asked her in. "What he told me made me want to puke."

"Why? What did he say?" she asked lightly, unprepared for the coming attack. Her brother was a cagy one, offering candy and small talk with the carving knife well hidden behind his broad back.

"To think a sister of mine..." he went on as if he hadn't heard her animated query. She expects gossip, he thought, maybe a juicy tale about an old boyfriend's malicious recounting about his memories of their time together. I've got her now. "Thanny, why did you just keep it a secret? How did you keep it a secret all this time?"

"Keep what a secret?" she asked, now becoming suspicious of his sudden deprecatory tone, the hurt look in his eyes. "What did Ben tell you?"

"Only everything.... Or at least most of it. I think he was trying to protect me from the worst of it even though what he told me was bad enough."

"What?!"

"About the dog," he told her calmly, biding, leaking the story slowly. "The thing with the German Shepherd back behind his garage. He said that you only wanted him there to watch. You promised him a roll in the hay, he said, and you made him get naked and then you hid his clothes so he couldn't run away so he'd have to stay and watch while you...." He shuddered dramatically at the thought of what he had heard and needed coaxing in order to continue.

"Watch me do what?" she asked in a much calmer tone, now very sure that she wasn't going to like what she was about to hear.

"He said that you got all horny getting the dog – Mrs. Caner's friendly old Alex – getting him all excited with..." Another pause as he tried to keep his gorge down. She slapped him hard on the arm; the sting forced the rest of it out of him. "...with your tongue on Alex's peeny while Ben stood by all naked and about to get sick, just watching...."

By this time her brother's serious demeanor had fully dissolved and he was chortling uncontrollably on the bed. He had tipped over backwards to lay on the Indian design of the quilt as he tittered out the last of his pornographic fabrication between gulps and snorts.

"You're the one who's sick!" she shouted at him as she fled the room. Her traveler's luggage was in her room, waiting to be filled and with hateful determination the job was done in very short order. Now I know why, she muttered to herself as she zipped shut the last tight compartment on the sack. She didn't need any extra push to get her going, *but thank you, Willie, for just being you. You little prick.*

All that was left was the actual going through the door and not looking back. The clock said six – suppertime – and the family would all be home for the evening. Her parents would be expecting her to be there. The only thing now, she considered glumly as she tucked her gear back into the far recess of her closet, was opportunity.

Night would be the best time, but also the most dangerous.

Chapter 9

"Here's a new thought," she prattled carelessly out loud to the warm evening air.

She crouched in the road on one knee, positioning herself so that her back was to the sloping lawn of the corner house as she readjusted the left shoulder strap of her pack. "Thought occurred to me," she said, thinking of her writing of the night before. "That I'm the one who walks all over me. No one else. Just me." The thought was not a new one, though, despite what she told herself. She had considered the fact that she had often put herself in the position to be made the butt of unseemly remarks, the victim of the fears and angers of others. What other reason to challenge Willie whose sense of humor, she knew from past experience, to be crude, childish and, more often than not, wantonly cruel? So was her forgetting to lock the door to Haven last night anything else but an invitation to her father to enter – as he did almost every night to investigate his daughter's reasons for not sleeping liker a good girl should at such an hour – and to find her so blatantly exposed? And didn't she know what kind of fellow Gerald was behind that gloss of charm and dash that he would not be fully satisfied with their intermittent love making on the wide, corrugate flooring of the bay of his van or in bed, on the odd occasion when his roommate could be guaranteed to be absent from their warm and cozy "pad"?

"Maybe," she muttered with a last tug at the sliding strap. "But who would have been able to figure what happened tonight?"

And that was a puzzle.

***

Her bags had been packed and she was looking for an opening, a means of vacating the premises without causing any undue stir. She didn't need another confrontation with either her father or her brother and the tears that surely would have been shed by her mother at any such outburst would only have done to weaken her resolve and put off the inevitable – her leaving was a necessity, she had convinced herself – for an indefinite period of time. Still, she would have to leave soon. It was only a matter of timing as to when that would be.

She had come downstairs from her room to get the lay of the land, to test the waters for comfort of movement. It would be a waste of time, trying now; there would be no way to get out while they were all awake. It was a nervous folly, these scouting forays for an early exit but she felt herself becoming desperate to leave, to get it over with and to be gone from that house, that maddening family. Her stomach felt queasy, her face flushed; symptoms of an oncoming virus, she would have said if she hadn't been aware of the real cause of her discomfort. She stood behind the couch where her parents sat, forlornly watching the gyrations of a cartoon soap bubble on the television screen as it shrilly told them of its innate powers to kill germs and make bathroom and kitchen tiles sparkle and shine and smell like a pine forest after a springtime rain. "Opiate," her mind buzzed and sputtered with concepts scraped from her textbook in a social science course she had just taken last year before making the decision against continuing her college career. "Mind fogger," she defined the programming her parents were watching. "Soporific clap-trap, shallow, dead headed garbage...."

"Harriet called," said her father, sounding weary. "She said something about a party, a sleepover affair. She wants you to call her back."

"What shall I say?" she asked, expecting a negative reply carried on the crest of his usual forbidding tone. Such had been delivered the reprisals and diatribes against her "shiftless" friends and their orgiastic shebangs for all of her life.

"Go if you want," he said, not taking his eyes off of the flashy network logo on the screen. "It can't do any harm."

Her mind raced with sudden precision after a slow start. Permission? What was this, a trick? Blessings on the venture now only to be denied at the moment of her parting? But no; that was her brother's conniving game. The elder Petár was a man of action and quick decisiveness the moment that he saw fit to put an idea in motion and, the decision made, he would not back away from it. His promises, though hard to come by, were always sound and never any regrets on his part for any decision he had acted upon. She saw her chance and, now having it, she decided to press her luck.

"I already talked to her," she lied. "The party's tonight and...."

"Do you want me to drive you?" he asked, casting a weary look over his shoulder, not catching the false pensive look on her face.

Was this really possible? Maybe he was feeling guilty about the beating he had given her the night before last. Even so it was not like him, a man who was repentant or regretful of nothing he had ever done, or so it had seemed thus far.

"Uh, no, Daddy. That won't be necessary. It's not that far, only a few blocks. I'll just walk it if you don't...."

"Suit yourself," he said, sounding relieved. Her mother nodded wanly beside him, giving her silent assent. "Better borrow Willie's sleeping bag if you're going to be sprawled out on the floor."

This was incredible. He was making it so easy. "Where is he?" she asked dazedly.

"In the kitchen," her mother answered before descending into a fit of spastic laughter at some asinine stunt she had just witnessed on the tube.

Willie was amenable, even kind. He dug the double sleeper out of its hiding place on the upper shelf of his oversized closet. It had to be a double, she mused acidly. As if he was married and would be spending his honeymoon camping under the open skies with his bride. Never know when the extra space will come in handy, he had told her that Christmas morning with a disgusting, leering wink. He had asked the folks and they had given into his pressures for the wide, light weight sack without question and had gotten it for him. She had to cajole and argue and demonstrate like a striking dock worker ceaselessly for a month just for the set of Tolkien books that were currently the rage in school. She got arguments; Willie got what was considered his due as the only son.

He threw in two sets of hook ended tie straps with lazy magnanimity and offered to help her tie the clumsy bulk to her backpack. Amazing, she later thought, that no one even mentioned the heft and size of the sack she was bringing on what was said to be a simple sleepover. She almost gave it all away when she refused his kind help in a dizzy fluster, but he didn't seem to notice her over-concern nor did he seem to care. He only shrugged and turned off the lights in his room as she heaved the sack into her room by herself and locked the door.

She had to rearrange the position of the pack on its aluminum frame so that the sleeping bag could be hung from below like a hibernating opossum, the snub ended duffel on top with the aid of the second set of elasticized bungee cords Willie had given her. She tested the weight of the thing and groaned. Fifty pounds or better, she estimated. But I'll get used to it. A last look around Haven's cramped space brought to eye a few more necessities: notebook and pens, a pocket-sized CD player and a few favored discs, a small box of incriminating personal correspondence from friends. Haven was barren now, for her, The posters on the walls – swans on a placidly rippling span of water, an orange sunset with a quotation from Kahlil Gibran, several rock and roll and hip-hop personalities, the a stylized ram's head of her astrological sign – they all could stay. They really meant very little to her, anyway.

Willie bawled a good-bye over the blare of his stereo as she tramped past his room. The back door had already slammed shut behind her when she heard her mother yoo-hooing. "Be good, Thanny. Have a nice time."

***

"Hey Sweetheart!"

She looked up from her wrestling match with the arm straps of her pack as a flashy red sports job with a rumbling muffler slowed down to a crawl on the other side of the street. "How'd I get to Calmore Street?"

She hooked her thumb in the direction from which the car had come. "Passed it about a mile back," she told him and with that and nothing else said he was off, going at a tire screeching clip straight forward where the nose of his sleek ride was pointed. Calmore was in the direction she had indicated but, along this street there were several detours and dead ends before you came to it. He passed her again, having made the U-turn at the next intersection, tooted his horn and waved to her as he sped past toward some commitment or other that was on a street he probably wouldn't find. Her vagrant thoughts wished him well as she made her own choice of an avenue of escape.

But which way?

That way led back to town, to home and the people she knew, to memories of dates and pettings, friends and long, useless conversations about where the future would find her once she and her parents had made up their collective mind as to what they wanted out of life for Thanielle. She turned resolutely around and faced in the direction that led out of town to farms and valleys and forests and glades and the hulking shape of the State Hospital in the near distance. That ungainly dinosaur of a building sat on a campus ten or more acres around. Its on-site power plant generated enough electricity that, in the distance at night that it looked like its own miniature constellation below the full moon.

That," she said aloud to herself about the state nuthatch, again for the benefit of no one to hear but the listener in her head. "That might very well be where I end up." She laughed darkly at the very idea. "My fate," she said, not believing it. "My destiny."

Chapter 10 – Instant Friendships

It was not an actual crossroads in the accepted sense of the word. The road remained narrow and did not fork, split or bisect another byway at a ninety-degree angle, giving drivers and walkers along this stretch of road a choice. It was a crossroads, however, even if Gordon did not see it until he was accosted with the fact of its very presence in his life.

He had been telling Vardis about himself, the turmoil and consequences by which he had arrived at the hospital. He had started by pointing at a low hanging mass of cumulus that looked like an airborne continent and he ask his friend what he saw.

"A mountain," said Vardis, making a face of concentration on the huge, puffy object in the sky. "Or maybe even a whole range. Maybe...the Rockies?"

"Don't ask, tell me. The Rockies? Okay then that's the Rocky Mountains up there. I guess it could look like them, with a little imagination." He screwed up his face, drawing the skin of his nose up to his sparsely haired brows and squinted tightly. "Yeah, right," he said, relaxing his face. "A mountain range. But my trouble, you see, was that it would quit being just imagination and then less and less an imagined, fantasized thing until I actually believed it and then if I really did believe that those clouds were, in fact, a mountain range – and I could talk myself into taking just about any moronic notion for the truth – then I'd get myself all worked up into a tizzy and start imagine myself climbing those mountains. See? Actually go into that cloud range and walk up and down the hills and valleys – see'em there, on the far right hand end? – And I'd stumble up the trails to the humpy peaks and down the other side. All in my head, mind you, but I had deluded myself into really believing I was there and I knew it for fact that it was all really what I saw it to be. Mountains in the clouds, man. Damn but was I ever fucked up!"

The clouds weren't the only thing. He told his friend at length about almost drowning in the bathtub, believing himself to be the commander of a submarine and his eyes were the periscope, peering across the surface of the water at some phantasmal destroyer or aircraft carrier that need to be sunk. Stoppage of breath was forgotten in his wandering brain and a deep breath nearly cost him his lungs. Vardis laughed sadly and said that if it had been him, he would have dreamed himself up as a frog or an alligator skimming across the top of some marshy pond in search of big old roachy bugs or water snakes for lunch but then he wouldn't have sunk into such a state while taking a bath. It would have been an "unrealness" delved into while fully awake, sitting in a chair or on the edge of his bed. The two of them commiserated, Gordon bearing the lion's share of the conversation.

It was during one such explanation of himself that Vardis stopped in the road and looked around. Gordon halted beside him and cut his spiel short – this one about the patterns on his bedroom wall when he was a little boy – and stood silent while Vardis walked to each of the shoulders of the country lane and surveyed the landscape from a number of vantage points. The right shoulder bordered on what was evidently the wide front yard of a farmhouse with a barn and several outbuildings scattered close and far like a child's toy blocks randomly placed on the living room carpet. Off of the left shoulder was a meadow several football fields deep and just as wide.

"Realness," he whispered, gazing far. Then, he almost shouted, "Maybe it's out there for me, Gordy!"

"What, Vard?" Gordy asked as he joined his friend at the split rail fence that separated field from road. "What's there?"

Vardis told him what he saw in his mind. It wasn't real, he said, but he was sure that he would find it and he pointed across the huge field and said, "There. That way."

Gordon shook his head. "Not there, pal. Realness is inside of you. All that's out there is grass and weeds and cow shit. Can't you see them? Look, they're grazing out there, by those trees way at the far end of this field. Can you see them? Just bulls and cows, that's all."

"It's out there, Gordy," Vardis said. "It's just waiting for me to find it." He climbed up and onto the top rail of the fence. He gestured with a stirring motion to the road. "This side, this road is a path to follow to my next spell of unrealness. That's all that's sure. But this side…." He turned toward the meadow so quickly that he almost lost his balance and would have pitched headlong into the calf-high grass but he caught his equilibrium in time and righted himself on the fence rail. Breathing rapidly from the sudden fright and rush of adrenalin, he said, "That's what's on this side. Unsureness. Adventure. Something new and different. I don't know what the hell it'll be but maybe it'll be better than what I got now."

"And surely it can't be any worse," Gordon finished Vard's thought on a sarcastic note. Vardis studied his friend for a moment, smiled and then went back to gazing out across the mammoth field with the cows and their sires dotting the land like dark stars in a green sky. "I understand what you're about with this, Vard. Believe me, I do. But why change course now just for the sake of a metaphor?"

"'Cause it's mine," Vard said as he climbed down off the fence and into the knee high grass of the meadow. "'Cause I don't know what to do and this looks as good as anything. And 'cause my mind's made up. You comin'?"

Gordon closed his eyes and shook his head in disbelief. So fast? Is this the way partings were supposed to be initiated? Just a "nice sharing the walk with you but this is where I get off"? Like dropping off a hitchhiker? When he opened his eyes Vardis was already walking. "Cows!" he called, suddenly frantic. 'There's a woodlot this way! Vardis! It's just as iffy going this way!"

Vardis kept going, even broke into a loping run for a short while then slowed back to a walk and trundled on. He turned once, continuing to walk backwards while he waved to Gordon and then skipped back to his forward gait until he was only a gangling speck among a sea of mooing, skittish specks on a wide expanse of green, green, green,

"Hope it doesn't rain tonight," Gordon thought out loud as he started on his own way, wondering how he could explain all this away if he was ever asked. *It was just the time for the way things were to happen,* he rationalized. *You go your way, I'll go mine. No ropes or chains hold us together and, besides, I don't care much for cows. And bulls scare the living bejeepers out of me.*

Gordon was a fast walker, especially when he talked to himself. It was a silent, secret conversation held between the two sides of his brain. At least that was the way he explained it to himself. The daydreaming stories and images that became his own personal reality was one aspect of his psyche that he had never attempted to categorize. He would gladly describe any such event if he trusted a person but he wouldn't dwell on reasons why or how that capacity for self-delusion existed within him. It was just there.

"And sometimes Gordon talked to himself about himself in the third person" he thought to himself and stopped in the road, listening to his mind's voice trailing off. It was like he was describing the doings of another person and not himself at all, and he had never tried to figure out why he did that, either.

He looked around and realized that he was no longer amid fields and farms. He faced the way from which he had come but could not see where the road had entered the wood. He looked up but the sun was only a broken cluster of fragmented light and twinkle in the budding branches above him. *Used to be able to give a good guess at the time from the sun,* he remembered, holding up his hand in an n effort to position it below it below the pale yellow orb. *Four fingers per hour, graduate down, counting until you came to the western horizon and that's how many hours there will be, more or less, until sunset. But where was the horizon in this dense wall of trees and which way was west?* He shrugged without using his shoulders and began to walk.

Lost, he would have said even though he had a general idea from where he and Vardis had started. But even when they began their trek, he had very little idea of where he was, what town was nearby, what landmarks to look for, even the hospital from which they had begun their journey. State Hospital was what he told the cab driver when he entered the dusty vehicle, and that seemed to be enough, even though he had no notion as to where that might be. He had slept most of the way in the back seat, so nothing would seem familiar to him now. Lost, he thought abstractly. But that's nothing new. Nothing like the two hours that Vardis had lost in his black-out "unrealnesses" but a whole life lost, it seemed, in those recesses and ditch falls and catty traps of his febrile mind. Places to hide, that's what they were. The need for hiding like that never seemed to have a definite starting place in his memory, in his life, if there ever had been a true need for it in the first place. It was just something to do to kill time.

He looked around as he walked, watched the trees pass him by as if they were projections on a screen to either side of him; they were moving, not him. But his legs were moving, his heart beating with the minimal stress and effort needed for walking, his lungs sucking air with practiced gulps. The brain hummed along without any voluntary help from him. It was its own thing, throwing ideas, memories, random thoughts and fancies on the brightly lit screen before him like there was another person there, in the brainpan, beside himself, making the decisions as to what was appropriate to think and feel at the moment.

And here was another one now.

Charlie Calderone. Ever since he had come to the ward Gordon had felt a special affinity with the boy even though the interest was never reciprocated with anymore sincerity or intensity than could be found in a cheerful hello or a casual request for chewing gum or something to read. Charlie was one who needed someone who would listen to his tales of his druggy life with an open mind, not someone like himself who would descend into his own world of fantasy and daydreams when the hard points were being made. Even so, he felt that he and Charlie were somehow alike. Both of them hiding, he summed it up. Just that he needs drugs to do it and I don't. I can find a tunnel in the ripple of a blanket thrown back after a night's sleep and burrow my way through there like following a rabbit to the funny lands where card carrying crazies exist to serve only their true king and red heart ruler – me. Or look out long and hard through the screened windows across the infinity deep lawn to the back gate of the hospital and watch the witchy women making mumbo-jumbo over the remains of dead snakes and spiders that lash up into a fiery dragon, devouring them before being done in by the laser cannon which I always carry with me.

"Always," he whispered to himself, patting an empty pocket as he watched the approaching figure in the distance. A stocky man in his forties with a sprinkling of grey in his scrubby beard. Carried his life and belonging in a heavily loaded gunny sack draped over his hunched shoulder. Maybe all the monetary riches to his name stuffed into the toe of a ratty workman's boot.

"Anything that way?" he asked Gordon as they met.

"Cows," Gordon said. "Pastures. Lots of grass."

"Well," said the man with a grateful sigh as he set down his sack and pulled a beat up watch from a jacket pocket. "Four o'clock already. Saw a clearing back that way, not too far. It'll be dark by seven and it's best to be camped down and get the meal ready for the fire by then. You had any lunch?"

Gordon shook his head. "And only a couple of handfuls of wild mulberries along the way for breakfast."

"Some stew, then," said the man, nodding decisively. "Got all the fixings in the sack here, even an extra blanket if all's you got is what you're wearing. And I'll guess that it is, isn't it?"

Gordon said that it was and then said no more. The man was rushing him, giving him no time to think for himself. Give the extra person in his head a chance to talk to him, argue out a decision of some kind. A few sentences, quickie questions without waiting for an answer and this guy had taken over, this stranger. Still, though, they were going the way the man wanted to go and, when they reached the clearing, Gordon did what he was told.

"Supervision is an art," the man said as Gordon hefted rocks for the campfire. A rotted log suited him fine for a throne as he directed his new friend – for that was how he termed this new relationship even if this nameless fellow hadn't come to that realization yet –in the fine points of setting up an open-air encampment. There would be no rain, he pronounced regally, so even a lean-to would not be necessary.

"When the stars begin to shine," he waxed drearily poetic in his ease. "We shall be smiled upon by the Gods of the skies, the Lords of Infinite Space."

"Mister?" said Gordon, interrupting the man's reverie. "How's this?"

"Hm? Oh, fine. Excellent. And kindling, too, I see. You know more than you say, my friend. Ever camped before?"

"All it takes is some common sense," Gordon said flatly as he stared with little interest at the gathered pile of twigs in the stone circle. "You gonna rub sticks together or something?"

"Why waste the energy for that when...?" The man quickly produced several books of matches from one of the several pockets in his jacket. It almost took all of what he had to get the fire going, but he wasn't worried. "A full belly and a good night's sleep will make tomorrow – er – worriless," he said, looking a bit perplexed. "Is that a real word, worriless?"

"Sounds good even if it isn't," Gordon said, growing to like this demanding, humorous man. "Gordon," he said, extending an open hand to this friend who was presently intent upon the contents of his bulky sack.

"What? Oh, yes, of course." He jerked the boy's arm roughly and smiled. "Jacob Rine's the name but you can forget the last. I'm just Jacob, or even Jake, if you like."

"Traumer's mine. Gordy Traumer, and where'd you get all that?" He gestured toward the man's sack of stuff. "Raid a grocery store or something?"

Jacob had spread out a blanket and was setting out the "fixings" for their meal: a quart jar of water, onions, tomatoes, potatoes (Idaho), string beans, apples, oranges hamburger meat (one pound), mushrooms (canned), pork 'n' beans, a box of dried prunes, cornflakes, tuna fish (three cans), canned cling peaches, jars of sugar, salt, black pepper, cinnamon sticks, a ball of soiled string and a large, battered and fire blackened saucepan.

"Raided? No, not really. Let's just say 'creatively acquired,' shall we? Then we'll see what we can make out of all this." He snapped open a gravity knife and began to peel an orange with slow, careful strokes, each of which left about a foot length of unbroken rind in his lap. "Would you care for an apple or an orange or some canned peaches for your first course? There's a can opener and some forks in the bag somewhere. Just help yourself."

Gordon reached for the box of prunes, causing another smile to spread across Jacob's lined and mellow face. They ate in silence, each man enjoying his own choices, his own decisions as to what a shared supper should be.

And so their first evening together began.

Chapter 11

"Morning found me waking up in a forest, dense enough that the sunshine coming through the upper reaches of branches lit the area where I was, greenly and soft with misty shadows playing off the trunks of the trees," Thanielle would write later on but that would be with the benefit of hindsight when what would come to pass on that morning was already known to her, the consequences already affectionately recalled as part of her personal history.

She had been gone from home for eight days. Even though she had rationed sparingly for each meal, her remaining store of food was still badly depleted. This had proved to be a particularly humid May as spring months usually go and all her clothing held the rancid odors of perspiration and body filth.

She had stopped at a grocery-general store the evening before, surprised to find one on such a deserted back road. The proprietor confessed that the majority of his customers were mainly visitors to the State Hospital, some five miles up the road. They mainly purchased such items that could easily be gotten past the guards and nurses at that place, either legally or by stealth, and that would be pleasing to their relatives or friends who were patients there. They all seemed to gravitate toward similar items such as tobacco products, chewing gum, fruit and nuts or candy, comic books or paperbacks or magazines, writing implements and stationery, toys and games, coloring books and crayons.... "You know," he said. "The usual loony-keep-busy stuff. I don't usually get much call for soap and laundry products like this except from the farm ladies that come in on weekends for their food shopping along with some essentials for keeping the car in good shape for their husbands, mostly. And then there's the occasional call for a girlie magazine or two – also for the husband, I guess. But you say you need shampoo? Stuff I got here's so old it'll prob'ly turn your hair green. Best you stick with the trusty old brown laundry soap. Travels better than that liquid crap and it's good for the clothes and the skin as well as the hair. D'oderant? Yeah, I guess you could use some. It's on the back wall there, next to the toothpaste."

His prices were truly exorbitant, so she only had a few pennies left over after her personal hygiene was taken care of. The owner of the place didn't mark any of the products on his shelves or behind the counter; he kept all that in his head which made her come to the conclusion that he was sure to have hiked the prices for a vagrant traveler like herself whom he would never see again. Since this was the only store of any kind for miles, he knew that he had her right where he wanted her and so she paid what was asked and put as much distance from the shady place as she could before choosing a place to camp.

The stream beside which she had laid out her belongings in her process of setting up camp ran swiftly, but there was an eddying pool a few steps down where the bank sloped. It was there that she kicked off her sneakers and waded into the chill water fully clothed. The big bar of laundry soap she had bought stung her hands where briar stickers had cut her when she had pushed through the underbrush the day before. She scrubbed at her shirt and jeans with the soap until she raised quite lather in the calm water until clumps and tendrils of it reached the swiftly racing water out in the midstream. She stopped to watch the blobs of white scoot away downstream like a regatta of little white sailboats. She washed her hair then, lathering it to a bouffant and then rinsed, repeating the simple process several times until her fingers squeaked against her scalp like rusty nails being scraped across a slate chalkboard. When she got out of the water she stripped to the skin and soaped herself from face to soles and, with a shuddering cringe, jumped once again into the sparkling water for a quick rinse. She got out of the stream for a last time and dried herself with the bath towel she had brought rolled up inside the sleeping bag.

With all this done she walked up the bank to where her brother's sleeping bag lay open and airing and laid out her clothes to dry and then, with a sigh, arranged herself on the bag so that she could gain the same benefit as her garments from the warm rays of the springtime sun. Clean, she let her mind hum as her hair fanned out on the spread bath towel. She felt like Venus rising from the sea all naked and lovely. The simple glory of just not smelling like the business end of a skunk, just to feel like this, light and lazy and fresh and drying and warm and relaxed and....

"Whoops!"

She folded the open sleeping bag over her, sandwiching herself between the soft, fuzzy linings as soon as she heard the startled cry issue from the trees. "Who's there?" she demanded. "Where are you?"

"Over here, Miss," said a voice at the clearing's edge just behind her. "Just coming through. I didn't know there was anyone here. These your clothes here?"

"You leave them alone!" she yelled, hoping that her unknown visitor hadn't gotten too much of an eyeful. "I don't want you to go and get them all dirty again after I went to the trouble of washing them,"

Good tactic, she thought. *Play it friendly but firm. Don't say anything about being naked or he just might get ideas to stick around for a show. Or maybe even something worse. Be nice but don't give into anything you might be regretting later on.*

"There's shirt and a pair o' drawers here that're dry," called the voice. "Smell nice, too. Amazin' what a bit of fresh air'll do for washing. And I can see a pair of – hem! – panties there, too. Cover yourself good and I'll bring'em over to you. Don't worry, Miss. I'm no rapist or anything like that. You can trust me."

She lay still, wondering how far she could trust him, this man that she couldn't even see. She listened to the rustle of his footsteps through the dead leaves on the floor of the forest and onto the moist grass of the clearing. He was behind her and she was sitting with her bare back to him. All he has to do is catch me under the chin from behind and throw the flap of the sack off of me, she thought morosely. A club or a knife in his hand would be all that would be necessary to ensure her cooperation while he took whatever advantage he might. She wouldn't be so foolish as to resist when her life lay in the balance. She rolled over onto her side and craned her neck to see him but her black and red plaid shirt blocked her view as he dangled it in front of her face. On her side her bare rump was out a bit to the open side of the unzipped sleeping bag; she could feel the chill of the air on her damp skin, giving her the feeling of complete vulnerability.

"Sorry to have startled you," was all the man said before lapsing into a momentary silence. She flopped back down on her back and looked up into his grizzled, friendly face. "I was out looking for firewood when I got to the clearing here, saw the clothes and then a flash of skin. You heard me 'whoops!' when I turned my back. I'm a gentleman, Miss. I can 'sure you of that. I'm no peeper. No, I'm not."

She said that she believed him even though she was not quite certain of what to make of him right then. She took her clothes from him with a whispered "Thanks" and shimmied into her panties and jeans under the cover of the sleeping bag. The shirt, however, posed a special kind of impediment to modesty. She told her "visitor" that she would have to bare herself to put it on and would he please turn around. The man, whose face was dirty but kind, promised not to peek as he turned away.

"You have a nice tan," he said as he looked off into the trees. "Do much sunning?"

"I thought you said that you didn't look," she said as she buttoned her shirt.

"Flash of skin, like I told you. Nice, soft skin it looks, too. Tan like honey. Out in the sun much?"

"The beach sometimes, when I could get the folks to take me – or my boyfriend. You can turn around now."

"Boyfriend?" He turned to her, friendly smile and concerned wonder on his face. "He here with you now?"

"No," she admitted, hearing the word spill, watching for the reaction. *I'm alone and unprotected; now what are you going to do about that?* "He took off on me a couple of months ago."

"Ah, abandonment! I know the feeling as well as I know the reasons."

"You've been walked out on too?" she asked kindly, knowing that perhaps it was too personal a can of worms to open when you first meet someone, but the fellow had provided the key. Why not be adventurous and go through the door?

He followed her around the clearing, traipsing happily after her as she checked the disposition of her litter of clothing. He even served as her carrier for the dry articles as he catalogued his list of entrapments, woes, near escapes, uncalled-for refusals, proposals, propositions (accepted and denied), abandonments, betrayals and heartaches.

"Both sides," he said, completing his lengthy tale just as they reached the spread sleeping bag where he dumped the ruffled load. "Both sides of the fight and neither of them is any fun. You know, when Estelle told me that it was over – she was the third that done it, remember – I was so shook that I swore to myself that I ever got attached to a woman again, I'd be proud sure that I would be the one to do the throwing over, not her. And I did – poor Amy – and it felt even worse doing it to another than me being on the receiving end."

"That's because you got a heart," she told him, feeling the truth in her words. He was an insistent man – she could look straight into his beagle eyes without any stretching or straining and she was five foot nine – but he was sweet and honest, human and kind. "Not like the guy I was going with. All smarm and love-dovey until our last date. You know what he did? Told me he was leaving for this big European holiday in one weekend and his prick was still inside me. Can you imagine that? Still pumping away while he's telling me he's going away and might never be coming back. To find out that way that I didn't mean shit to him. Didn't even ask me to go with him and didn't even have the balls to tell me until later that he probably wouldn't see me again at all after he got back. Nothing at all about all that until I had to drag it out of him. But get this: while we're fucking and he just laid this bomb on me, he tells me to squeeze him hard with my twat because he's just about to come. Like I cared about him getting his rocks off after that little announcement. Oh damn!"

Tears aren't supposed to be a part of it, she thought. *This was supposed to be like the writing, this trip, this running. To get away from things like that, that made you cry, like Gerald.* This was to be another way to retreat, to escape and forget. The man's clothing smelled like the earth, all musty and caked with the dust of the road. She sniffed and snotted on his shoulder, felt his bear's paw patting her back in a slow, soothing rhythm. She apologized, smeared the snail trail on his jacket with her hand and then started to laugh when she heard her voice bounce and quiver with the pleasant pounding of his big hand on her lungs and spine.

"All right, then," he said softly, hunching a little to look into her face which was still tilted forward to rest against his sternum. "We've just traded something, you and I, that's all. Yours is just a mite newer than mine and still pretty tender. C'mon, Prettyface. You'll get used to it just like I have. It won't hurt so bad as time goes on, no matter what it was he did to you. C'mon now, okay?"

She looked up into his face and nodded, then smiled. She shed what little water was still trapped in her hair onto him with the motion. They both laughed. He gave her an apple from his grimy pocket, told her she looked like she could use a bit fattening up. Flattery, she huffed as she crunched the fruit. This is where it all goes, she told him, indicating her hips and thighs. He shrugged and said that was what made a woman attractive to him: a big behind, wide carriage and strong legs. They sat for a while and talked about what they seemed to have started here, then about their lives and why they were there in that forest clearing on the fast-moving little river.

"Now," he said as she rubbed an exploring hand over the sleeping bag's cotton lining. "Everything should be dry, I think. How about packing up and come over to my camp so we can get a good meal into you? I got a friend there I just know you'll like. He's a soft-spoken guy, as shy as I am outgoing. About your age, I'd guess, maybe a bit older. You'll shine to'im, I just know it. Wha'dya say?"

They loaded the few damp wet pieces of her clothes into her duffel, the rest into the pack and strapped it all neatly together and slung it onto her shoulders. As they headed for the trees, the man held his hand out to her and was not too surprised that she almost immediately took it. "Trust me," he said, needlessly.

Amazing what can be accomplished in a morning when you put your mind to it, she thought. Clean yourself up, do your wash, meet a new friend. She looked at him quizzically, realizing that, for all they had given one another of themselves in the short time of their acquaintance, the one trade which had not been offered was that of their names.

Small thing in light of the load taken off her, she would later write, using the third person singular. *Who else could she have told all that to and not have been slapped down for it? Surely not her parents or her brother. Her friends would have been horrified and embarrassed by the admissions she had so easily made to this man. What was his name? But what difference was that – a name – in the overall scheme of things? Why bother with petty inconsequential?*

He was her friend and confidante and for her, that was all that mattered now.

Chapter 12

Lunchtime drizzle; a lean-to hastily erected; a fine way for new acquaintances to get to know each other, Jacob thought disappointedly as he steadied the crossbar between two sturdy young saplings.

The roof of the new shelter was originally supposed to include both vertical struts angled from the main crossbar to the ground as well as mini crossbars graduated between each of the vertical struts. In order to speed up the process in deference to the sprinkling rain, however, the mini crossbars were eliminated so that pine boughs could be quickly lashed in place with bark strips by Gordon. Thanielle was busy trimming low branches off trees in the vicinity for the roof and sides of the lean-to with the aid of Jacob's gravity knife. Both she and Gordon were inexperienced, but patient and thorough in their work. Early to mid-twenties, both of them, the older man figured to himself as he watched them work. Well-tuned machine, perfect match, a lovely couple; he was satisfied.

He knew his own eager propensity for meddling, his enthusiasm to see things turn out right for people who deserved their lives to be happy. That wasn't everybody, though. He had seen and met and had become intimate with people who deserved much less than they received in light of the little which they gave to others. Those ones – Estelle of his wet dreams lay on top of that heap of memories for her cross attitude, her critical, uncaring eye, her trader's values on human emotion – usually just passed by his attention with little more than a vague nod of recognition. *I see you*, his mind seemed to consider, *but you are not even worth that much from me.* His critical eye: he kicked himself for it but at least it wasn't just for the way a person looked or acted. He gave each man or woman a fighting chance to prove him or herself in his estimation before the claim was made either to the positive or the negative. Some took longer than others to be given a final verdict. *Now, the boy there*, he thought. *For all his calm reserve and shy reticence, he's proved to have fingers sensitive and nimble enough for the intricacies of lashing wood to wood and have the job hold together so well it was as if it had been accomplished by more experienced hands than his own. He had an ear attuned to the slightest change in a speaker's voice and the good sense and compassion to alter his reactions to suit the speaker's pitch and need. And the girl, hacking strongly but erratically at the tough tissue of green timber like she was wielding a machete instead of a dull bladed hand knife showed the ambition and determination that the boy lacked or, at least, which he did not see fit to display. She could be mellow when she chose, could carry on a civil conversation when the topic was to her interest or liking. Let it change to something for which she held an opposing opinion, though, and she would sure as well let you know what it was , loudly, coarsely and with an edge to her tone as blunt as a note from a carelessly tuned cello. In that same conversation the boy would become all but invisible, his head stuck in the bushes of his private maunderings like an ostrich fending off an attack of preying dogs with the old head in the sand ploy.*

Something each could learn from the other and damned if Jacob Rine was going to let any opportunity for the good of these two kids pass him by, or in any way go to waste.

Well-oiled machine, he thought again. *Perfect match; lovely young couple.*

"You two do such splendid things together," he commented on their work in his best praising, meddlesome voice. "We all ready, then? Then let's get inside and eat. I, for one, am sure ready for it."

The saucepan served as a catch for the one leaky spot in the pine and maple roofing. Water pattered the blackened bottom with a bubbling drumbeat that soon slowed and steadied, quickened and rolled with the unseen intensities of the misty afternoon drizzle. The line of the drip from the ceiling formed a boundary in the makeshift shelter with Jacob and Gordon on one side and Thanielle on the other, each of the three quietly forking up mouthfuls of tuna fish and tomato and a canned fruit cocktail, which was Thanny's contribution to the meal.

Even though the silence of the meal was soothing and conducive to digestion, Jacob found the lack of talk, as well as the seating arrangement, to be rather unnatural and definitely not to his liking. They sat cross-legged in a semi-lotus style, eating quietly like frat-house cronies after a big bash was over and all conversation was now superfluous, nothing left to say or do but each to nurse his or her own hangover thoughts and regrets. The lean-to was filled with the sounds of chewing but nary a word was spoken to break through that masticatory sound barrier.

Unnatural, Jacob thought. *Let's get this party going!*

"You know, Gordy," he began on a picky note. "When this young lady and I first met I could see by the look in her eye that she thought that I was some kind of pervert freak and that I was surely about to rape and ravage her right on the spot. She was bare-butt naked at the time, so I had my chance and she damn well knew it. What puzzles me is how I persuaded her – rightly, I think – that my intentions were nothing but those of a gentleman, honorable and friendly."

"It didn't take long to see," Thanny said, sucking an errant piece of fish from a rear molar. "That you were really only just a nice, harmless chatterbox."

Gordon agreed with her and that was where it began for them. *I'm to be the focus, then,* Jacob silently noted the emerging pattern of what would follow. *Well, all right then; got to start somewhere. After all, I'm the one who just opened that particular door; might as well go on through it. I can always shift the perspective later on, I suppose.*

"Harmless?" he piped, affecting the rising tone of one insulted. "You should talk to Amy. That girl thought the sun rose out of my belly button and set in my ass."

"Ouch!" Gordon yelped, raising a laugh from the other two. "What an awful case of the piles that would be!"

"You told me about her," said Thanny and turned to Gordon for verification. He nodded his confirmation that yes, he, too, had heard this story. Three days on the trails with a man leaves not much more to do that talk and trade life stories. "But I still don't understand why you threw her over."

"Devotion," he said, summing it all up badly before the story was even begun. "She needed so much more than I ever could give her. She made it so that she was always with me, never a moment's rest or time for myself. I had to always be attentive, affectionate, responsive.... Not that I'm not all those things, mind you, but not all the time. And she engineered her time so that, outside of the work I was doing then, I had nothing to spare but for her. And add to that the fact that I had sworn to myself that the next woman I became involved with after Estelle would get the old heave-ho from me...." He became pensive, a sudden moodiness entering his voice like a chill blast of air from some long forgotten, buried source. "It seemed that one excuse was as good as another for me," he muttered uneasily. "I've never forgiven myself for that."

The lean-to became silent again but for the drip in the pan, a sound becoming more liquid, less intrusive as the water level reached the vessel's halfway point. A keening wind swept through the upper branches of the trees with a loud whisper while Jacob's attitude slackened from self-aggrandizement to a more animated temper as he began to elucidate for his companions on the landscape in which they were waiting out the weather.

"Bulldozed and beaten for farmland and industry beginning more than a hundred and fifty years ago," he began his extemporizing, sounding like a professor before a class of bored students. "The Interior Department snatched up enough of the unposted land to keep a fair amount of acreage unspoiled and in a relatively natural state. Clearings like this one are the result of a resolution about fifty years ago when logging concerns were allowed in to strip out 'old' wood and give new trees a chance to flourish. With the supreme wisdom of the land management in this area at the time, though, no new shoots were planted and the forest, being naturally slow to regenerate itself, hasn't managed to push very far into this glade or the one in which I found Miss Petár so bewitchingly sunning herself this morning."

He leaned forward, cocked his head in Thanny's direction, omitting Gordon from this new, oddly connected thought that he wished only to share with the pretty young woman. "And I tell you, deary," he said in a growling low voice. "If I were just ten years younger, you wouldn't have found me so damned 'harmless'."

His change in tone from instructive to mock lascivious brought a short burst of nervous laughter from the two younger members of the trio. Despite his efforts at confidentiality between Thanny and himself, Gordon had also heard his admission of physical attraction to the girl. Jacob struggled to free himself from the apprehension that his two new friends would certainly start building him up to be in their minds as some kind of sublimating lecher without the guts to admit his preference for much younger flesh as that of his own.

As he waffled and stuttered, fought back a rising anger at his own inability to sound anything better than merely foolish, Thanny rested a hand lightly on his knee from her side of the shelter, wetting her shirted arm under the trickle of water from the leaky roof.

"Don't try so hard, Jake," she said. "We don't judge you that harshly. We like you." She looked over at Gordon who was concentrating on whittling a root with the gravity knife. "He doesn't say very much," she commented after some consideration.

"That's because he's deep in thought."

She leaned across the little lean-to past Jacob, dampening her brow as well as her shoulders under the lessening dribble. "What are you thinking, Gordy?"

The young man smiled, moving only his eyes from the growing pile of shavings in his lap, his head remaining rigidly fixed on his neck. "About how silly you look right now," he said and reached forward to brush a thick strand of wet hair away from her right eye. "And that you must be a very kind and trusting person to throw in with us so easily."

"When I've been shown this much hospitality, I can't help but be trusting," she said, backing away from his ministering hand. "You've both given me good reason to be."

"Well, then!" Jacob chirped, suddenly animated again. "A family, then, all trust and good feelings. Is that what we're to be?"

Gordon shrugged as he gazed with warm interest at Thanielle. "Looks that way, Papa," he said tonelessly. *Truth needs no punching up.*

Oh dear, worried the elder man. He turned from one bright young face to the next and back again. *Why do they both smile so? What do they expect?*

"The rain's finished," Thanny announced with a hand sticking out of the lean-to into the open air. "Do we move on or stay camped for the night?"

"Why ask me?" he snapped petulantly like a child in need of a nap. *Just because I'm older only means that I've had more chances – and I've taken a few – to make mistakes, to be a fool and an ass. So, what do they expect of me?* He felt a wave of confusion, a need to escape, to have some answers as to what exactly was expected, needed, wanted of him. Instead, he asked on a subdued and amiable voice, "What do you two want to do?"

Chapter 13 – Realness

Just when they all thought that they had had their fill of the flicker of light and dark filtering down from the upper branches of the tree canopy over their heads, they found respite. They had been hiking along, the three of them, for two more and then the thickness of trees, trees, trees slowly started to thin out and give way to sparser foliage, more shrubbery than trees, more maple than pine and fir. Shrubs and deciduous means "we're coming to a meadow or a farm or something open and sunny," Jacob told them as if he knew what he was talking about.

There were things that he could teach them from the experiences he had learned from his peripatetic life on the road and rails and trails. There were things that he did want to teach them but, of course, he knew that they would have to find out much of it on their own, whatever they would, in spite of what he could tell and show them. Four years on the road for him minus a month or two--that had to count for something, give some amount of credit to his name to accept students of the road. But then there was the question: road to where?

His own had led from the open door of an apartment building in a city to which he had not since returned. The woman with whom he had been living "in sin" (her words, not his) finally "saw the error of her ways" (much given to epigrams and clichés, that beautiful, misguided woman is what he would tell any hobo, wayfarer, friend or shopkeeper who would listen). They had argued through something like two thirds of their relationship for an hour or more every night he came home from his job in a local restaurant as first assistant manager.

He insisted that their marrying would only be a formality after the fact; being man and wife was a state of mind and lifestyle not governed by a piece of paper or a ceremony but by the way the two people felt about each other. He understood her convictions, though, and would have married her in a minute if that would have assuaged her guilt feelings in the matter. But he knew that it would not.

There would be no erasing a sin already committed, a sin that her beliefs made hers to bear. She should never have agreed to let him move into her apartment and live with her as a husband when he was really nothing more than a favored suitor. There was love shared, that was true enough, but it was an unholy love not smiled upon by heaven. He would become irate at this and question her clairvoyant knowledge of what heaven did or did not smile upon. Her response was automatic, always the same with very few exceptions. Out came the Bible. She quoted passages with a quivering voice, rubbing a slender finger under each minutely printed line and verse as she read, leaving blackened tracks below the more favored lines from numerous such exhortations. "Praise be to God," she would intone as she closed the massive tome with a resounding thud. "I am a sinner and I must atone."

This sort of guilt-ridden show of defiance against their "unholy" union continued steadily each night for more than two weeks. "Eighteen days," he had told many in those four years of his wandering, having kept a close and exasperating count before he had finally departed. The emotions of that departure were a little harder for him to categorize or even amply define. It was all unequal parts of frustration, confusion, anger, despair, disgust, sadness, jealousy, torpor, and loneliness. He was truly lost. In the end, he would see that the underlying matter for him was a need that he could not put his finger on, nor even find a single word he could say to her, or to anyone. Whatever it was, however, he was sure that it was there within him, "hidden somewhere," he said angrily and sarcastically at the same time, behind his heart.

"I don't think it's been fulfilled as yet," he told them as they sat resting in yet another clearing in the light filled forest edge. "Need for love, maybe. She certainly didn't supply that, at least not so you'd notice; not toward the end anyway."

"But there must have been something to begin with," Thanny commented bitterly, though she had meant her remark to sound empathetic. "You said there was love there."

"Yes, I loved her," he admitted, unabashed as he spit out a seed from the last apple in the sack. The skin of the fruit was dry, its meat already going brown as he cut it, just this side of rot. "But I've told you about the end, not the lovely times we had, the bed that we shared, the evenings of just sitting with her in her tiny living room, holding her. Affection," he mused, talking to himself aloud. "We had been dating for six months when the lease for my apartment came due for renewal. They were going to raise my rent way out of my reach. I suggested that I might stay with her until I could find more affordable digs. She jumped at the chance. I could almost see her physically pounce at the idea of having me with her always. She agreed. Now, we had slept together many times through our dating. I'd spend nights at her place and she over at mine. That was when the loving was really at its fullest. Like the moon was shining its blessings on us. Mphh!" He frowned as he grumped. But he was just reacting to his own lousy metaphor and said as much. "But we were the best, the closest, the only. Know what I mean?" Both Thanielle and Gordon murmured their sympathy and nodded their understanding,

"I only lived with her for three months and it was all a build-up the whole time until the final blow-out. Even that spread itself out pretty damned wide. It seemed that we never did anything on the spur of the moment anymore, she and I. Everything was planned out. We had met through friends we had in common whose purpose I later found out was to get us to meet. She and I remained just friends for weeks before even venturing out on our first date. All very friendly, just hand holding and necking. It wasn't a great physical explosion between us with the relationship blossoming later on. We worked on it, had been going out together for about a month before we started getting all gropy with our necking, hands all over the place over and under clothing, getting each other all hot and horny until we just knew that we had to get naked and into bed together.

"It was the same with the breaking up and my leaving; it was something we had to work into slowly. I'd get home, all dead tired from work and there'd she be with dinner all set out and we'd be eating in an uncomfortable silence when she'd give her first little dig like 'We shouldn't be sitting here, eating like this, you know. Married couples eat like this.' And I'd try to be flip and tell her to pretend that we were married and let it go like we did when we had sex before we moved in together and…. But I'm getting too close to repeating myself, aren't I?"

"Not exactly," said Gordon, being polite. "Sounds like you're just getting ready to back track and then keep going, sort of."

"Well, then, you know the rest, pretty much. Just so much bitch, bitch, bitch you can take before you feel that you want to sock her one, or just leave. And I'm not one for violence, so…."

He sat back against the knotty trunk of a thick beech tree, shaking the branches with his weight, and sulked down, pressing his stocky hulk into the soft earth. He reached under the frayed covering of his jacket and pulled out two yellowed pages which had apparently been torn from a book, and began to study them. They were creased at the folds, tattered at the edges, dog-eared at most of the page corners, and badly wrinkled throughout. He smiled when he came to a passage which he found humorous or insightful, but mostly his expression remained thoughtful as he read, and rather dark.

Naturally he was asked what it was that held his attention so thoroughly and he handed over the mangled sheets to his friends. "It was the last thing I took before I left her," he said. "Kind of a spiteful thing to do, really. It was her book and I just tore out the pages I wanted and left the rest of the book there. I did it right in front of her, too. But it was what reminded me of her when we were first dating – all the time we were dating, in fact. That," he concluded, pointing to the pieces of paper Gordon and Thanielle presently shared. "That is the way I want to remember her, not as the harpy I walked out on."

The top of the first page showed Page 143 of a novel called *Tectonica,* a book which Jacob described as "a total piece of shit from which I was lucky enough to extract this hidden jewel." Gordon turned over the first sheet to Page 144. Down at the bottom Jacob had highlighted in yellow felt marker pen the last paragraph on that page, which continued on Page 145 on the second sheet in Thanielle's hands.

She lay in the darkness of the little room and watched the ceiling as the first shock wave caused the house to undulate and tremble violently. It had finally come to pass. It was really happening, just like the man on the television had predicted. But she was not afraid. "I might die here," Adele thought, fully realizing her circumstances at that moment. "This may very well be my very last thought." Courage was her main suit, as well as her indomitable spirit, in view of the manner in which she had dealt with that young mugger in the alley only an hour ago. Her jaws firmly clenched, her eyes unwavering as she watched the cracks form themselves and grew along the ceiling, like the trail of some unseen, scurrying animal, she bravely awaited her end. "Untimely," she thought, envisioning the obituary which would surely appear in the town paper the next day. If, of course, there was enough of the town left standing tomorrow to warrant there still being a newspaper. "Untimely. But then what death is ever 'timely'?"

Thanny thought that it was awful; Gordon shrugged, said that it didn't impress him at all, neither in a positively nor a negative way.

"But you had to know her for this to mean anything to you," said Jacob as he tucked the pages reverently back into the inside pocket of his jacket.

"She was in an earthquake?" Gordon asked. *Dumb-boy*, he thought, realizing the naïve stupidity of that question almost as soon as his mouth had said it.

"No, but if she was, I am sure that she would have reacted in much the same way. Brave, courageous – a bit of a pessimist, actually. The worst thing could happen to her and she would just take it in stride, as if she had expected it to happen. When anything good happened, the delight shone through every pore of her being. A gift of dandelions picked along the highway would be treated like a diamond ring if the giving were a sincere show of the way you felt about her. And she could tell if you were sincere or not just with a glance. Really uncanny, her instant judge of character."

He became quiet with that, mulling over the facets of his lost, last love. "People change," he said with a tender finality. "That was the one thing I couldn't account for in her. That sudden, scary change in her personality."

"Maybe she was just afraid," Thanny conjectured, trying to be helpful. "You know... of commitment."

"Maybe it was the moon," Gordon offered laconically. The others looked at him wonderingly. "Full moon," he continued, feeling encouraged by their silent interest. "Does funny things to people. Just like it did to the...." He caught himself right in time, realizing that neither of his travelling mates knew where he had come from, how he came to be there with them. A lot of little realizations coming up today. "Well, it changes people, anyway."

"I think I read something about that," said Thanny, raising her haunches off the ground and scuttling crabwise to her right to position herself closer to her friends. "Yeah, a couple of weeks ago. I'd just left home and I saw this newspaper headline telling about something that happened on the moon."

"I saw it, too," said Jacob. "It was an earthquake. But that only happened very recently. It wouldn't account for my girlfriend's changes that happened over four years ago."

But she wasn't listening. Thanny had taken the ball and was running with it in her mind. Her family, she prattled explanatorily. Her father's temper, her mother's weepy acquiescence to Thanny's old man's irate will, her brother's careless cruelty; all blown away one evening, all of them degenerated to zombielike civility and indifference. Could the thing she had read about in the paper, the volcanic activity in the crater – Posidolia, was it? – the quaking of that glowing, smiling night ball that several of her boyfriends had used as a porchlight by which to find her mouth for their good night kisses, have been the cause of those unexplained changes?

Jacob listened with vague interest. It was a story – Thanielle's story – which he had not heard before but he had enough of his own store of wonders and worries to give much credence to the girl's impassioned raving, her excited chatter about the home and family she had left behind.

He watched Gordon's face shine with intrigue, listened to his attentive queries about Thanny's family, the first such questions that Jacob had heard from the boy that weren't laced with a somnambulistic drawl and shrug. He was truly fascinated. Thanielle had a captive audience and the young man didn't mind being so held at all.

But what of me? He thought selfishly. *What am I doing, leading this Children's Crusade to nowhere? True, they're in their early twenties, young adults, but innocents, too, both of them, no matter how you cut it. So what do they want of me? Why do they stay with me, tag along as if they were puppies and I had a pocketful of treats? Why do I encourage them?*

I don't fit into this picture, he concluded to himself sullenly. A wave of the hand, a raised eyebrow and a new notion was there, unbidden, and insistent: *they expect nothing of me; they have all that they need without me to lead them.*

Chapter 14

"If I were to try to come up with a single word to describe our relationship," Thanielle would write in her thought-journal later on – for she was the writer of the two of them or, at least, the one who made the distinct effort to record her thoughts and feelings at the time – "It would be 'suddenly.' All of the important things that happen or come up all do with little or no notice. No real warning, just boom! and it's happened, or it's done, or it's said. Just the way Gordy and I react to each other, I guess. We each affect the other spontaneously. Spontaneity.... Maybe that's the word I'm looking for."

A case in point happened later on that day.

Jacob had glimpsed a gas station on the other side of a cornfield whose produce, so early in the season, was still only a sprinkling of pale green shoots laid out in even rows across the wide brown field. Gas stations in such an agrarian area as this, he told his companions in less elevated terms (redneck was the word that he used, not agrarian), usually stocked foodstuffs and other supplies. His sack of goodies and necessities was getting too light for comfort; time to refill the larder.

"More 'creative acquisitions'?" Gordon asked, a note of censure creeping into his voice.

Jacob didn't take the note of disapproval, only answered the question with a sigh. "We get what we need the best way we know how. Thanny, open your duffel."

She did and he loaded what was left of what they had into the canvas handled tote, and he left with an empty bag across the open field, leaving the two younger member of the party to fend for themselves. "Don't do anything I wouldn't do," he called back to them with a chuckle.

Out of sight and earshot, Jacob was not privy to the first real test of friendship between Thanielle Petár and Gordon Traumer.

"Something's bothered me about you, Gordy," she said matter-of-factly. "I know that I like you, that you're nice and friendly and quiet and sweet and I enjoy being with you and talking to you. But I don't know anything about you."

"About me?" he asked, sounding concerned. "Like what?"

"Like where you come from, for instance."

Quiet, she had said before. What she really meant was too quiet, even moody. What was inside him? Jake was right when he said that Gordon was a deep thinker. That was evident from his taciturn attitude more often than not. But what was it that he thought about? Maybe that was the question she really meant to ask, but was unsure how to broach it delicately. *Where do you come from?* That was an innocent enough beginning. Then, maybe, go on to *Why did you leave there? What was it like? What is it like here, for you, with Jake and me? Why are you so quiet all the time? What is it that you think about? Who are you, Gordon Traumer?*

But first he shrugged (it seemed to be his favorite gesture) and answered, "Not too far from where you met me and Jake." She could hear the wariness in his voice, as if he were paranoid and conscious of the possibility of a trap being set, as if he were hiding something.

"But where? The only real place near here is the town I come from. I'm sure I would have seen you around there sometime. It's not that big a place."

"Maybe you just forgot," he said. *Nervous*, she noted. *He is hiding something.* "I've got the kind of face you take for granted and can easily forget. It's just too.... Typical, I suppose, too forgettable."

No, she thought. *Not that face. Childlike, serene, boyish. Four days she was with him and Jake and look at him: only the barest trace of stubble on his chin. Virginal innocence in his eyes, trust and guileless charm written in the smooth texture of his skin. Lovable. I would have remembered that face if I'd seen it before, that's for sure.*

"Where do you come from?" she insisted sternly.

A light blinked on in those calm, baby browns of his like sparks. Mischievous. "A long way off," he fabricated. "Where the air glows like tinsel in the sun and cleanses your lungs as you breathe. There's a church there where nobody prays, nobody attends services. Rituals are just pretenses for the socializing that follows and for the community whose people are integrated into themselves and the lives of all the others that are there. That sort of pseudo-theological tripe isn't necessary. Like a brother/sisterhood there. Only love. Only love and understanding and respect and compassion. It's all beautifully laid out, the town I come from, and gloriously predictable. Have you ever gotten lost walking in familiar surroundings? The roads wind and snake around there so much that it's easy to lose your way even if you're a local but there's never any need for fear. A house will be nearby, somewhere along the way and you can get a meal, a bed, company and friendship anywhere that you stop." He halted a moment to gather his thoughts, construct his fable further and then, changing direction and theme, continued softly, "All the women are gorgeous and all the men likewise.... I suppose."

He stopped again, this time out of embarrassment, blushing a little at the thought that his aesthetic judgment on masculine attractiveness might be construed as a comment on his own sexual preferences. Seeing that this was not the way in which it was taken, that she was just listening – half-smiling, taking it all with a large grain of salt, but still listening all the same – he went on with his impromptu description.

"I've never heard anything mentioned at the town clinic about any venereal diseases being reported and maybe it's the air or something but the women all swear that contraception is unnecessary, that their bodies seem to produce an enzyme of some kind that inhibits conception unless it is wanted. Perhaps it's some unconscious, psychological thing that, when a child is wanted--the sex is being used as a means of reproduction and not only for enjoyment or to express love-- then the woman's body adjusts itself accordingly. In a town of such universal love, of course, there would be a lot of instances where contraception would be necessary if it weren't for that one biological – umm...."

"Aberration?" she suggested.

"Yeah," he said with a wink. "That's a good word for it."

"Sounds like a real Utopia."

"It's called Mishmálaca," he said, throwing syllables together at random, stressing the second one, giving the end of his fiction an ungainly flourish. He wondered where he had read that name or where he had gotten its parts. It had to have come from somewhere. He knew that he hadn't made it up out of whole cloth.

As he pondered this, Thanny waited. Having learned that this was Gordon's way, she expected nothing. She watched as his face seemed to go blank, all trace of the excitement he had previously exhibited while telling his odd little tale now gone from his attractively structured countenance, lost again in his own little world.

"Gordy," she said after a short spell in a near whisper, breaking into the wonder train he was riding by himself. "You're not going to tell me, are you?"

"Didn't think you'd buy it." He sounded dejected. She rested her arm on his broad, sloping shoulders, an affectionate and friendly gesture, she hoped. "I tried, though," he said.

"It sounds perfectly lovely," she assured him. "Your Mishmálaca. If it were real I'd ask you to take me there. But it's not. It's too beautiful to be real. So why not tell me the truth?"

"Because I want to keep you as a friend."

"And telling me the truth about where you come from would make me not want to be your friend?" She was incredulous, wariness raising the pitch of her voice almost a full octave. What was it that he was so afraid to tell?

His answer was abrupt, telling all, surprising her even though she had expected to hear something like it, if not the specific place it turned out to be.

"Nuthouses have that effect on people sometimes," he said, looking directly at her. Then, to clarify even further: "The State Hospital."

"Escaped?"

He nodded sagely. "But not dangerous," he assured her, holding his arms out to his sides as if to be frisked for weapons. "Call it 'creative exiting,' if that sounds better. But then there was really nothing creative about it at all. It was all so easy."

He paused, she waited; neither of them gave an inch. *Does he want me to prod?* she wondered, resting a hand gently on his arm. This seemed to be the trigger.

"Not dangerous," he said again from someplace far away. Then, his eyes met hers and he looked at her calmly, feebly as his voice said, "You want to hear about it?"

Of course she did. As she would later write, "My response to him was swift, an unpremeditated yes."

Smiling happily that his confession hadn't chased her away as he had feared, he began telling her about the taxi cab ride with Vardis to the hospital, his signing of the admission papers in a haze of confusion and half realized resignation to the fact of what he was doing, and where he was going to be for an indeterminate amount of time.

Chapter 15

Jacob returned from his foraging foray with a full sack, the haul this time truly prodigious. It was getting late, he told them. He had been gone the better part of the day. When they finally found a suitable place to camp for the night, then he would break out the goodies.

In the distance was another wood or a continuation of the one from which they had just emerged that morning. It seemed that the forest was a perpetual thing in this territory, with chunks of it cut and burned out to create arable farmland. Old pioneer land, Jake said. All the little farms of a hundred and more years ago finally grown together to make one huge, sprawling valley of cultivation which they should come to in a few more days of hiking, at the very most.

"That way," he told them, pointing in the direction from which he had just returned and from where he had garnered their refurbishment store of goods. "Behind the gas station-grocery store is some of the most beautiful timberland you'll ever see. I even saw a deer. A doe, I think. Gone in a flash, mooning me with that white flap of her tail. I didn't see any antlers, so it must have been a doe."

"Or a young buck," said Gordon in a happy mood, not meaning to sound arbitrarily discouraging.

"Possible," added the older man thoughtfully. "I didn't see any balls, though."

"Then it was just a deer," was Thanny's sprightly reply. She giggled and then, coughing herself to a more somber mood, asked Jake if he thought they could make the wood by dark.

"Don't know. All we can do is to give it our best." He looked around him, stretching his sight as far across the plowed and seeded field and cow cropped pasture as his slowly lessening vision would allow. The two of them were inside a ring, he realized, and he pointed this out to his companions. Forest is best gauged in square miles than in acres. Farmland only here and there in sizable slabs like the one at whose periphery they were. Irrigation sprayers hissed and clanked over new shoots of corn to their left, alfalfa to their right with a tractor path between the two, Father on was a well-used pasture for a small herd of cattle and then weed choked meadows and a hamlet or two. The gas station Jake had just returned from was, on its own, one of these hamlets, a combinations service/filling station, luncheonette, grocery store, bus stop and Post Office, as well as the home for the middle aged couple and their family that ran the whole affair, which had the rather unlikely name of Taragon. In the majority, however, in the maximum, the utter supremacy of land area around here was virtually untouched, unspoiled, primeval forest.

Jacob stopped his banter, realizing he was talking a bit too excitedly. "Perhaps," he concluded more calmly. "I will re-evaluate my opinion of land management in this area. After all, a couple of logged out clearings are a small price to pay for so much beauty to be allowed to remain."

"Yeah," Gordon, devilishly agreed. "And some of those clearings are almost big enough to build towns in."

Jake didn't get Gordon's sarcastic tone and so answered his young friend's comment with one of his own. "Of the size that we had passed through several days ago?" he said, making sure he understood Gordon's reference. "Yes, I suppose they would be able to accommodate at least a small settlement."

"It'd be nice to try."

Jacob laughed, a short bark. "Oh? And what would you call it? Taragon-Two?"

"Mishmálaca," said Thanny without a moment's hesitation. Jake blinked at the automatic reply, as if she had the word in mind and only had been waiting for the right moment to spring it on them. He looked at Gordon and realized the young man was in on this little presentation as well. He looked back at Thanny and then at Gordon, then back again, swinging his head in rhythm to his practiced stride as he paced two steps north, then two steps south with his young friends occupying the east and west points of this impromptu compass. *Smiles again? What have I missed, being away for so many hours?*

"Sounds like a lake in Wisconsin," he said, not knowing what he was getting into and well aware of his ignorance. "Is there really such a place?"

His answer was a snigger from Thanny and a yawning evasion from Gordon.

"Where is it? I mean, if it really is a place."

"Don't know,'" Gordon said. "I've only heard about it. Beauty in abundance there, like you said." He looked around him, aping Jacob's broad observation of their wide open surroundings. "Who knows?" he finally said in a voice that was ready to break into laughter, but he held his composure as he raised his eyebrows in mock alertness, drawing another snicker from Thanny. "We may be right in the middle of it right now."

"Aw, c'mon, guys," Jacob pleaded teasingly. In fact their evasive playfulness was wearing thin and becoming a bit irritating. "What is this Mishma-whatsis?"

"Mishmálaca."

"Yes, yes," he snapped suddenly, a rasp of exasperation at the edge of his voice. "So what is it?"

"Nothing, really."

"It's sort of...well, a private thing, Jake," Thanny said, breaking the spell. "You know, between Gordy and me. You understand, don't you?"

"Oh," he said softly. Disappointment, a small wave of annoyance coursing through him but that was nothing. "Sure, no big deal. Why'n't you say so in the first place?"

Private jokes, verbal intimacies, sharing, whatever, he told himself. *It was all theirs and theirs alone. Nobody would breach that particular wall of theirs, least of Jake Rine. Considerations, decisions,* he thought, coming to where he wanted to be, inside his own head. It had been building in him these last few days, a nervous disquiet, a rutting discontent, a place that did not particularly please him – the air was rather stale in there, the sound of the blood in the veins and arteries very disquietingly percussive – but a place with which he not unfamiliar, one which he had inhabited many times before. He had taken the shortest route to get there this time, though. Things usually took a lot longer for things to get brewed enough to get him to this far a point in the journey. Decision time already; the mind had come to it too quickly, but there was no going back once that pass had been crossed.

But now: implementation, the hardest part. I'll do it, his head said. And he knew that he would as he always had in the past once the choice was made, or was made for him. It was no longer pending, but a certainty needing only the time to make it right.

To make the break a mutually amicable one.

Chapter 16 – Separate Ways

It was the second lean-to that they had built since the three of them were together and was just as well constructed as the first. This time, however, the rain had been no mere drizzle but a series of torrential downpours, one following momentarily by the next, each one lasting from ten to forty minutes in duration. The single amusing leak that had dribbled Thanny's hair to the visage of a drowned Afghan hound on that first afternoon, and which had them all giggling like children, this time had done the same to them all--and worse --throughout the course of the night.

The following morning, as the sleeping bag and blankets hung heavily from the makeshift clothesline strung between the low branches of two gnarly oaks – the rope for the line being one of Jacob's "acquisitions" of the day before--the three travelers wearily broke camp.

"Lousy night," Thanny bitched, aiming an accusatory glare at the now clear, morning sky.

"Lousy lean-to, too," Jake commented dryly. "We really could have done a better job of it, kids. We had plenty of time to get a lot more covering for the shelter and get it done right before it started to rain."

"We? Hey, Jake, don't go handing Thanny and me all the blame here."

Thanny and Jake both stopped what they were doing at the reproachful tone of Gordon's voice. They watched as he kicked peevishly at the ring of stones that, but for the night sky's recurrent expulsions of its overflow from the clouds, would have contained the ashes of a fire from last night's meal and comfort. His foot plowed through the unlit pyramid of soggy kindling, sending it toppling over the rocky bounds of the unused fire pit. Cold green beans, tuna fish, ham salad and cling peaches, all canned, were the contents of the previous evening's meal, which had been filling, at least, but certainly not appetizing. The morning meal of fruit salad and server handfuls of dry cereal wasn't any better. There wasn't even coffee to help them wake up from the previous night's fitful dozing.

"You just sat there on your butt and gave orders," he said to the trees before turning quickly on his heels in an exquisitely executed about-face that stood him directly in the line of sight of the accused. "You could have been a lot better help, you know."

"Supervision is an art," was Jake's lame reply. *Unappreciative, snotty, insubordinate,* he thought, haughtily compiling a list in his head of the negative attributes of his campmates, feeding fuel to his resolve, not that he really needed any at this point. It was all just a gesture, what they were engaged in, just a game. *Can't even build a decent lean-to,* he rattled on mentally. *Listen: even my shoes are completely soggy, squishing like bare feet in river muck. I'll probably come down with a case of double pneumonia because of these damned kids. Aagh! What am I going to do with them?*

The answer to that, of course, had already been decided.

"Example's an art, too, Jake," Gordon told the older man crossly as he wrung a few pints of rainwater from Thanny's brother's double bed sleeping bag. "If you see that we're doing something wrong, then show us. Don't just... just sit there like a...." He couldn't find a suitable descriptive word in his limited vocabulary, so he said no more, just went on to do what he saw as necessary to get the little troop moving on.

"Leave the bag alone and let it dry by itself," Jake instructed after a while. "Wringing it out like that will only bunch up the down at one end. Then it'll be useless when the nights really get cold."

"It's not a down bag," Thanny said. "It's fiberfill."

"Oh," Jake said. "All right then."

Doesn't take much to shut me up, Sister. I hear you, loud and clear. Brassy dame for one so young, that one. I shouldn't have been so nice and taken her along. The kid and me would have gotten along just fine without her. Now, they shine to each other – I predicted it, didn't I? –

And then they set on me like wolves on a hobbling lamb. What did I do? Try to teach them something about camping and living out in the wild and this is the thanks I get. They think they know so damned much? Then let 'em have it. I sure as hell don't need this shit.

"How are the blankets doing?"

Gordon gave each one a cursory feel and proclaimed all three of them to be dry.

"Take them down then and pack' em away in my goody bag. We'll squeeze what water we can out of that fiber stuff and let it dry out the rest of the way on the trail. Should be good enough for sleeping by tonight, I should think."

"Yassuh, Massuh, Suh!" Gordon growled, rolling his eyes, causing Thanny to look at his angry little performance with an aghast sort of wonder. "Aye-nuh-thin' yo' say, Boss-man."

When they were ready to go Gordon hoisted Thanny's pack onto his shoulders minus the duffel bag which was secured to her back with clothesline rope. The trudged the hundred yards of widely spaced trees to the road and stopped there for a moment on the muddy shoulder. They picked their direction, the one which they had been following the day before, where the road showed a shallow though definite upward grade, and they set off at a slow but steady pace.

Prior to the last night's abortive camping, the road they had been traveling – macadam at its center with asphalt gravel on the rain softened shoulders – had skirted the low foothills of the mountains that, past the farmland and forestry as far as the eye could see, were a bumpy, misty mirage over the clouded horizon. Now the road veered westerly across the rolling entry to the range. It was not large in the sense of the Alps or the Himalayas or the Rockies but to the unaccustomed body of the wind-sucking neophyte to hiking, the vista gifts that would be acquired at its peaks would be had at a rather large and unexpected physical price.

The highlands that they saw before them, however, were only the hillocky rise to the east of the main range which would, at their present rate of hiking speed, take them several days to traverse before the truly steep part of the trail into the range of square topped mountains would be reached.

"Who could have seen what was to come?" Thanny asked later in her thought-journal as if she had a handy answer. "We would have had to have been able to read Jake's mind to know that he planned to leave us stranded out there in the middle of the woods. He did it with all the kindness he could muster, make it seem that the idea was all our own. It was so well orchestrated, down to almost the minutest of detail that it's hard to recall how it all started – how he had started it. So smoothly done that it wasn't until much later that Gordy and I were able to piece together enough of the facts to realize that it wasn't something that just happened, that was decided on the spur of the moment, but had been Jake's plan all along that it should come about in the way that it did, at that ugly little fork in the road."

Where the road that they were on widened as it approached the split, Gordon said that it reminded him of pictures he had seen of the devil's two-pronged pitchfork. Thanny gave a one ha laugh at the description; Jake made a noise in his throat but said nothing.

The road spanned out to twice its usual width for about fifty yards before it split unevenly, the left route wider than the right. The sign there angled only to the left, showing that to be the main road which would take them to Corliss, Sunup, Blazer, Honeysuckle (with the thickest print of all the names on the sign) and Taragon. It was apparently a roundabout route through some of the smaller hill and mountain communities in the county. The road forking off to the right was an unpaved logging trail, double rutted by the wide treaded tires of trucks and off-road vehicles that would lead them to more isolated territory, straight to and through the mountains beyond.

Thanny and Gordon, for their mutual part, preferred the more mundane, easier camping in the lowlands. Jake opted loudly and adamantly for the right-hand fork. They argued for close to half an hour. It came down to camping right there, one of them said, until their differences could be resolved... or just part company then and there, and go their separate ways.

"I'm an honest man, children," Jacob said, drawing smiles and stifled laughs. "And so I will not lie, especially not to such good friends as you two. I know these woods like a beaver, and I tell you that this is the way for me. That road may be the way for you, granted, but I tell you now that this is the way I will go. There are vistas up this way – and I know it for sure, even though I haven't been on this trail before – vistas and overlooks and panoramas to take your breath away and give it back to you fresh and exhilarating. Colors of the rainbow in every budding green thing, seen from an eagle's view, hawk sight, angel's lair, God's sight up there, I tell you. The road will be steep, and I expect we will have to stop many times along the way. Not so much for me – I'm an old hand at this sort of thing – but for you it'll be leg cramps, aching lungs and backs, fatigue to make you think you're dying and maybe some little bit of well-earned fear. But I'll be with you, stay with you all the way to see that we do it all right. Take the road to Flyspeck and Cowflop and Pansypot if you really want to, but you'll go that way thinking of me as old Jaky-boy Rine on the trail that we were too chickenshit to try. And that's all I'm asking of you – try and see if I haven't been telling you the God's honest truth."

He was both playfully inviting and almost threateningly cautionary as he sketched out the high and low points to be had along his chosen route. Even as he spoke, Jacob silently hoped that he was not elaborating too well on the beauty of the landscape and the overviews that might make them want to continue their partnership in travel with him. This was the decision he had made the day before. An effectuation of freedom, he would have called it, if he had had those particular words at hand. Other young people with him to share his camps, conversations, bed and ease could be easily found, he knew. Thanny or Gordon alone would each have made excellent choices for campmates but taken together they had become insufferable. This is what his mind and heart told him and had been the basis of his decision, rash as it may have seemed, even to him.

He emptied his sack of about half of the merchandise he had acquired on his foraging trip into Tarragon. He would never go back there again, he had sworn to himself--another reason not to take a road that circled back in that general direction. The present circumstance of the parting of the three was one reason he had come away from there with so much. His planning, short term by someone else's measure, was far reaching and nearly prophetic in his way of thinking. Oversupply yourself, dump half of it all and still have enough to take you through a good four or five days, maybe a whole week if you ration yourself meagerly enough on meals. It was shaky logic, certainly, but it suited his personality, one which thrived on incongruous associations. The present one with these two young hiders from themselves, these two runners from reality, though, was not working and hence, had to be brought to a smoothly anticlimactic end. He would later be proud of himself for the slick and seamless way in which he had managed it.

They traded things – spam for spaghetti (canned with sauce and bite-size meatballs), artichoke hearts for mixed vegetables, peas for pumpkin pie filling – but all of what Jake dumped on the ground was all for them, he told them after he had picked through the foodstuffs and essentials.

He also left a softly rumpled, pillowlike cloth flour sack among the cans and boxes, the contents of which he quietly designate as "a gift."

He hugged each of them for long time. He thumped Gordon on the back, kissed Thanny on the curtain of her tawny hair that covered the side of her face and, whispering a private word of farewell to each of his young friends in turn, he slung his gunny sack over his shoulder like some seedy looking Santa. He took his leave of them down the right hand road with a jaunty little dance to start him off and then to sing a quick time rendition of "Skip-To-My-Lou" in time to his tarantella inspired gait that would have been beyond the stamina of someone many years younger than himself.

Chapter 17

In several ways, Thanielle and Gordon felt that they had been lied to. They rambled through all that they had gotten from Jacob Rine throughout the relationships that had grown among the three of them over the past couple of weeks—theanimated conversation with the man, how he had led them to believe that the three of them would remain together through thick and thin like Musketeers, Stooges, and the Fates for the rest of their days. Nothing specific along those lines was actually said, but the unspoken direction their talks had taken made them both assume that that was what was being inferred. They wrangled on the steady uphill of their route about how he must have seen their break-up as a certainty, that they would have had to part company sooner or later. There was nothing in either of their recollections of the man to hint at the fact that, from their first meeting in their drippy afternoon shelter, the parting that they had just come away from only hours earlier had been meticulously planned by their now absent friend.

After an hour of walking, the recognition of the second lie, one which they had been unconsciously telling themselves, dawned on them simultaneously. The signpost at the fork in the road had showed their chosen way as being that which would take them circuitously back to the bosom of civilization or, at least, to its rural outskirts. Back to the valleys, the farmland, the flat plains sprawling with the homey business of small-town life and activity. Humanity-- they would no longer be alone. But this road, they found, just like the loggers' trail that Jake had taken, led through deepening forest and inclined ever upward with only short respites in glades and dales cut into the foothill slopes by the occasional unnamed barren wash or trickling brook. They talked of Sunup and Corliss as if each place would be a bustlingly active township; Blazer a village built around the industry of a mill or a factory; Honeysuckle a miniature city thriving on the income derived from the camper-hiker-hunter-fishermen trade or else an artist colony with craft shops, galleries, book stores and markets in which to spend their time, energy and meager economic resources. The idea that each of these little settlements would be a mirror image of Jake's description of the Mom and Pop lunch-wagon, rest-stop of Taragon, a miniscule waystation of civility in the midst of the wild only occurred to them sometime later.

They had been lied to by a friend, by a road sign, and by their own willingness to accept the possibility that the choice they had unadvisedly made might have been the wrong one, that the only real certainties that they had at hand were themselves. Singular, lonely, self-contained and self-absorbed, both of them. Also, of course, they had each other.

Thanielle's frequent pee stops began to rankle a bit on Gordy but he tolerated the assumed fact of her incontinence with a shrugging prudence. She needed a nature break twice in one hour after she had only stopped once for a drink at one of the many little streams and brooks that they had crossed, either jumping from stone to stone or wetting their sneakered feet. Who could figure it?

What does he think? She wondered as she leaned against the mottled bark of a felled oak out of sight of her companion who was waiting with their gear by the trailside. *Two days and my bladder gives out so I can't hold my water, that's all it took? What does he know but what I've told him? Like I can't think when I have no one like him to talk to, that old vagabond who runs away from us like I ran away from home, but him all loveless and blind to another's feelings? It happens in threes, I've heard, but with me the threes spread out over months, not all easy one, two, three in the same day like most people get it. Who will it be next to walk out, catch me with my pants down, my guard broken by sweet talk and confidence who I can tell my soul to only to have him say, "That's all, Toots, it was nice but I'm leaving now?" Will it be you, Gordy, so quiet and shy and flighty that I'll have to make a full turn-around adjustment to see you as you want to be seen? No, I won't let you get that important to me. You can walk away today or tomorrow or any other day, for all I care. I won't cry like this for you. One, two, three – maybe. But you won't be the third. I'll either hate you or ignore you or call you my buddy but there will be no love held between us. Make that a promise from me, then. I can wait long and patiently for number three to come along, that third walker to take his insensitive way away from me. But he won't be you that does it, Gordy. It damn well better not be you.*

She dried her eyes as best she could on her shirt sleeve, wiped at the dampness between her legs with a handy oak leaf, then blew her nose like a ditch worker, thumb closing off one nostril and sending a stream of snot flying to the ground from the other without having to wipe her face afterward. *One, two,* she thought as she cleared her nasal passages like that, one at a time. *One, two and coming up on the long path to number three.* She saw him sitting on the ground waiting for her, using her pack and duffel piled behind him for back support. *Languid, easy as sitting in front of the TV set in the living room at home,* she thought. His smile showed a touch of a frown, a shadow of concern.

"You okay?"

"Fine," she said. "That one should be the last of it for a while."

He got up and slapped the dust from his pants, lifted the pack back onto his shoulders, and cinched the waist strap tightly around his slim hips. He helped Thanny with the duffel, securing the ropes tautly about her waist, over her shoulders and under her arms. They lifted their legs high to clear the top of the rutted ditch that lined that side of the ill-kept trail and, back on course, they climbed to the next rise. They hoped to come to a flat plain rather than the continuing uphill struggle that had been the mainstay of their panting, gasping hike for the major part of the morning. They were quickly disappointed, however, with the top of the hill proving to be only a brief width of shelf in the hilly ridge.

On and on, Thanny thought gloomily. *It will just go on and on with no end, just heaving and hiking up and up and up. No rest....* Her breath came in gulps and wheezes, sighing and whining with alternating breaths as she looked around her in something near to panic. Exhaustion, disappointment, uncertainty, fear. Her eyes began to fill with water and blur her vision. Green became diffused to yellow and slate blue, the blue of the sky blanched to a steely grey. This was a new worry, this insecurity, this panicky unsureness, these color hallucinations. It all must be closely tied to that other, that anger at being abandoned, betrayed, left her own devices. And she found that she had pitifully few of her own "devices" which she could rely on.

Gordon's arms were strong, hampered as they were by the broad padded weight of the shoulder straps of her pack. He hugged her tightly, whispered his there-theres, saying that he was there with her, no need to worry; they would get through all this together. Mishmálaca would be their goal and it would be just them, the two of them all the way until they found it.

She squeezed him hard, whined and whimpered as her eyes rose to meet the darkened sight, past his close cropped head, his pink, translucent earlobes, of the abstract view of the aluminum tubes of the pack frame on his back like the stanchions of some cantilevered bridge, crisscrossing over the thickness of pale green beyond his broad left shoulder. She studied the thongs that supported the pillow of the dolled and still mildly damp sleeping bag behind his head.

"But there is no such place," she complained, squeaking in a voice that reminded her of a cartoon mouse she had seen on television when she had been sick with some long ago childhood disease.

"It's only a matter of where you look for it," he said. His hand rubbed her back under the duffel bag with short, gentle strokes, a hypnotic rhythm up and down her spine. "Only a matter of wo you're with when you look. Not even a matter finding it at all, really."

She heard the promise in his words, the tone of need and commitment there. She pulled back to look find the pupils camouflaged at the center of his dark brown eyes. "You and me, 'til we find it?" she tested.

"Even if we don't," he promised. "You and me."

Her breathing evened out. Here was the security she needed, she thought. The promise is real, not imagined or supposed. He had said it.

"So, which way?"

"The same," he said, pointing the steep way ahead. "You sure you're all right?"

"Better now," she assured. Then she kissed him on his boyish cheek. She liked his smile, that face. *No, I'll never forget that face*, she thought happily and kissed him again, this time quickly on his closed and wryly smiling mouth. They started out as she meandered through the back trails of her mind and took his hand.

So, she thought, that's how solemn promises to yourself are broken. One after the other, his for mine, mine for his. A trade, somehow – nothing was said about it; it was just done – and it makes me a bit richer, that trade, as if it was me that got the better part of the deal.

She smiled and squeezed his hand. He squeezed back as they started up the next steep section of the trail. *Yes,* she thought, *so much richer than before.*

Chapter 18

They no longer had Jake's pocket watch to guide them through the hours, to tell them "when" they were – much less "where" they were, of which they hadn't the faintest clue – but the terrain was high and open enough for Gordon to employ his Boy Scout trick of using his hand held at arm's length and positioned so that his index finger was underlining the sun. Each finger would equal fifteen minutes, all four fingers would then be an hour's worth of time. The real trick was to count the number of hands down to what he had to assume was the Western horizon concealed behind the stand of trees. Calculating quickly, he confidently announced that the time was approximately one o'clock. Confident in his visual calculations as he was, this pronouncement was still rather heavy on the "approximately," for he wasn't positive of the hour of sundown. He had made a guess for it at six o'clock which, he told Thanny, would be dinnertime at the ward.

Neither of them were really hungry, but being that it was midday or thereabouts and the clearing in which they had stopped was on level ground, the sky bright and the air pleasantly warm and without wind, they decided to stop for lunch. They dug out the edibles from both duffel and backpack but nothing there appealed save for Jake's final offering of good will. Thanny kneaded and shook the flour sack like a child on Christmas morning, trying to decipher the contents of a present before giving way to jubilant curiosity and shredding the colorful paper with unabashed joy.

"Soft on this side," she said, squeezing z corner of the bag. "And over here, it's...." A quizzical expression developed on her face. "It's kind of hard. A box, maybe?" Gordon punched a starter hole in a can of tomato purée that he had chosen from the dumped items and worked the can open without cutting himself on the ragged edge of the lid that the gouge-type can opener had produced. The tomatoes sagged on the fork and dripped a watery, plasmatic fluid on the dry dust of the open hillside as he gobbled up several meaty lumps from the can. He offered a forkful to Thanny but she refused, saying that she would wait until they camped later in the afternoon before she would eat. Gordon finished the contents of the can, then drank the last of the fluid from the dangerously serrated open edge and belched resoundingly.

"Want to go then?" he asked as he stuffed the drippy empty can back into the backpack.

"I'd rather sit for a while, "she said.

"All right," he grumped as if in pain as he got to his feet. "Then I'll go."

"What?!" Her voice jumped in time to her stiffly rising to her feet. "But I thought...."

So soon? So soon? I at least had a month and a half wait between Gerald and Jake, my one and two leavers out of three but two happening in one day.... So soon? Tell me no, tell me not to worry, tell me that you will be back and commend your life, your soul, you balls and dick into my hands in the event that you don't return. But please don't do this, please....

He could see the anxious way that she moved as she rose from her lotus posed seat on the dusty ground, lurching toward him as if to strike a blow. Their bodies met with a jarring force that nearly bowled him over. He stuttered an open promise to come back, safe and whole, for he knew that she needed to hear that. He pried her hugging arms from around his neck, wondering what had brought that on. Had they become so close so quickly and he was too dim witted to see? He kissed her hands, touching his tongue to a knuckle as he did so. He tasted vanilla from her skin mixed with the astringent, salty sting of dried sweat.

"I just want to see what's up ahead," he explained. Then, after a pause, he added hesitantly, "I just like to be alone sometimes, to think."

Gordon began his walk, the first one he had been alone since his first meeting with Jacob Rine. He looked upon his time in the hospital and on the road with Vardis as being ostensibly lonely, introverted times, even when he was with Vardis. What had been shared between them but fantasies and daydreams that had been the focus of much of his life anyway? But striking out on this new journey, he had stroked Thanny's back affectionately and said words of reassurance and endearment that he wasn't sure that he truly meant... but then, he thought, deep down he surely must. *Words don't come from an empty chasm. There has to be some basis, even a lie,* and he knew for a fact that he wasn't a liar.

So I must be willing to come back, he told himself as he walked away, turned on his heels as he went to give her a little wave, something like the one he had gotten from

Vardis before his friend had taken flight over the meadow grass and bovine leavings like brown islands in a pea green sea. *But then I knew that he was really leaving, never to come back. She wants me to be with her to continue this journey like I was sure I wanted Vard to go along my way with me, but he had his own ideas that I couldn't fathom just like she doesn't know me from Adam's ass. I never got a chance to know Vardis all too well either, but that was because he ran off too fast for anything to really be said between us. Unrealnesses, black-outs, believing you're a snake, a bear, a hawk or a goat. What does that tell me? Where does all that come from? Shrug your shoulders, boy, 'cause you'll never be able to figure that one out. Just take as something that just is, that's all.*

Dead and gone, past and recalled, mulled over and wondered about. Come back, Vardis. There's so much more I wanted to ask you, to tell you. But no, no longer. Scream at the wind and it'll steal your breath and mind away and give back nothing. Chances taken and run away with; that was what he did. Stole our chances – thief in the night while my eyes were closed. Got clean away with the goods and the bads: himself, his life, his voice, his ideas, his unrealnesses, himself.

So now I got a new one and look at me. Look into her scared pretty face and I melt, want to run away myself. Hey, I came into this with nothing and I can go out just the same and I won't have missed a thing.

Nothing but what I might have or even could have had.

And I want to know what might have been if I do run. Scared, unsure, lost in myself, the old Hider. That's what I've been and now she's found me. The question is, do I hide again or stand up and face her? Talk to her? Listen? That's the key, G.T. Listen and you might find what you want, what you need, through another person's voice. Who are you" What do you need? Why do you stare? Why is that boulder off in the woods there like a king's castle with a phalanx of guards ringed around it for the coming attack? I sit here and stare for hours if I weren't just passing through, searching for a better place to lay down a mat for sitting and staring. I would sit and watch the coming troops, the massed squads and divisions and platoons in neat medieval rows through all of these trees, every archer a man of great stealth and skill, every lance man at ready with his deadly spear honed to a sharp glinting point. Shields bearing the crest of the red dragon holding the black sword of victory. Purple plumed helmets and hammered iron breast plates. Ready for the charge on Rock Castle. The tramp of marching feet in these woods suddenly halt, leaving a palpable silence hanging on the air. Then, after a nerve-wracking pause, the sudden and thrilling ta-RA! of the ram's horn and the arrows commence to fly from the bows of archers hidden in the treetops. Castle guards fall at their battlement posts as the phalanx of the king's trusty retinue move haltingly forward to meet the charging, battle screaming lance men. The drawbridge rattles and thunders on it ratcheting hinges. The counterweight used to hoist the castle gate hits the ground of the castle's inside courtyard with a crash that opens the portal that will spew forth the rumble of cavalry hooves across the ancient bridge timbers to meet the challenge.

What challenge? Lance men and archers of some regent's army vying for the castle keep, the crown and its attendant lands? No. To waste the time of the conjurer who has better things to do with his thoughts and imagination than to envision mythic battle scenes out of the textures and shadows of a rock that he passes by in the woods.

Come back to it, man. The thought was there a moment ago, real as breath and spit and piss and walking on warm sands in August. Come back to it, yes. That's right. There is something to be missed – her name is Thanielle Petár – and she stands with me as the choice, my choice, whether I will or will not let it slip by. She, now, is my choice. Goodbye now, Vardis. That was your voice speaking, not mine. I would have chosen otherwise but you found another way to go without saying how or why. I hated that, that lack of caring, absence of reason, just to say it's there. But where? I don't know but you saw it then and then the next think I knew, you were gone. Your choice not mine. Goodbye, then, Vard. Adios, amigo. 'cause now I think of Jake and his choice of that road less taken – another goodbye. And I could do that, just keep walking, away, away, away…. But I won't. I can't. Call me foolish or call me brave or headstrong or willful or just naïve. This is me and I want to know more than just stormy skies that fly in the face like dust in a stiff breeze. Real, yes. I want to know myself outside of my head, in another person's eyes, in the words of a friend who is real and knows herself to be genuine, not the product of hours and days lost in the netherworlds of foggy, wondering daydreams.

So, that's it, then?

Yes, I guess that it is. At least it seems so, doesn't it? It's all been said. The decision is final and clear. Good.

"Now," he muttered, turning his head left then right, pirouetting slowly to see in every direction there was. "Now," he said again to the trees, the air, himself. "Where the hell am I?"

Chapter 19 - Presents

"Thanny? You asleep?"

Gordon had returned, having been gone for only a little more than an hour on his solitary walk, to find Thanielle stretched out on her stomach on the open sleeping bag. She had changed into shorts and was topless. She had fallen asleep lulled and comforted by the sound of the breezes brushing the feather hairs on the nape of her neck and the warmth of the sun's rays on her bare back and legs. Her shirt lay just beyond the reach of her cradling arms near the zipper toothed edge of the splayed open bag.

Gordon nudged her shoulder, wondering what name to call, maybe to whisper to her that would rouse her from her nap. "Baby?" he tried; there was no response. Something different was needed. He raised his voice slightly and made a bolder attempt. "Honey, you better get up if you don't want to get a sunburn."

His voice had been low and at its softest register, but it gotten better results – which he could not have known – than if he had shouted at the top of his lungs. She lifted her head wearily from her crossed arms and tilted a sideways, slit-eyed, scrutinizing face at him that seemed to show something of disgust in it. But that impression was probably drawn from the narrow, single-eyed way in which she stared at him, the sun searing her eyes as she squinted, giving her the demeanor of scorn and derision. She lifted her upper torso while craning her neck even further around for a better look at Gordon, who was now behind her and a little to her left, before she said rather bitterly, "Don't ever call me that again."

"Honey?"

"Baby." She said the word distastefully, letting it slide out of her mouth like a ball of rancid fat. "I'm not your baby, so don't call me that."

He surveyed her thoughtfully, not knowing what more to say, quite cognizant of how sorely remiss he was in the ways of decorum in situations of this sort. Apologize? Assent? What was expected? He did not know, only continued to stand a little while longer, caught like a child who has done something wrong out of ignorance, has been faced with the error of his ways with sudden chastisement and does not know how to respond.

Thanielle broke his cautious mood by flinging an arm in the direction of her shirt, only to find that she had tossed it well out of her reach. She sweetly asked Gordon for his assistance. Gordon circled around her, slowed when the angle of his approach brought into his line of sight a glimpse of Thanielle's bare breast. *A navel orange*, he thought lewdly, determining the size from what little he could see. The nipple was hidden behind the heel of her left hand, but even so he was completely mesmerized. His feet locked into the dusty soil for a moment as the nipple peered out from behind the hand like a child's widely staring eye. He was awed at the pert roundness of the whole, the sleek, soft way that it lay on the fuzzy lining of the open bag like a diminutive, sleeping baby. It lay back down again with Thanielle's exhaled breath, hiding its mottled cordovan eye in the dent in the fabric it had caused, becoming once again just a soft ball of flesh, an intimate part of a friend's body, a friend who had lately looked at him with warm affection.

"Gordon?" Her voice came as an intrusion, a reminder that she was still there. He said that he was sorry, that he had felt a little dizzy there for a moment but not to worry, he was all right now. He handed her her shirt and retreated to a safe distance where he turned his back on her until she called to tell him she was decent.
Then he came forward, all anxious and excited as if he had only just arrived, all embarrassment and chagrin forgotten as he began to tell her what he had found. In mid-sentence, however, he stopped and became coy.

"No," he said. "I think I'd rather just show you."

"Show me what?" she asked suspiciously. He seems so sweet and nice. Don't tell me I've gotten myself hooked up with some strange wilderness flasher.

"It's a place along the trail. It's like a gift from the gods." He saw the change on her face and said, "I know that sounds kind of weird but you'll understand what I mean when you see it. C'mon, please. Let's go."

"Is it far?"

"Maybe a half hour to get there at the most. It's great, really. You just won't believe it when you see it. We'll have a roof over our heads tonight. It's even got a...." He put a finger to his lips, shushing himself. "C'mon. Let's pack up and go. Please."

They re-rolled the sleeping bag and strapped it to the pack, reloaded the little that was left lying around – canned goods, the jeans which Thanny had changed out of earlier in the day, Jacob's flour sacked gift to them – and, trussing themselves up in their gear once more, the hike continued.

The fact that their destination was a secret which Gordon scrupulously kept, despite her joking pleas for him to tell her what to expect, all acted on Thanny's nerves in such a way that, by the time they were on the final stretch before the surprise, the forty minutes which they had been hiking seemed to her to have taken hours to pass. Her sense of perception was at such an electric peak that, when they finally reached the spot in the road at which Gordon meant them to be, her only reply was a disheartened "This?" It may have had the ring of disappointment about it, that single, almost sneering word, but behind it were bunched all the positive emotions of delight, wonder, awe and gratitude.

It was an old-style lunch wagon, having been carted by truck or car or whatever conveyance was used when this type of diner was in vogue and set down on its concrete slab foundation. The awning which shielded the front and its row of small windows and now boarded entrance had long since been torn away, lost in the shrubbery along the road or perhaps a rotted until it was now a part of the soil or else had been sold to the highest bidder for whatever value striped canvas may have had at the time. But its support pipes were still there, growing out of the front of the place like solid tentacles held up by rusting pipes of the same diameter and tenacious quality from below, anchored into the ground as if rooted there. The windows were largely unharmed, only three of them having been covered in plywood and carved with the initials and dates. "J.M. and M.T. 1972" stood out on the one like a ragged gash. The rest of them, reaching around the sides, numbering fifteen in all – nine in the front, three on each short side – were opaque with soot and dust and grime but twelve of them were still whole.

A sign above the small, decrepit establishment – actually a small billboard supported by a trellis of gangly two-by-fours – bore the abbreviated legend, "___ ___ ___ LISS DINE___." And below this, in smaller print, though just as bold, "HAPPY TO SERVE YOU."

"Corliss?" Thanny extrapolated. "The first town?"

"Maybe," said Gordon. "Maybe it was something like the gas station that Jake went to in Taragon. Only this one couldn't make a go of it, apparently."

Gordon took her hand and led her around to the back of the boxy little building, pointing out the windows, the water tank on the roof amid the timbers of the sign supports like some formless insect caught in a web, the large, sturdy, shanty-like addition to the main part of the building. Inside, he told her, were the living quarters, a bathroom, a bed, even a shower stall but the water tank was empty and, besides, the water heater was an old propane thing that he didn't want to monkey around with, but the thing that most appealed to him was....

He shooshed himself again, said nothing more as he led her the twenty yards beyond the old diner through the trees to the bank of a prettily burbling, rippling brook. No more jarred water for them, he said, as long as they were there. Slaked thirst, clean bodies, shelter, a bed, warmth, even a wood burning old Franklin stove for cooking; the place was ideal. True, the old refrigerator, long out of equitable service, stank when you opened it from the few pieces of rancid and rotten meat and fish that had been left there, but that seemed to be the only real drawback. And he drew back, again leading her by the hand – a liberty which she didn't to mind his taking – to the rear entrance to the place that opened directly onto the living quarters.

If seen from above, the entire structure formed a lopsided pentagon with the diner itself serving as the bottom line. The attached outhouse to which Gordon had referred as the "bathroom," jutted from one of the oddly slanting walls like a square carbuncle. A chimney poking out of the ground nearby was the vent to allow the gases generated by the breakdown of human refuse in the septic tank to escape, thereby minimizing the peril of the immediate area forming an immense fireball and setting several acres of surrounding forest ablaze. From the outside, the living quarters were but a shack attached to the more professionally designed and constructed diner, a well-built hovel meant for temporary habitation.

Once inside, however, Thanny was assailed and charmed by the homey interior. A fire showed its florid face in the grating of the old Franklin stove next to the protruding box of the shower stall. Strange that she hadn't noticed the smoke from the roof chimney, she thought. The wallpaper had yellowed with age to a deep ecru, highlighting its friendly pattern of vertically arranged orange carnations. The lines where the strips of paper met were a little uneven at points, giving the room a rather uneven effect if one gazed too long, but that, for Thanny, only added to the charm of the place.

On the wall nearest to the door to the diner was a poster which proclaimed the faith of the former owners. "PLANEPATORIANS: KNOW THY CREED" it yelled in huge red letters across the top. Below this, in a much smaller. but in a font size still easily readable from ten or more yards away, the poster also declared "OSVALDO PLANEPATORA HAS BROUGHT THE TRUTH TO THE WORLD. Smaller still were paragraphs that dealt with Osvaldo Planepatora preaching to large, raptly attentive crowds, as well as the rest of the poster's text dealing with the "truth" that had been brought to the world and to all Planepatorians by the prophet and soothsayer from Uruguay. No Christian, Jew, Hindu, Moslem, Buddhist or Atheist, it said, would be able to accept this marvelous man's teachings, so revolutionary were they.

The main point, from which all others sprung, was simply that the Messiah has already come to Earth many times. It is not in the nature of things that one Messiah should take on the sins of the world, as the Christians believed, but one was needed – and did come – approximately every hundred years or so. Each century had its own Messiah, expunging the sins of the world since the last coming, doing so by the grace of his – or her – violent and untimely death.

The twentieth century had already seen but would not recognize its savior. People cried and mourned and gnashed their teeth at his crucifixion (of sorts), affected by a bullet through the brain, removing a portion of the skull as it passed through, splattering blood and infinitesimal bits of brain and vein matter over the interior of his armor plated staff car as it passed through the open section of downtown Dallas, Texas. They saw – the entire world was the horrified witness to the event – but they would not see, as Osvaldo Planepatora had seen, that this man's death was an act of global purification. It happened on November 22nd in the year 1963, and the man's name was John Fitzgerald Kennedy, the Messiah for the twentieth century.

Thanielle laughed and hung onto Gordon for support as her knees gave way. She rose back to her full height still hugging tightly, and read more of the teachings of the Uruguayan teacher. Her arm vised about his waist was causing Gordon some confusion again as to the propriety in such a case, but he remained still and stalwart until she had finished the last part of the tract, tittering her way through the small print.

"All Messiahs in the past have met their end in the prime of their lives," said the poster in its final inches of text. "Have died violently and publicly, either by design on the part of the authorities or by those unscrupulous persons bent on the elimination of that man or woman for his or her power, personality, teachings or charismatic hold over the populace. In the future all assassinations, executions and bizarre, fatal accidents involving religious leaders and/or heads of state should be thoroughly investigated so that we may be able to recognize the next man or woman who shall be the one to die for our evil, animal ways.

"Remember: God is infinite, eternal and omnipotent. God did not have only ONE son but MANY. Let us applaud and revere them all as is their just and deserving due."

Thanielle had to lie down to compose herself, to stop laughing. She had even laughed at the photograph in the middle of the surrounding print of the poster – the dapper, balding, square shouldered man with an imperious mien and a Hitler moustache, standing in front of his palatial Montevideo villa overlooking the Rio de la Plata.

Such a display seemed rather disrespectful to Gordon. After all, the man was only someone with courage enough to expound his theories and convictions and if he gathered a few disciples to his "truth" along the way, was that any cause for laughter? Gordon didn't think so, though he did admit the picture portrayed Planepatora as a rather pompous looking bird but, he reasoned, the last man to wear his lip hair in that fashion, bunched in a two finger width expanse under the septum, also looked a bit too proud of his own worth and he certainly proved himself to be of no laughing matter whatsoever.

Of this man's stated "truths," though, Gordon could give no creditable criticism for, in truth, he simply did not know. What could he say but that they sounded false? In the universe, where man's understanding took in so little and swore so much, perhaps this odd sounding prophesy – if that was truly what it was – might be the truth or a part of it, but who could reasonably say? Philosophy, in Gordon's opinion, was a lot of unfounded guesswork anyway.

By the time he had all of this figured out and was pretty sure that he could verbalize his thoughts, Thanny had stopped laughing was off of the linenless bed and digging in the pockets of her backpack.

"I feel sleazy," she said as she pulled out her trusty bar of brown soap. She continued to paw through pocket after pocket, looking for something else until she could find it. "Grubby, grimy, yucky," she muttered as she dug. "Two days, right? And nothing but hiking and sleeping in our clothes and feeling like something's crawling in your crotch and armpits, like you're wearing something even when you're naked.... Ah! Here they are!"

Sandals were what she had been looking for. She shed her socks and sneakers and curled her toes under the straps. She was going to take advantage of the stream for a body bath – no dunking but for the rinse. She would leave the preparation for the evening meal to Gordon, if he didn't mind. Or, she said, at least for him to replenish wood for the dying fire in the belly of the stove so that they could have something hot for supper. Cold beans and canned fruit for another night, she said, and she would just vomit. He said that he would do his best, told her to come back fresh as a daisy to a toasty, warm, heaven scented den of culinary relish.

"Just hold the mayo," Thanny teased, snapping the beach towel she had hastily drawn from the bottom compartment of the stuffed pack, causing the balance affair to topple on its aluminum legs against the wall. "Heavy on the ketchup."

"We don't have any ketchup," he called after her, but the door had already slammed shut.

"Now," he said to himself. And that was the last word he spoke for quite a while. He was on a mission that would stymy even King Arthur's Knights for its skill and audacity: a quest for the palatable meal. Out of this bed of mediocrity? The list of possible ingredients for the meal included canned pork and beans, tomatoes, beef stew, corned beef hash, creamed corn, string beans, lima beans, spinach, several cans of a variety of fruits as well as boxed and wrapped packages of macaroni and cheese, mini boxes of corn flakes (both frosted and plain), soup, greens, and a bag of pretzel rods which had become nearly pulverized in their close quarter trip with so many canned goods surrounding it in Thanny's duffel bag. No wonder the corners of the canvas backpack and the seams of the duffel were beginning to fray and tear. He looked at all of the cans lined up on the floor before him like a regiment of limbless robots. Gross tonnage, he thought, laughing at the absurdity of the exaggeration. It was a lot, though. Too much to lug around, especially seeing that hiking was supposed to include the art of packing efficiently, travelling as lightly as possible-- living the Spartan life.

With a roof over their heads, he reasoned happily, and with the larder so well stocked, they could afford at least one good belly blasting meal. He didn't have to convince himself any further. He had already picked over the cans, choosing the stew, macaroni and cheese and a selection of vegetables, and carried the whole gathered lot of it, seven cans and one flimsy box in all, into the diner to be laid out and opened. There were enough pots, pans, plates and glasses from the cabinets above and below the counter to help make the meal seem festive if not truly toothsome when completed. He sighed over the unworkability of the old commercial-use grill and griddle behind the counter; dead, he found, for the simple reason of the absence of the kerosene fuel on which the old relics needed in order to operate. He located seven large canisters of the stuff but none with enough juice to cause a flicker along the fire jets under the grease caked grill. To allay his slight disappointment in this (what had he expected in a diner so long abandoned to the wild?) he busied himself emptying cans into pots, mixing corn and string beans with the gluteus broth of the stew, crumbling in the pretzel crumbs for their salt content as well as for added body, mixing cherries and crushed pineapple together in a bowl for an improvised fruit salad, dumping spinach and lima beans into a separate, shallow draft pot and setting the two dishes to be stirred and heated on the hot plates that lined the shelf behind the small pot-bellied stove like miniature manhole covers.

Preliminaries done, he went back to the storage cabinets to rattle around for anything he might have missed that would add something more to the meal. In a high, concealed cupboard he found answers for which he had not been searching: a half-full quart bottle of blackberry brandy. The cork was sugar-coated, the neck smelling piercingly of alcohol. The label, purpled with dribbled hooch, said fifty proof, but with time, he reasoned, it surely had had a chance to ferment to sixty or better. At least that was the nose wrinkling impression given with just one quick whiff. He placed the bottle on the table by the window which he had chosen for the meal, found silverware as well as candles and candlesticks in the busboy's cabinet near the boarded over front door. He carefully set the table with forks and spoons on the left, knives on the right, a roll of dust covered paper towels in the middle of the table in an old holder he had found in a cabinet somewhere to be used as napkins. He set the towel holder – ceramic in the shape of a bread loaf – in the center of the little table, sandwiched between wine bottle and one of the tall candlesticks.

Now, all that was needed was heat to cook the food. The one he had set in the stove before he readied himself to go to the clearing to collect Thanny served this purpose, had warmed both the living quarters and the diner, and made the place feel like home. But now, since he hadn't known how to bank a fire properly, the one in the old pot belly round gut was now only ashes and charcoal. He dug the sooty remains out of the belly of the bulbous beast with a rusty shovel he had found, and then went outside for more firewood. An axe would have been a Godsend but miracles were in short supply after his big find of the day. Wits at a sharp edge, he was busy searching for a reasonable alternative, when his attention to the task was totally deterred by the one unforeseen element of the day:

Thanielle.

She was perhaps twenty yards away, squatting with her bare back and buttocks to him, looking to be the size of a foot-high doll at this distance and perspective on the high bank. She stood then, and he could see the shadowy division between the buttocks like a smudge of dark finger-paint on a seamless white ball, the manner in which the thighs flowed in a curved line from each of the round cheeks dribbling brownish grime laden suds into the sluggishly flowing water of the little stream. Then, in an instant, she jumped and there was a splash but she was out of the water in a flash, shivering as she bent forward for her towel. He momentarily glimpsed the breast he had spied before which had peeked at him from behind her concealing arm and its sheening twin sister, though the one which he had silently called "friend" was the slightly larger of the two. That much he could tell, even from such a size reducing perspective at which he had been standing. But no more, for she had seen him, standing there motionless with his feet growing roots into the dry earth. Sher ducked behind a leafless, budding bush and hurriedly dressed, then rushed at him as if from ambush cover, barefoot and livid.

"What the fuck are you anyway?!" she came screaming at him. She barreled into him at full tilt, wet hair flying, whipping his face at her sudden, heel digging halt. "Get your jollies spying on women taking their baths?"

He couldn't speak, rendered defenseless by a sudden rush of fright, guilt, gratitude and a festering confusion all rushing over him in a single, jumbled wave. She looked at his baby face and felt pity swallowing her anger at the sight of that simple-minded, frozen stare of bewilderment. She wanted to pet his hair, tell him to never mind, but she was determined to maintain her truculent stance if only to teach him a lesson. So, she yelled at him like a drill sergeant, called him a peeping-Tom-pervert-creep, poked him, shoved him, slapped at him to provoke a response, but only succeeded in working herself up into a new rage, though this one without any real focus to it. She made him silently cry with her cursing, her taunts and accusations that he was a dangerous freak who wasn't fit to be with people, that he should be locked away and the key deliberately lost so be wouldn't be a danger to others anymore. He sniveled, sobbed, apologized with the choked explanation that he had only been curious.

"Curious?!" she screamed, cutting him off. "You ogle me like some goddam creepo rapist just 'cause your curious?! What did you think I looked like naked anyway? A horse?"

"I didn't know," he sniffed, the tears now flowing freely. "I've never...."

For some reason this set her all over again. *He never! Oh, no, don't tell me, she thought angrily. Don't tell me.... A virgin, that's what I've got here. A pansy-assed, no-never virgin boy. God! Of all the luck. Curious like a dog in heat, I'll bet. Well, we can fix that, can't we? Here, honeychild. Here's your curiosity for you. Take yourself a look. A good, long look.*

He stared like the victim of a mesmerist as she unbuttoned her shirt, undid her jeans and dropped her panties and held open her shirt for that good look. "Boobs, bush and buns," she said, pounding the ground with her bare feet as she pranced about in an awkward little circular dance step, hampered as she was by the waist of her pants and panties bunched up at her knees so that he could get a decent round robin view of all sides.

She redressed quickly, an inconsistent twinge of shame showing on her face. If all the emotions she was feeling at that moment could have been expressed with one look, the curve of the lips, one slant of the eyes, she wouldn't have been able to later untangle her facial muscles for a long time thereafter. So, she settled for crossness, a slow boil, the look of a cat cornered and ready to spit.

"Now," she hissed, seething calmly, her voice an abrasive growl. "You show me yours."

As she said it, she was almost immediately sorry for it. He had heard her quite sharply and clearly. With a swift about face he was off and away from her at a dead run.

Chapter 20

He had run for maybe fifteen minutes before finding the tree, a thick trunked oak, and he slumped against its rough bark. Time telescoped and fattened, spread itself thin until he didn't know, didn't care how long he had been sitting there. His back ached, his buttocks had numbed against the ground, his mind waddled along on its own little wave of conjecture and defeat.

Gone, he thought morosely. *Everything down the tubes. Should never have made that pact, left hand to right hand, the voice inside, that pact with the world as if it really meant anything at all. It was just foolish, that's all. Compatriot, soul-mate...pah! I'm the only one, the only one to talk to. What's that called? A solipsism? Something like that. Anyhow it's just me to me that's important. Who else? Look at Thanny. She rants and screams, gets all out of whack just for my being a normal guy and just looking, never understanding the fact that I've never before seen such supple sleek smoothness of female skin over hips and butt, breasts and whatever's hiding under the matted hair there just above and into her groin area. Her face doesn't smile but screws tight into a mask like horror-anger-rage, woe-is-my-life for the likes of Gordy T. She becomes blind and resentful, pity-proud and prudish like a hooker on Sunday like I hear tell from Charlie Calderone's serial stories in those smutty anthology mags about women who do it all the time but hate themselves for it. So what if I made a mistake? Just tell me and I won't do it again. I'll change. Concede to my ignorance, to a fellow who's maybe a little dim at times, slow on the uptake now and then. Turn rocks to water in your heart and drink hearty, me lassy. Just be kind enough to offer me a sip.*

And what the hell does that all mean? Maybe I'll figure it all out if I think about it hard enough. Of course it's also a good possibility that I won't.

But back to it, I say that I'm the only one; I know what to do, what to say, to answer even before the sight is seen, the question asked and the idea right there out in the open. I know me and that's all there is to it. Teaching another person about me and all that I am, and I'm about is really too much to ask. And the learning about another is a new challenge for me that, right now, I sure can do without. Only me and that's enough. So just let me be, let me dream, fantasize, sit here and dream those silly, fantastical, irrelevant things – frogs that talk to me and explain Einstein's relatives to me in a croaky

voice; men in black armor stalking the gates of Nuremburg Castle and me the keeper of
the gate watching the oncoming, incoming hoard stealthily slithering into siege position;
taking a piss and falling into the toilet flushing myself into a world where alligators run
the sewage-usage plant turning shit into granola bars and mermaids run their tendril
fingers through my hair. Let it all remain with me, in me, of me, mine and mine alone. In
peace.

The ground under his ass shuddered beside him, the tree at his back shook with the new weight, a hand on his arm, warm breath in his ear. "Gordy?" He started, a deafness breaking in his ears, in his mind. That deafness had suddenly been there as soon as he had sat down beside the tree with its bark rasping lightly at his back, that deafness shouted into his head there and plugged over the drums by his thoughts; his sight obliterating, ear stuffing daydream world of *wonder why, wonder how, wonder if and when and where and who.*

"I'm not going to show you mine," he said as he came back to that fear of what had been ceaselessly demanded of him. "You can't have that."

"That was just my anger talking," she said, the hard edge on her voice lost, the lines on her face now even, soft and gentle again. "You made me feel cheap and humiliated and I hate that, hated you for making me feel that. If you make me feel that way again, I guess I'll hate you again, even knowing that you don't mean to do it. It's just the way with me. One thing leads to another. Some things I don't want to do – or to feel – but they come on me and I just explode." She squeezed his arm with her right hand and with her left took his face and turned it toward her, forcing him to stop looking away like frightened child, to really look at her. "Forgive me?"

It was more a plea than a question. He nodded and said yes, that he forgave her for her anger and hatred. He deserved all that, though not so much of it all at once. But for her feeling that she had of being cheap – that was beyond his forgiveness. She wasn't cheapened by his mistake. Didn't she realize how lovely her body looked to him, how beautiful she was in his eyes? She looked into his eyes and saw that place where he saw her, that place from which he had felt that deep yearning, that passionate appraisal. She gazed long and deep, and she blushed. *Yes, she saw.* There is nothing cheap in beauty, he said, physical or any otherwise you might name. That was all that his eyes had made of her: something fresh and desirable, not dirty. Those thoughts, the lewd, lascivious, the salaciously outlandish ones, took a practice at which he had not had very much experience.

Forgiveness with a shrug – why not? It would help preserve something for which he had been hoping almost from the first day Jake had brought the two of them together. And friendship needed a bit of hardship to help strengthen it, he told her. But that was only an axiom he had heard somewhere and had never really tried. But it sounded good in theory, and maybe it worked.

"It needs more than just hardship to help it along," she said. "You don't really understand, do you?"

"So tell me," he said with an arm that had snaked itself around her so he could pull her closer to him so that their legs touched, thighs fused together into one, combined, denim blue, elephantine sized muscular bulge.

The tree branches shook and creaked above them, squirrels chattered and squealed, cavorted and made their rat-like sounds in the boughs, dropped fluttery, pastel green poly-noses gathered from nearby maples onto their hands and laps and bombed them with the spherical elm tree seed units that his grade school friends and he had called "itchy balls." One of them landed sharply on his knee, causing a reflexive jerk. Thanny giggled and pressed closer to him, feeling more comfortable with him now that the worst was over, apologies out of the way and accepted.

Gordon sneezed, causing a dribble of mucus to exit his left nostril. *Hay fever season*, he thought, following what seemed to be a logical deduction. He recalled having the choking feeling in the throat, the annoying omnipresent tickle in the sinuses, the watery eyes, the runny nose, the gagging feeling that precipitated a bout of sneezing. Would something like that make a dent in her understanding of his past imprudence, maybe bring back her anger, the hurt, maybe more belligerent denials of the good times they had spent, the confidences they had shared? He shook the thought away, shivering as he rose to his feet.

He listened to Thanny's humiliating tale about Willie, her little brother, and his lack of respect, the dirty minded, snotty-cruel attitude of someone who got it all and expected more all the time. He gave her all the privacy of an animal in a zoo. That kid learned how to silently jimmy the lock on the bathroom door so that he could barge right in whenever he pleased. He had become so proficient that he barely made a click when he opened the door, catching her with her pants down – literally, she told him. While you were peeing, she said, using the second person indicative form, distancing herself from the reality of those times that her memories brought back to her. Or taking a crap, she went on, or brushing your teeth, putting on your make-up for a date or even taking a shower. He'd whip back the curtain like the *Psycho* knifer and flash would go the Polaroid. Blind and naked as a newly hatched chick and just as helpless, there you were. Once he even brought along a friend. Quiet as mice, the two of them. Not a snigger or snort out of either one, just two faces peering at her bare behind under the sluicing spray, waiting for her to turn around and give them the full frontal view before running away, screaming obscenities as inventive and dirty as any sailor. They were twelve then, she seventeen.

She mentioned other things, further indignities, instances of his playful barbarity. Peepholes bored into the walls of her bedroom, various voyeurisms through the window with and without the assistance of collaborating friends to hold the ladder steady as they waited their turns. Rumors came to her attention that copies of some of those bedroom and bathroom snaps had made the rounds in Willie's school and had been sold for a tidy profit.

They walked quickly up the embankment of the stream and through the woods, propelled by her voice, her myriad of tales of invasions of privacy and affronts to her dignity and peace of mind. He understood, didn't he? It was as if it were happening all over again as she told him. When she found him watching her as she got out of the little river and was drying herself, it was Willie again, back with a new face – a kind and friendly face this time – but up to his same old tricks. Couldn't blame her flying off the handle with a reason like that, now, could he?

"Of course not," he said as they stopped to sniff the air.

"What's that smell?" she asked. "Supper?"

"We're getting close," he said. "I hope the stew didn't burn on in the pot."

"Burn? But where did you get the wood?"

"Behind the house, a whole stack covered with a tarpaulin. You must have missed it, you were so busy bitching me out."

The diner/house loomed before them, all odd angles and comfortingly cumbersome looking, white smoke puffing from the pipe-chimney on the roof, its conical hat askew. A warm, invisible glow of radiant heat spread from its bare outer walls in pleasant waves. At the door, by the light of candles he had set throughout the diner and living sections, he could see that she was blushing a sedate rose color up from her chest to her chin and the roundness of her smiling cheeks.

"What?" he said, reading her silence.

"Well," she muttered. "Did you really think that I was...? You know... attractive? That my body was... Is...?"

He smiled brightly as he held the door for her. "Beautiful? Is that the word you're going for? Oh yes, let me count the ways," he said, quoting someone, knowing that he sounded as aw-shucks tongue-tied as any fawning schoolboy with an immense crush on the sweet faced, cuddly girl in the desk next him.

But he didn't care.

Chapter 21

After the meal they let the pots and dishes sit in the tepid sink water to soak. They walked, hand in hand, to the living quarters, still trading chatty flirtations that were readily said and then dropped just as easily. The ease in which they went from one subject to the next with such easy fluidity was a wonder to Gordon. *Where is all this coming from?* he asked himself. *Was it the drink or the physical attraction between them or maybe the fact that a real bond, a real friendship was in the process of being forged?* They each only had one glass of wine, both of them finding it to be too strong and bitter to either of their likings so it couldn't be that. He decided to adopt a wait and see attitude in hopes that, whatever was the reason behind this wonderful *something* that was growing between him and Thanny, that it would continue to flourish and keep on going until it became whatever it was in the process of becoming.

As they walked through the diner and into the living quarters, they blew out the candles that Gordon had lit as a romantic touch to their meal. They laughed at the fact that no matter how lovely the ambiance the candles created, they also were a great fire hazard that had to be quelled right away. When all the candles were out and each raising a thin tendril of smoke there was only one that they left burning, the one on the nightstand next to their bed that was so oversized that it took up more than half of the space of the bedroom. Thanny begged off for just a moment to use the john. Would he be a sweetie and set up the bed? He saw her to the outhouse (inhouse?) door noting that she carried something with her but he wasn't able to see what it was. Clothing of some sort. He drew a belated, uneasy chuckle from her with his promise not to drill any holes in the wood or take any incriminating pictures of her on the crapper.

While she was indisposed – the word occurred to him as a curious euphemism – he unstrapped the sleeping bag from the pack frame and unrolled it onto the bare, stained mattress. The springs creaked and chattered under his weight as he spread the roll out neatly and zipped it wide open. He took her oversized and still slightly damp beach towel, rolled it tautly into a long, soft cylinder and laid it down the center of the spread open bedding to give each of them his and her own designated sleeping space. She will appreciate this, he thought, having calculated the relationship to be about where he saw it to be and where neither of them would be intimidated by it. At least he hoped that she was of a similar mind in what they meant to each other; platonic, friends, non-sexual. That was how he saw it and told himself he wanted it to be.

She emerged from the little toilet shed as he was emptying out Jacob's sacked gift to them so he could use the sack as a pillowcase. He dumped the baled clothing on the floor in a daze at what Thanny was wearing – panties and a t-shirt and nothing more. Her small breasts were enticingly revealed under the thin lay of cotton fabric, each looking like something to be picked off a tree.

"This is how I sleep," she said and pulled the rolled-up towel off of the bed. She lie down on the splayed open sleeping bag and zipped it along the bottom and halfway up the side thus covering herself from the waist down. "What's all that?" she wanted to know.

The clothes on the floor, the first half of Jake's flour sack present, tied together with twine, bore a scrawled note: "For the man with only the clothes on his back, wear these in good health. Love, Jake." Gordon cut the string with a serrated steak knife he got from the diner and catalogued the contents of the bundle aloud: "Three pairs of socks, three pairs of tighty-whitey underpants, a brand new starch-stiff pare of blue denims, a white t-shirt and a lumberjack plaid work shirt."

Then, there was the shoebox, sealed closed with cellophane tape and labelled "Possible Necessities" in the same scratchy scrawl as the note attached to the bale of clothes. The box contained a band aid box first aid kit, a roll of toilet paper, nail clippers, a snake bite kit, aspirins, a jar of petroleum jelly, injector type razor blades with holder and an aerosol can of shaving cream emblazoned with a black marker penned question mark, lip balm, antacid tablets, calamine lotion, a box of a dozen condoms and his trusty old gravity knife.

"Probably stole a new one for himself," Gordon reasoned bleakly, throwing the knife back into the box. Thanny picked through the items one by one and thought of Jake in a warm, new and pleasant light. He didn't forget, he cared, was thoughtful, she said.

"But what kind of thoughts?" he asked, holding up the box of prophylactics.

"About human nature," she said, watching him take off his lived-in clothes. It was the first time he had bared any portion of himself to her. He was slim, long and lanky, the muscles of his stomach radiating lightly out from the center vertical line of navel-to-sternum under the taut, white skin. His legs the color of beach sand looked healthy enough but not too strong and were peppered with a mild rash of acne along the backs of his thighs. Nice, she thought as she studied him. Not the best I've seen, but nice.

The room was warm but kind of chilly. He got under the cover quickly and zipped himself in. The candle was beginning to gutter behind him as its wick burned into the last of the bees' wax of its long ago making. Gordon rolled onto his side to face Thanny.

With his body blocking the direct light of the candle one side of her face was thrown into deep shadow, the other into bright relief. He was surprised when she unzipped her side of the bag and, propping herself up on one elbow, began to stroke his hairless chest, feel the ripple of his ribs, roll the muscles under the thin layer of fat there before retracing the line she had drawn back up past his chest to rub the meager bristle on his chin.

Platonic, he thought as his breath began to come in labored huffs. *Friend, confidante, non-sexual, hugging and hand holding....* She said that she was sorry for the nasty way she had done her little exhibitionist strip earlier, the angry demand she had made to him. She wanted to make it all up to him. She wanted....

Want, ran her thoughts as she sat up. *Desire.* She ran the flat of her palm over his chest down to the elastic band of his boxer briefs under the warm cover. *Want.* She leaned over and kissed him lightly once, twice, then with the third she thought, *I have you* and with that third kiss he opened his mouth just slightly but enough for her tongue to slip between his lips and teeth and find his tongue. *Acceptance.* This virgin man knew instinctively what it was all about and so he didn't have to be taught. Not much.

Experimentation. Their tongues wrestled excitedly; they breathed hotly into each other's mouths and so shared one of the fundaments of life in their serious playfulness.

She sat up and removed her t-shirt in one, cross armed, sweeping motion that spread her shoulder length hair high and then rained it back down from its apex to pepper the shadows around her with freckles of light like sunbeams broken by the spidery branches of budding trees. She took his hand and pressed it to her left breast, told him to feel it, to press and knead it, to pinch the nipple until it felt hard to the touch, to kiss her there and run his tongue over the pink, hardened point and she felt the heat of his mouth, the pressure of his sliding tongue on the raised mammilla when she told him how best to use it and felt the little electric twinges shoot back from the nipple and rise to touch her face with a gentle and invigorating heat. She lay her torso at an angle across his and they kissed again.

Platonic, prattled his mind, but he wasn't listening.

Two weeks ago, she thought, and a night like this with any man would surely have reminded her of Gerald and have started her crying. But she knew that this man was not Gerald, that this was a man whose touch was gentle but unsure. His hands on her made hypnotic, reassuring patterns, broadened their reach gingerly to the soft firmness of her buttocks, kneaded there and explored with kneading hands and fingers probing deep into the fissure before going back to massaging her spine. He had to be shown what, how and where, and he was eager to learn. Gerald had been so sure of everything in his sexual ministrations, she mused, and yet he really knew so little.

She lay on her back, changing positions with him so that he hovered over her, playing inquisitive games with his hand sliding from breast to abdomen and back to her left breast, then right while kissing her hungrily. She guided his hand to her groin to burrow in the woven mat of hair over what she wanted him to find. She was curious as to what his fingers would do when they slid along the crest of the slickness that edged her labia. She could feel the tremor in his fingers. She coached him as she lay back and told him softly what she needed, of her preferences, called his name from deep in her throat so that it sounded as if it were coming from a long distance away in the forest as his fingers found the spot in which she loved to touch herself, felt the finger's insistence at the spot as if it knew that there was something immediate here that needed more and it continued its curious probing until it slid inches below and slipped into the vaginal opening. She felt him roll the clitoris under his thumb, rub the slippery lips of the labia, said "Sweet, sweet Darling" as she began to climb the steep wall that would bring her over the edge, a way that was tortuously long and wonderful. She groaned his name three times, her voice catching on the hard G with that fourth sing-song of the litany of his name over the harmony as a lone finger continued to busy itself there, yes there, there, Sweet Lover, while that tongue, that gorgeous tongue softly abraded her left nipple, giving her the dual pleasure, running tickling ripples up and down her skin, raising goosebumps on her arms, running with a deep heat radiating out, growing, spreading a fan of flame and blossoming explosions in her groin, sending incendiary flashes through her chest and head where the world spun and spun and with a lurching flash of a destruction of what felt like cosmic proportions, made the whole of her personal world, her universe, become stock solid still.

She pushed him gently away when it was so sadly finished in her, told him to unzip the bag and reached down for his mouth with hers as she pushed back the cover, listened to the bedsprings creek and complain with her movements as her hand breached the band of his shorts, found him hard and ready, slim and rigid as she stripped him bare, and stretching and reaching for the strewn items of Jacob Rine's gift to them, she found what she wanted. She came back to Gordon and kissed the head of his erect penis and rolled the condom into place. She removed the sticky-damp panties and threw her leg across his hips. As she squatted and straddled him, reached down to position his member – she called it his member – at the opening of her vagina, she told him to prepare to lose his precious virginity. The only time that it had really been precious to him, he reflected later on as she soundly slept, was when he was just about to lose it, just a moment before he felt his "member" slide deeply inside her. Afterwards, he felt gratitude for what she had done for him, what she had given to him that night...but that small bit of thanks was lost in the flurry of the many things he felt for her in the coming moments, minutes, and past the time for counting out what and how much and why. Cuddling up behind her, he was soon lost in slumber as his chest lay against her back, his groin into the curve of her buttocks, his knees hooked behind the angle of her own as they achieved the fetal spooning position favored by lovers, newlyweds and twinborn infants.

Chapter 22 – Interludes

Thanielle awoke during the night twice, both times feeling the pleasant warmth and pressure of Gordon's slender body nestling against her spine. His knees locked loosely in behind her own, his breath buzzed faintly at her neck, his left arm draped over her side under the fleecy lining of the bag, he slept serenely and soundly. She disengaged herself from him the first time and got up to use the "indoor toilet," as she and Gordon jokingly referred to the indoor outhouse. On her way back to bed, she stopped for an unsuccessful attempt at restoking the dead fire in the stove but only managed to effectuate the merest flicker of red among the soot and lumps before the whole black mélange of ash and crumbles went back to its dark sleep. She had to practically climb over Gordon to hustle herself back under the cover of the sleeping bag to get back to her previous position with her bare back pressed to Gordon as she pulled his arm over her like a protective shield. She went quickly into a warmth induced stupor which floated her back into a deep, dreaming sleep.

There were animals there, chattering and chuckling in her ear, telling her that there was a man for her, didn't she know? Tall as a telephone pole, he was and just as thick in proportion. Hand to hand to suckling breast, mouth and tongue to her drooling twat with that thing of his there that throbbing thing between your weakened thighs pounding away where the fingers had found those tenderly responsive spots there that makes your body sing; he's the best at that and you know it, girlie, you damn well know it. The animals talked dirty, using words that she would not normally use to describe those areas and parts of the body which derived the most intense of pleasures. She nodded her assent, though, admitted her understanding and agreement with the wise duck and chipmunk voices of the varmints.

When she turned her head, owl-like, a full ninety degrees to her right, there was the angel of her mind, flapping its white wings and smiling sweetly with Thanny's own face. Then, a 180-degree swivel of the head to the other shoulder and there was her devil, all sunburn crimson with an arrow-headed tail, pointy horns on its head and a self-confident sneer on its handsome face. The devil leered and winked at her; the angel smiled serenely and fluttered its snow-white gown. Facing forward, she saw the both of them as if looking into a mirror, one on either shoulder but between them, where her head and neck should have been, there was only a pale blue void. The two little people of the best and worst places that stood on her shoulders, each having what she considered to be her own face – her personal property, that face – shrugged their respectively white and red shoulders, cocked their heads inquisitively to one side and nobody said anything. The voices that she had heard from the animals had been her own – and then they disappeared, giving her back her face and head with its clear skin and high forehead, the broad jawline and frowning mouth, the aquiline, ball tipped nose and the deep set eyes and thick brows.

She awoke that second time feeling a burning in her groin, a horniness that seldom occurred for her in her sleep. She hadn't recalled ever having a "wet" dream before, but this time she awoke feeling a decided dampness, a sensuous fluidity lubricating the inner portions of her upper thighs. And Gordon was there, pressed to her, knee to back of knee, hip to hip, his mouth to the nape of her neck, like a part of her. She inched backwards on her side, pressing her back and haunches more firmly into his front. She raised her left, topmost leg and cocked her knee back over him and rested her calf on his thigh. She huffed slightly as she reached down between her legs, cooling her back in the cold air of the unheated bedroom as she pulled away from him for just a moment, and found his flaccid penis. She began stroking the head of it with her thumb, wondering at the unique sensation of having it slowly growing in her hand.

Gordon woke with a startled grunt. By the time he was aware enough of the situation to work out the proprieties to be observed here, she had already pulled the damp crotch of her panties aside and placed his hardened member at the well lubricated, hair hidden opening. She nudged herself back onto him with a momentary twinge and with a wiggle and a manual shove she had him inside of her. She pressed persistently on him, feeling him sliding easily in and away, in and away, to and from the deep and shallow her. At her fifth push backward and as she was pulling away with a low rolling, exquisitely sensuous rumble rippling through her as she rocked away and back, away and back while masturbating herself to near climax, Gordon draped his arm over her and reached down his sleepy hand to help however he could. He licked her ear, whispered something endearing, the sound of which she immediately loved and as quickly forgot.

In the morning, not long past dawn, after Gordon had restored the fire in the stove and went to fetch water for whatever brew they could muster for breakfast – they had no coffee but were hoping to locate some abandoned teabags in one of the diner's many cupboards – Thanny lay dozing, half dreaming, then alternatively wondering and dissecting the reasons for last night's two heady instances of love making.

The one she knew, or at least could somewhat account for. The reasons were several and obscurely connected, but they were known, to a degree: to learn him, to teach him, to know him physically, to break the stranglehold that Gerald had had on her needs and libido all these past months, to make a commitment, to fall in love. These were the pragmatic, concrete reasons which she had outlined to herself. (Fall in love? Pragmatic? At least she thought so).

There were others that were less distinct, almost like poorly recalled memories of the odors best loved in childhood, ones of which she was, for the most part, totally unaware. But they were there too, of that she was certain. But how to explain that midnight snack of sudden lust and the sheer necessity for it, for him, so specifically? That vaguely recalled dream couldn't have had much to do with it; that was too weird and disconnected from anything to have been the cause. It was as if a fever had suddenly swept over her, the knowledge of the cure a sure thing in her mind. Not so much frantic as it was an ache that had to be rubbed to be gotten rid of. Nothing like that had ever happened with her on any of the sleepless, torrid nights with Gerald.

Puzzled and alert, she lay there, letting her mind wander, her vision to form bursting color patterns on the insides of her eyelids, her ears to take in the mutter and burble of the water of the sluggishly racing little river outside. *Bubbling*, she said to herself, hearing voices there. *Now I know what they mean by "babbling brook."* It whispered and gargled, tittered and blubbered, spoke to her without meaning, without words, though it said things now and again, nothing wholly intelligible, only a word or a syllable here and there. It said *whuppah* which brought a smile to her face, sad *cood* which made her wrinkle her nose and brow in concentration for the next sound which was *foosh*, quickly followed by a clearly enunciated suck that evinced a whoop of delight right out of her like a belch after a quickly chug-a-lugged can of soda pop. She couldn't tell if the next one or the one that came right on its heels were actually the voice of the stream of her own imagination playing tricks on her, using the faraway sighs and chattering of the rushing water as meat for the associations she was making, but she did not wait to find out. *Shlush* reminded her of the greenish bruises she still carried on her hip from the beating she had taken at her father's hands, and she threw off the cover, laying naked with an uncomprehending look on her face. Laying that way, just as she had when her father had come into her Haven, brandishing his anger and his rage. *Tarap* rang in her ears as the sound the strap made when it came into burning contact with her bare and vulnerable ass... and she was off the creaky bed in an instant, pulling on her panties, jeans and t-shirt, and heading barefoot out the door.

Gordon was sloshing up some kind of muddy colored paste in a bowl that he identified as breakfast. He pointed to two ready prepared glasses of an icy orange drink that he had distilled from several packets of powder. Water was already simmering on the Franklin for hot lemonade – the best that he could do in lieu of any of the more acceptable hot beverages of the morning – and, once his bowl of slushy corned beef hash, powdered eggs and beef stock from last night's meal was beaten to a suitable porridge-like consistency, it wouldn't, by his figuring, take too long to heat up and be ready for consumption. He hoped that she was hungry, he said, because this muck really looked shitty.

She guzzled her orange drink, spat out sandy bits of residue from the bottom of the glass and waited silently, watching Gordon busy himself. She listened to him whistle happily through several variations on a tune that she could not quite place. Her eyes watching with easy affection, she began to talk, to ask questions, elicit responses, felt the air about them quicken with rapport as it was stifled by the steamy heat from the stove. They ate their goopy breakfast, seared their gums and palates on the thin brew among the amiably thrown off jokes and serious commiserations. They both found Gordy's ersatz "porridge" to be much too bland, well in need of seasoning and body.

They washed everything that was in the cauldron sized sink with scalding water left in the pot that they hadn't used for their unsweetened lemonade, using the scummy white soap left by the former owners, and put everything where they thought things should go. They borrowed, did not steal. Where would they pack the dishes, the silverware and half full bottles of hooch in her backpack or duffle anyway?

Breakfast finished and the morning started, they worked out an itinerary for the day with a silent agreement between them that they would stay at least one more night before moving on. The itinerary was a simple one: relax, kick off your shoes – Gordon did, Thanny didn't have to – and take it easy.

They took the towel and the sleeping bag with them out to the sandy bank of the rushing stream. Here the voices were loud, too loud for words or even indistinct syllables to come through. Here it babbled too roughly and insistently for it to be troubling or to sound like words being murmured in secret behind closed doors. Here the voices were a stadium roar, a deluging shout that made no sense. Thanny undressed to the skin, rather surprising herself to find that she felt no shame or embarrassment at being nude in front of this man with whom she had twice made passionate love but who, really, she did not know at all. Giving this thought little credence in her mind, Thanny stretched out, belly down, on the opened sleeping bag and closed her eyes. There was nothing shameful in it. It was a spontaneous thing. She was a little disappointed upon opening her eyes, however, to see Gordon stripped down only to his boxer skivvies and no further. They lay side by side on their stomachs, elbows cocked, palms cradling chins, their elbows touching. They talked of the soft lining of the open bag, of their own and the other's arms, of the eye of the other that could be seen with the slightest tilt of the head.

"Was it awful?" she asked, pursuing the line of query they had begun during their tasteless meal. "I mean, your father had died and your mother was...." She searched for a word that would be sensitive and yet correct. He had described such an unusual person in his mother, though, so that no one word used to define her would seem tactful and true at the same time.

"Nowhere," he said, helping. "She was nowhere. She couldn't say a word without being reminded of my father. She cried all the time, wasn't any good to herself or me or anybody else. There would have been financial things to think about, a job to get, assets to liquidate – Dad didn't leave much in the way of insurance, barely enough to cover the funeral expenses – but no, she was useless; a complete basket case."

"Then came the slew of foster care places while your mother was away," she said, continuing the story as he had told it earlier now that his voice had trailed off to an uncomforting silence. It was a goad, Thanny knew. *Say the right word or phrase and it would all come spilling out.* And she did want to know; to know whether this connection she felt with him was really true and right; whether he was right, the kind of person she would be able to trust and, as she had learned from her own past, how far she would be able to trust him. To know if his promises were real or simply words and, if real, whether she wanted them or not, Mishmálaca come to be or be damned.

He rehashed what he had told her before, using different words, different scenes and points of reference than he had used over breakfast, telling her about the year spent being shunted from nice elderly couple to an orphanage –he had been ten at the time of his father's death – to the crowded home of a family of six children that took in "the needy," to several faceless institutions to the matronly, smothering arms of his father's oldest sister, his Aunt Madge.

He had always been her "onliest li'l boy," even when his father was still alive and they were all together for the family's infrequent outings to her suburban Cape Cod home on the outskirts of a small city just off the Massachusetts mainland. Perhaps it was the same one from which Gordon had taken off four years ago. Her little boy, her little man, her joy and love was Aunt Madge's needful proclamation in telling little Gordy who and what he was to her. He always had been, always would be and was, in her dark and steely, red flecked eyes right up until her death at age seventy-three when Gordon was sixteen. He hadn't cried, had absorbed enough of her enthusiasm for the afterlife to almost feel glad at her passing, much as he missed her.

Six years ago that was, he mused and – *what month was this? May?* – then it was two years and three months ago that he had checked into that hospital on his own recognizance and between leaving his aunt's happy/sad bungalow and entering that happy house of kindred losers, there had been a three year and eight or nine month long pall of odd jobs, hitch hikes, loose knit comraderies, occasional girlfriends and whores, sometimes whole days spent being where his mind saw fit to deposit him: on a mountain peak, conversing with a hermit sage of the ancient clan of the Sun; running naked through the springs that poured forth from the spirt of mankind; standing invisible and intangible among the dragons of their cold, melting past as they lumbered over and through his ghostly body on their inexorable way to their collective, mysterious demise. He had been everywhere and nowhere and all in between. But it was all a fog, that peripatetic time of ranging, rummaging, wandering and just being, a useless time that should have been better spent. The only thing keeping him from doing something more meaningful with his life were the facts of his wondering sense of reality and the fact that he did not know how to change that seemingly evil proclivity in himself.

"What I need," he said, trying to come up with an answer to this quandary, "what I need is...."

He lapsed into silence, letting his voice evaporate as if boiled and steamed while Thanny rose to her knees, crossed a leg over his lower back and sat with a bounce on his buttocks that forced the breath out of him. Her hands worked firmly into the tenseness at his shoulders, felt them relax and flatten as she gave him a substitute for that need which he could not name. She followed the back muscles down the left side to the waist of his shorts then slowly, methodically back up to the shoulders again to work slowly down and up the right side after which she blended the two together as if she were kneading dough. She tickled his ribs maliciously for a few moments to signal the end of her treatment. He asked if he might "do" her, then, to which she replied that he had already given her the best massage of her life last night. She let him have his pleasure at trying, though. His hands were strong. The effect of the warmth of the sun and the sensuous divining of his hands along her back, shoulders, neck, buttocks and legs soon lulled her into a tranquil doze.

She woke once to find the towel laid over her like a blanket to keep the heat of the sun from burning her tender skin and Gordon gone. But she dozed off again, waking the second time to find him sitting by her fully clothed, her notebook thought journal in his lap.

"I didn't read any of it," he promised without any provocation. He held up the spiral bound book as a mugging victim might offer his wallet, both hands held up to the ears. "The Private" label had stopped him from looking any further than the cover but he had been wondering, he said, if she had any blank pages she might let him have.

"Gonna do some writing?" she asked before giving her permission for him to take what he needed from the back of the half -filled book. The pages being ripped out of the book sounded like an exceptionally large and loud zipper being wrenched open.

Writing, he said. Yes, he would be writing, though he wasn't at all sure what it would be. It was still morning, though, close to noon, telling what he could from the sun – or was that west over there? Anyhow, he had to do something to kill the time. Can't just sleep the day away.

She rubbed his thigh with a throbbing grip and worked her hand up to the seam below the fly on his jeans. "I can think of something," she said.

He smiled at her, stroked her head and lay down beside her. Eye to eye for another uncounted set of minutes, her hand on his back, his creeping under the towel to the backs of her thighs, moving up, squeezing the soft flesh gently as it slid up to cup the gluteal curve, all four fingers to breach the cleft until the middle finger lay right on the sphincter and stayed there, ready to obey the order to penetrate. Thanny felt the intrusion and sidled closer to kiss him again.

"Secret?" she said.

"What?"

"You turn me on like no man ever has or could." His response was non-verbal, only an inquisitive furrowing of the brow causing two rippled lines to appear above the bridge of his nose. She kissed him again, letting her tongue slide surreptitiously into his mouth for just a few moments before she pulled back and nipped at his nose. She wondered at the lack of movement of his hand on her rump. "No lie," she said.

He kissed her fervently, then pulled his hand away from its suggestive position and rose to his feet. Now, he said, he knew what he was going to write about. Crouching down to squat beside her, he drew the towel away from her shoulders, peeled it slowly down as he patterned a series of kisses from her left shoulder down her side to the hill of the buttock, across both cheeks and narrow cleft, murmuring *love, love, love you in the afternoon* before leaving her in a snit of wonder and frustrated stimulation as he trotted off back to the diner, flailing the notebook and loose pages like a banner and shield.

Chapter 23

After lunch Thanny was alone, resigned to leave Gordon with his writing whatever it was that he was writing until that time when he called to say that it was finished. He said that he would let her know, rebuffing each nosy query of "Soon?" with a crotchety "I'll let you know," "Almost done?" with "Give it time," in the manner in which Michelangelo told the Pope to buzz off while the Sistine Chapel was undergoing a one man refurbish.

She walked for a while, tracing a portion of their hike back toward the clearing and the fork in the road where they had left Jake but a sudden rainshower, lasting long minutes, chased her back to the diner. The little downpour had drenched the ground enough to preclude any more sunbathing on the riverbank. The hours – uncountable using Gordon's hand to the sun method – pulled themselves along at their own snail pace. She wished that Jake had included a paperback novel in among the bag load of potpourri – anything to pass the time. She looked in on Gordon, busy at his writing, scribbling out, mumbling and cursing through several torn out pages from her notebook – he had already come to her twice for more pages to destroy – as his little exposé or whatever it was that he was spilling from his eyes and hand to the penpoint across the page took the semblance of shape. Then it disappeared under an angrily laid down veneer of scribbled ink beneath which he began anew.

She sighed. Would he never be done?

She lay on the bed feeling itchy, wishing for a book, a magazine, a newspaper, a radio.... Up and at'em, she dug in her pack for the little, aged transistor she had unthinkingly packed, so small that it barely hid in the palm of her hand as she held it. Excitedly, she turned it one. *At last!* she thought as the static buzzed through the tiny speaker. *Diversion!*

"I can't seem to find the right lie," sang the calmly soothing baritone in counterpoint with the tremolo de-de-DA of the alto guitar chord which accompanied.

"I can't seem to find the right lie.

Insanity's horse

Ado-o-orn's the sky.

Can't seem to find the right lie."

She flicked her thumb over the tuning wheel on the side of the little white box causing a jet of broken dialogue, sounds, chords, notes and laughter to flutter through the little speaker. She stopped now and again for news, weather (increasing cloudiness, 30% chance of showers into the night, cool and humid tomorrow), advertisements and a few music stations – Classic Rock on one, Country and Western on another – before turning it off. Nothing appealed. Boredom again. How had she managed a full week alone with no one to talk to before teaming up with Jake and Gordon? Well... not no one, really. But that lady did all the talking, non-stop and then there was the hitch hiking buddy named Jim something or other who offered her a night's stay at his "crash" if she wouldn't mind the fact that their room would only maybe be big enough for just lying down in. She yelled at him in much the same manner in which she had chided Gordon. Scotched her chances there that night for a roof over her head, and glad for the quick-witted decision to leave the presumptuous turd. She slept in some little town park that night, crabbed herself to sleep with ranted expletives against Jim and his colossal nerve, temerity, hubris to think that she would.... And what, then, had made her say yes to Gordon, to eagerly, aggressively demand the same thing of him? She might as well have stripped naked and begged him to fuck her. She could think of several reasons for doing as she had done with him that night together on the bed in the sack, when they had just started out talking, none of which would she have cared to explain, say, to her father.

For a moment she considered marching right into the diner, prance right up behind Gordon where he sat at the counter and use whatever means available to her to wrest his attention away from his writing. In short: seduction. Kiss his neck, lick his ear, stroke his arms and chest, massage his neck under his collar, around and down to his belt buckle and under his pants to his crotch where she would rub and cajole to elicit an immediate and spontaneous response.

None of this was necessary, though, for he was up and coming to her, all bright eyed and bashful at once, holding his scribbled over sheets of ruled paper – she had to check her laughter when she saw it – to his chest like a schoolgirl caught braless by her brother in the bathroom. She shuddered at the analogy as she held her hand out for the finished masterpiece. He refused to hand it over. Not for the content, he said, but for his lousy penmanship. He said that he would rather read it aloud to her if she didn't mind.

She shrugged; it was no matter to her. But was his handwriting really all that bad?

"Like a chicken doing its death dance in the sand," he said, crinkling the lined sheets. "Ready?"

She smiled kindly, warmly alert, nodded, and peered at him expectantly.

"Draw me a picture of us," he began hoarsely, cleared his throat, coughed, then continued tremulously. *"What is the picture you see? You-Me, friends and lovers joined together by a bond we cannot touch or name, only feel. You-Me, a unit, a whole made of separate parts, coming together to form the entirety: a new entity.*

"Draw me a picture of you, alone: all your faults, foibles, guilts and memories intact. They are the only things you have made out of your past, made up of actions, words and thoughts of what has passed. Show me, then, what you see that shall be. A dream picture of a life of just You-Me, together in our own Mishmálaca in the hills. Tell me that it will someday be real.

"Draw me a picture of me, who you see me to be and what you need for me to give you. Be sure that your perceptions are correct. There may be those things that you see that are not there, real and concrete, though only that which your mind has given you out of its own hopes, expectations, and desires. Perhaps illusory, perhaps not. (Some word for me to be bandying about, don't you think? Illusory?)

He stopped for a moment, smiling, looking up to see if she had caught his little joke. She asked him if that was all, said it was lovely. Not much more, he said sheepishly and coughed again before pushing on to the end.

"Now draw the pictures together – us, you, me – and overlay them and align them so that the edges are one, our eyes become those of a single person. Pull it apart and put it back together a few times so that it becomes two people (you and me), then overlaid together again (You-Me). Tell me, then, which makes the better picture, the whole person, which would you rather be? Take your time. Now it is your turn. I leave this part up to you."

He looked up, searching her face for a response there. He couldn't see anything in her usually expressive eyes as he had hoped. He had expected at least a smile, a thoughtful look of pleasure, a reassuring nod of approval. But her countenance was like a wall to him, an opaque cloud of expressionless meditation.

He picked the notebook pages he had dropped on the floor as he had trudged moodily out the door, his feet sucking in the muddy earth outside. She wanted to chase after him but decided – wisely, she thought – to allow him his sullen disappointment at her lack of reaction. He would come back. She shuffled through the pages and found that amid the scribblings, scratch-outs and write-overs and despite his admonitions against the chicken-scratch illegibility of his script, she could read his inelegant handwriting very easily.

Chapter 24

Comfy-cozy, lazy-crazy, lovey-dovey, toasty and homey. Evening arrived without notice, for no one was looking.

Earlier Thanielle had followed after Gordon for a second time since they had found the diner. She had begun to worry about him being out there in the forest for so long, had begun to wonder about this ultra-sensitive man with whom she had gotten so seriously involved in so short a time. She approached him at the bank of the wide stream as he gazed disconsolately into the shallows of its rushing surface. He apologized without turning to look at her, as if he felt that her quiet presence before she had a chance to say anything. He said that he was sorry for rushing out the way he did, that he shouldn't have run away from criticism like that but....

"What criticism?" she said, pulling him roughly around to face her. "I didn't say anything."

"Well, you were going to; I could sense it."

"Yes," she admitted. "Something. Something nice, something complimentary. You use words in a very truthful way. You ask questions that need to be asked and to be answered. They say things about us – You-Me – in a way that I wouldn't have thought of, but it's all real. Feelings are always real. Mine, too."

His look was a quizzical one, delighted and puzzled at the same time. Here was another one who mixed emotions in a single facial expression. His mouth twitched, trying to smile but not quite succeeding. "Your feelings, too? Like I wrote it?"

"Not completely," she said. "But the gist was there. You've got to admit that it was a bit sketchy."

"Hmph," he grunted. "Criticism. I told you."

"You said what you said very well," she defended. "But you ended it in a kind of question, said that it was my turn now. All right. I'll draw you a picture of you for you. That's what you said, didn't you? 'Draw me a picture of me'? All right, but mine will have one quality to it that you don't have right now, and one that's easily fixed"

He didn't know what to make of all this, but he asked anyway: "What quality is that?"

"Cleanliness," she said. "Stay right there."

She ran back to the diner and came back a few minutes later with the brown soap, the bath towel, deodorant, the flour sack of new clothes and her sandals.

"Now, Mister," she said, her voice as commanding as that of a Master Sergeant barking out orders. "Strip."

That was when the clock speeded up, the day raced swiftly to its end. He wouldn't let her stay near while he undressed – too modest, he said – while he washed in the chill water of the stream and changed. She didn't go very far away but was always moving from place to place, as silent on her feet as a lioness on the prowl. He wrapped the big towel around himself when done, cast furtive glances around each time he heard the shrill, tweeting wolf whistle issuing from the bushes or the trees. The laughter at his expense followed the occurrence of his usually exaggerated reaction as if a dryad were watching from the wood, gauging this mortal as a candidate for her bucolic nest. He knew the real cause of the sounds, of course, and couldn't help laughing along with her for her little revenge, no matter the uneasy embarrassment it caused him.

When he returned all slick haired and spanking new in his stiff jeans that bagged at the back as though he was carrying a pillow there for padding for the hemorrhoids that he didn't have, his feet concealed and catching in the sloppy roll of the cuffs, he paraded his new outfit for her smiling delectation. The short sleeves of the t-shirt caught in his armpits, making the garment mimic the outline of a tank top while the white of the t-shirt showed between the straining buttons of the long sleeve flannel shirt in the shape of little half-moons. One look at him as he came into the diner and Thanny found herself wishing that Jake's thoughtfulness had included a sewing kit in his box of "necessities."

"At least the socks and underpants fit," he said, shrugging painfully. "The t-shirt's a little tight, though."

She had some money, she told him. They could probably get someone to fix up his new wardrobe in one of the other towns or hamlets – Blazer, Sunup, Honeysuckle – that they would come to along the way. In the meantime, she handed him the soap again and pointed him back toward the door to wash his old threads while she prepared what she could for dinner. Somewhere between three and four, the sun said; a little early for dinner, but he didn't complain.

They slung the clothesline from a nail on the outside of the jutting outhouse to a drunkenly tilting tree a couple of yards away and, after the meal was done, they packed the holey socks, boxer shorts, new shirt, t-shirt and jeans in with her assortment of spring wear, packed in the last of the food except for what they planned for the morning meal. Afterward, they scoured the diner for whatever forage they might find: only a few books of matches, a roller type can opener which Gordon thoughtfully replaced with the old gouge and gash model that they had been using up until then, and a few thick beeswax candles, all of which they packed away and zipped securely and tightly into several of the side compartments of the back pack.

They took the mattress off the bed and laid it on the floor before the old Franklin, propped their backs against the wall under the Planepatora poster and warmed their feet by the open fire door of the stove. Thanny melted some candlewax onto a plate and stuck six candles in it. "Last of the lot," she explained. "I've been saving them for just this occasion. She lit them all for a makeshift reading lamp which she rested above Gordon's head on one of the counter stools which she had brought in from the diner counter.

Toasty, comfy, cozy, he read the single sheet of paper she handed to him which had been torn from the now much thinner notebook.

"*I have drawn a picture of a man,*" she had written in a graceful cursive style. "*Who lets me see only one side of himself at a time. Let me count the ways:*

Quiet, soft spoken, tender and gentle as a puppy's lick, full of warmth and generous humor. His eyes dance for me when I touch him, his hands brush away my fear that he may not be here tomorrow. He is ingenuous; I trust him implicitly (this side of him, at least). I draw a picture of a man steeped in sorrows he cannot (or will not) explain or define; sorrows that have driven him to search out a land which he, himself, has constructed with a word and a dream: Mishmálaca. (I hope I spelled it right). A man who I will follow, be with, stay with whether he reaches his goal or not. But that is my need, not his. I hope that he will need me with him, as I need to have him (this side of him) near me. I hope that, when he finishes reading this, he will turn to me and kiss me the way I love him to, the way he does how he does it that makes me tingle all over and feel loved by him."

Toasty, comfy, cozy, warm and homey. It takes two people to make these words more than just letters strung out and bunched up forming words and sentences spaced across the page and making sense. They did as she asked of them and made sense of what she wanted to say. He was impressed and she was proud of what she had accomplished. Their judgments about each other's piece were similarly positive with very few negative complaints or criticisms. She had one about the way he had ended his with a question that put the onus in the hands of the reader. His main complaint also concerned something at the very end of her piece. In fact, it was in regard to the use of a particular word.

"Love?" he asked incredulously.

Chapter 25 – Bastions

The argument that they had the following morning began in joking good fun but soon snowballed into something much more serious. They had made the last go-round of the place to make sure they hadn't left anything behind or overlooked something that might be useful to them on their continued journey. They were ready to leave when Gordon commented that it would be a nice place to live; a simple, unadorned statement, nothing to take to heart, just a chance observation.

"But where would we go to find work?" Thanny asked, as if the statement connoted a real wish rather than the idle chatter that it was.

Gordon said that they wouldn't have to go anywhere. The diner itself would be self-supportive, given some work and time to gain its clientele.

She grudgingly picked up his growing enthusiasm for the idea no matter how silly it seemed at the time. He had always seemed to be one to latch onto things easily, she had come to realize and, just as easily, would blow them out of proportion. By the time they were a mile away from the diner they had built their little hideaway in the woods into an exclusive club for matronly dowagers and froggy old nouveau-riche bachelors out for a turn on the highly polished parquet dance floor, a bit of the bubbly and a taste of the famous cuisine of Chateau Mishmálaque. Their *clienteel*, as Gordon pronounced it, would be profligate with their spending, sparing no expense at the pretense of being "in" with the fashionable good taste that overflowed the walls of the elegant dining and night spot with its brocaded curtains and flashy chandeliers reminiscent of a richer, gladder time. The hotel by the river, on the other hand....

But this was where Thanny broke off the reverie and began to nitpick again. Hotel by the river? Really! It was so out of the way that no one would ever find the place let alone make it a basking spot for the rich. Where would they get the financial backing for such a venture, even if they decided that the scheme was even remotely feasible? Which, of course, it wasn't. She had only seen tire tracks from a single car when they were about to leave the area. It seemed to have parked there long enough to deposit ten or eleven empty beer cans onto the barren and still muddy apron beside the diner before pulling out. The idea was a stupid one; no matter how nice it sounded or how much fun it was to make up stories about what might be.

As she spoke one thing had begun to nag at her mind. Even as she pursued her little tirade about how foolish it was to even consider the old diner for such a costly and ambitious venture, something had begun to bother her. Those beer cans....

Of course, Thanny couldn't have known that, because of the out-of-the-way location and the vacant state of the place, the diner was an ideal and popular make-out spot for the youth of the area and was often frequented on weekends for just such purposes. From her own experience she was aware that, it being the first really mildly weathered month of spring – as May usually tends to be – the adolescent rutting season was in full swing in high schools and colleges throughout the county. Neither of them could have known that the night before as they slept off the heady, exhausting effects of their own love making, a large sedan of hybrid make and design (body by Fischer, engine by Ford, muffler and tailpipe by Midas, bumpers nonexistent, interior upholstery by the Honeysuckle Custom Car Shoppe) had pulled onto the muddy apron, pebbling its undercarriage with a rattling volley of crunchy gravel. The four occupants of the vehicle – boy, girl, boy, girl – had emerged and with practiced gaiety sashayed to the rear of the place and opened the door that led directly into the living quarters. The lead Lothario, the driver of the car, shined a flashlight into the dim interior, skipped the hazy beam across the naked, rusty springs of the bed, into the corners, to the cooling stove down to the floor where Gordon's nasal snore and Thanny's somniferous muttering had caught their attention. They turned around and tiptoed out. Their party had to be postponed until these two could sleep off their love hangover. Among the young of the area, it seemed, there was such a thing as lovers' courtesy. Let the other couple have the chance to do what they were doing in their own good time. Worse comes to worst there was always the car, the lap blanket, and a case of frosty beer in the ice chest. Not too bad, all things considered.

So that was where they stayed, necking furiously in offbeat time to the music from the car radio. No screams or curses, admonitions or denials issued from the half open windows, front or back, even though the driver did attempt to take some liberties with his date on which she wasn't too keen. She simply removed his hand from that area of her person which she did not wish to have manhandled and so answering his hangdog, questioning look with a sweetly mouthed, "Give it time." The beer flowed, the empty cans flew out of the windows one after the other like dud hand grenades. At about 2 A.M. by the faulty electric clock on the dashboard, they concluded that the couple inside was planning to make it an all-nighter. The two car couples left then, digging the balding rear tires into the soft ground, all of them pleasantly sated but somewhat disappointed. They talked on their way back to the highway and then on toward Honeysuckle and home about the sleepers in the diner, commented wryly among themselves of the kinkiness of laying the mattress out on the floor when there was a perfectly good bedframe right there in the room with them.

Neither Gordon nor Thanny had known any of this, of course; they had slept right through it all. The sight of the pile of beer cans littering the small sector off to the side of the rutted trail adjacent to the diner hadn't registered as something unusual with Gordon on their way out, and Thanny had something more personal to worry her at that moment. That concern – the beer cans – was a fleeting one, an unsuccessful attempt to camouflage the dull ache that lay over her eyes like some demonic little lizard digging its hot claws into her brow, the queasiness in her intestines, the sharp pains creeping in her lower back like worms winding up her spine, spinning fire in their wakes.

The day would be like this, all the way, she knew. She had used the tampon applicator in the toilet before they had left as a precaution. At least that was one thing she wouldn't have to wish that Jake had included in his box of goodies, though a bottle of Midol would have been greatly appreciated right about then. She considered herself to be fortunate when it came to her periods. She had known girls at school who were completely incapacitated when they were visited by their "monthly friend." The "curse" and the "dread" were other words she had heard used. For her, it was only a nagging inconvenience. No cut classes or days spent laid up at home in bed in unspeakable agonies. She had been told of such things, had seen the empty seats in school, made excuses at summer jobs at the luncheonette for friends who had to take an "unexcused" sick day. She was thankful that at least she was ambulatory even through the worst of what she had to put up with.

It had begun sneakily enough, as usual. First there was the excusable headache over the right eye, just under the hairline, mild enough to seem like it would soon go away, given a little time. By the time they had set their sights on the wonders of proprietorship of their castle of courtly splendor in the woods, however, the realization of what the headache, nausea and cramps nesting over her buttocks were all about had finally come to her. She had always been fairly regular with her periods and had timed it perfectly to the day. She had inserted the tampon that morning as a precaution and now she was glad for it; the only thing for which she presently felt anything positive.

Still, her back made for problems in carrying the rope-rigged duffle bag. She had to stop and rest every half hour or so and risk piquing Gordon's curiosity, which it eventually did. She verbally shrugged it off as the cumulative effect of close to two weeks of continual hiking and camping. He was stronger than her, she said, giving him his unearned, macho due. She hadn't wanted to bother him with her petty complaints, didn't want to be bothered herself, just to be left alone until it had all passed. Until then, she knew, she would be a roaring bitch to be with. Luckily her cycle was a reasonably short one and the painful, uncomfortable, griping portion of it should be done with by the next day, at the latest.

Gordon was only put off by her "cumulative effect" rationalization for three of their sit-down stops. On the fourth he began to press again, become solicitous, querulous, concerned, and nosy. Finally, in exasperation, she told him the truth, watched as he became thoughtful and nodded at the news. "I guess I thought so," he said, a definite note of relief in his voice.

"And what's that supposed to mean?" she snapped, reacting to definite sighing in his voice. Almost immediately she apologized for her sour mood, explained how she felt physically ("drained") and emotionally ("overwrought") and how long it would probably be before she was "normal" again, surprising herself for equating such a normal, monthly occurrence with something abnormal. If normal is something else, she reasoned, then I must be sick. She felt at times that there was something sick about menstruation, the fact that it happened to you each month, a few weeks past the full moon, something gross in the fact that special concessions had to be made – tampons, belts, pads, Midol, the pain and nausea and discomfort – delicate explanations handed out for a simple, normal biological function that only meant that her body was gearing up for yet another bout of fertility. This was the first time she had voiced those thoughts to anyone, even if it was only an obtuse reference to getting back to "normal," as if she were recuperating from an operation or waiting out the doldrum days in a psychiatric ward.

"Anyway," she said, calm now. "You made it sound as though you were glad that I'm having my period. Was I hearing things or was that a sigh of relief I just heard?"

"Maybe it was."

"Why?" she asked though she could pretty well guess the reason.

"Because," he began sheepishly and this was the way, she had learned, that she could tell that he was going to say something that he didn't want to say, something he didn't care for which troubled or embarrassed him: his pouting, childlike, aw-shucks manner. "Because now we can still be free and won't have to worry or maybe have to make decisions about what to do about.... about.... about – ah-hm! -- let's say what could be a regrettable situation."

"You mean my being pregnant."

"Yes," he said, his eyes downcast-- ashamed or just abashed, Thanny couldn't quite tell.

"That bothered you? That maybe you'd be a father?"

He nodded with his head still down, not looking at her.

"Well, I could have told you not to worry. I do use protection, I mean."

"Protection?" he said, livening. "The pill?"

"No, a diaphragm." She patted the duffle to show where the thing was. "Take it with me wherever I go."

His look of incomprehension moved her to explain further, to describe it, the manner in which it worked, the means of folding it for insertion using the spermicidal cream, how she had hidden the dusty blue colored plastic case in her night clothes on their first night at the diner. Sharing your sleeping bag with a man involved certain possibilities for which one had to be prepared.

"But last night," he protested, still a bit confused. "You didn't have time."

"Before dinner," she said, letting him in on her preparedness. Toasty, comfy, cozy warm, and homey and then the lovey-dovey part, foregone conclusion or not, had to be planned for.

"So why'd you roll a rubber onto my dick if you already had the diaphragm in?" he asked.

"That part," she said with an evil little smile, "was just for the fun of it."

Watching his face take in all that she had related and then brighten as the confusion was dispelled, her mind did an odd turnabout that brought on a rankling understanding of where this had all been leading before they had gotten off of the main topic and started in with this half-baked course in birth control.

"What?" she asked touchily, "would you have done if you had gotten me pregnant?"

He stood away from her, backed away as if suddenly frightened by something he had just noticed in the expression on her face. A mole with a face of its own, maybe, or a hair visibly growing out of the white of one of her eyes. "I don't know," he said hesitantly and then, quickly before he had time to second guess what he was about to say: "Marry you?"

"Tell me, really" she said. "Is that what you're telling me you would have done? Proposed to me?"

"It would seem the thing to do," he said, almost whispering. "We just, kind of, put the honeymoon ahead of the wedding, is all."

The idea, once it stopped being a punishment for hypothetical sins, appealed to him. In his usual glib and rambling way, he let it all spill out. He drew her a picture of Mommy and Daddy Traumer with Junior (or Juniorette) in a pram, strolling through Mishmálacan streets, accepting invitations into friendly (always friendly) neighbors' homes for tea and talk and games, the mommies and daddies just sitting, watching their respective offspring play with their toys and one another. He made it sound stiff, like scenes from some staid nineteenth century English novel of manners. Lovely, ever-summer weekends strolling through streets and parks, down to the sea and the amusement pier, weekdays of Daddy Gordon away at some nondescript job or other while Mommy Thanielle tended hearth and home and a brood of an indeterminate number. All very quaint, very unreal, just like Gordon to come up with something out of the past to give to the future and with no imagination whatsoever on this score.

"I've had that kind of life already," she reminded him. "Or, at least the real, unidealized kind. I was the baby in that pram, and I don't recall it all being so goddamned idyllic. No, Gordy. If that was one of the choices, then I'd definitely have to opt for something different. You see, I ran away from that.... But you know about that. I've told you all that about me before."

Her voice was beginning to crack, her edginess turning into frustration and an annoyed, unfocused anger. She didn't want to talk about it anymore. She let Gordon hoist her to her feet, didn't say anything as he roped the duffle and sleeping bag onto the top of the aluminum rack that held the backpack, and took on the full load himself.

"You ran away from three particular people," he told her as they got back onto the trail. "Not from a place, not even from a real home from the way you described it. Home would have been a place where you felt wanted and needed."

That was all, his sage contribution. She liked the sound of it, the thoughts that it engendered. But thinking just increased the insistence of the dull headache and sharpened it. The knives that turned as in hot butter in her sacroiliac dug deeper with each step as she walked. She just wanted to get a respectable distance down the road and away from the morning's starting point before she had to call for another sit-down rest stop.

What she really wanted was a warm, inviting bed and painless, dreamless sleep.

Chapter 26

The Blazer Rest Motel looked like any down at the heels roadside hostelry. It had a small restaurant at the south end of its square horseshoe arc which seemed to have been planned as the focal point of the little establishment, even though it did not occupy the central position in the building. It did, however, sport the blinking neon monstrosity that identified the place as one of business, a sign that--though a decade or so newer than the one that squeaked its trellised joints above the now defunct and decrepit Corliss Diner-- was, nonetheless, just as dated and weatherworn. The L in Lunch in the window of the restaurant tended to flicker spasmodically and the M in Motel listed away from the rest of the word, but at least all was readable for all the good its decipherability did the place, situated as it was off the beaten track of the rush and flood of any travelled road. This did not bother its inhabitants or proprietor, however, as the transactions of the hostelry and restaurant businesses were not the main order of existence for Blazer or its eponymous motel. Like Taragon and several of the other puddles of humanity in the vicinity along this circuit of quaternary back road, this was the entire town.

The restaurant occupied the farthest forward position of the southern arm of the open ended rectangle, jutting far enough forward of the northern arm that it was the first portion of the building to be seen from the road; an eye grabber in its heyday but now, with its muted shades of magenta and ochre, it sent the discerning eye glancing back to the myriad greens of the forest to find rest. Good, was the considered opinion of the management. Let them look elsewhere. What do they think this is anyway? A hotel? Making it look the part of a roadside stopping point for travelers was part of the plan for its façade, but also to hide its true purpose.

There had been money enough to do all this, to build access tunnels between the two arms of the place under the open court of the parking lot, to reinforce the rooms with lead sheathing and fire proof them with amorphous silica, to strengthen the foundation with cinderblock and concrete casings, plan and execute extensive, self-sufficient power sources (primary and secondary), sewage and garbage disposal processing plants, water storage and purification facilities and detoxification machinery.

There was more than enough money to purchase the hoarded foodstuffs, fuels, medical and surgical supplies, a library amply stocked with all the pertinent reference and guidance manuals from Aaronic source works to Zymurgy, as well as an equally extensive (2,500 volumes at current inventory) library devoted to fiction, drama, poetry and philosophy, from Confucius to Mao in the East, Beowulf to the Beat bards of the fifties and sixties in the west. Literature of the seventies and later were being collected slowly under advisement of several critics employed by a number of news services, each under a freelance basis. There was also an entertainment collection of movies, music, recorded books, electronic games, and teaching tools with all the necessary paraphernalia to exhibit these modern-day additions and supplements to art and literature. A laundry room serviced the small community's meager needs in this area, predicated on a scale equal to that of a fully staffed, professionally run laundry and dry-cleaning establishment of the mass market variety in a medium size town. That is to say, the equipment was all there, but not the legion of staffers to operate it all. Hence, only one or two of the many machines available for use were actually employed and then only once or twice a week at best.

Gordon and Thanielle came to this place conveniently located along their route for a bite of lunch or a cup of coffee, depending on the prices, but mainly for a rest and maybe some convivial conversation with someone pleasant, sympathetic and, above all, human. Thanny needed the understanding more than Gordon and was glad to see a female face hovering over them as they looked over their menus and noted the absence of prices for any of the items.

"Not too busy, I see," Thanny noted. They were the only ones in the restaurant. The woman said that their trade was usually pretty slight but that things would be picking up later in the month. Seasonal, you know, she said.

Having ordered an extremely reasonable chef's salad which she and Gordon intended to share, Thanny asked where the ladies' room was. She wasn't feeling too well and just needed.... She didn't have to go on about her situation but she did, stirring the curiosity and sympathy of the large, buxom woman until, drawing the waitress away from the table toward the cash register, she confessed her complaint with as few details as she could. The woman was commiserative as she led the way to the "little girls' room," abjuring all the way against the horrors of the "monthly meanies" as she used to experience them. She inquired if Thanny had an ample supply of "stoppers" for the duration and, taking her affirmative answer as the last of her nosy needs, she pushed open the door marked with the frontal silhouette of a faceless, skirted figure for Thanny, saying that if she needed anything at all "just to let Jessi know."

Thanny remained at the open door to the ladies' room, clearly ready for the conversation to continue. "Jessi," she said appreciatively. "A very pretty name."

"And I was even prettier than the name once upon a time," said the woman, pulling at the sides of her wide, pleated skirt as she performed a little side-to-side curtsy step in way of demonstration of lost youth. She looked to be no more than forty or forty-five, but she had spoken of her "monthly meanies" in the past tense, as if they were no longer a part of her life.

Still, Thanny conjectured, maybe menopause had come to her early, maybe she was only in her forties. Wouldn't do to ask, though; it wouldn't be polite. She did ask if there was any chance that she might obtain a Midol to help ease the effects of her own mild misery. Jessi said that she would check with Helena. She was the resident physician and health care specialist for their little project, she said.

"Project? You mean the restaurant and motel?"

"Oh no, dear," said Jessi happily, chuckling a deep voiced flutter at the misunderstanding. "A project, child. Like the ones the government takes on. You know: build this and build that, whether it's needed or not. Only this is a privately funded concern. My late husband's – God rest his soul – pet project you might say, for want of a better phrase. Obsession might be a better word for what it was to him. But you go and do what you have to do. Have your salad when you come out and chat with your boyfriend. He's waiting for you. Doctor Skelstein – that's Helena – I'm sure will have the medication that you want. And later, I'll be happy to show you around."

As the door hissed closed on its hydraulic stop Thanny heard the woman say softly to herself, an afterthought most likely not meant for her to hear: "Lunch and fun and then bye-bye, kids. We can't have you sticking around for too long, can we?"

Doctor Helena Skelstein, an attractive brunette in her mid-thirties, conducted a tour of her own through the numerous rooms that made up her combined living and working space, the largest suite in the complex. She had at her disposal a complete laboratory for diagnostic studies and tests as well as a fully equipped examining room complete with an x-ray machine connected to a computer programmed to show the stark imagery of its making on the large monitor that took up one of the entire short walls of the room, like an entertainment center. There was also a complete dentist's array of gadgetry and equipment; Doctor Skelstein confessed that she feared she was miserably remiss in this area of endeavor and was not sure how well she would fare if called upon to even just drill and fill a simple cavity, let alone perform the more complex and involved tasks of extractions, root canals, orthodontics or denture and bridgework. She was more than amply equipped and supplied for such work, but it was a discipline for which she had little or no practiced skill. "But I'm sure I'll get the hang of it all when and if the time comes," she said, trying to sound confident as she handed over an unlabeled bottle of pills to Thanny.

The medication had come from the nearly inexhaustible supply of medicinal and surgical needs. A door at the east end of her examining room led to a staircase into a tunnel under the parking lot between the two arms of the building (restaurant and office) which led directly into the storage area for all the necessities of the running of the Blazer Motel's infrastructural facilities. No sense going outside when the weather might become unlivable, she said. Remember, the reason for such a complex to exist at all was to allow its inhabitants to survive the worst circumstances that man's or nature's wrath might cause.

After her quick tour of Blazer's medical facilities, Thanny asked Jessi about what the good doctor was referring to when she mentioned such "circumstances." What kind of circumstances were the folks at the motel geared up to face?

Jessi smiled sweetly and told the girl that no one could be sure, but it was a certainty that something was coming and that the Blazer Motel was ready for the worst. Who knew what it would be: something to do with climate change, a shift in the earth's orbit or rotation, a catastrophic meeting with a comet or meteor, or even the result of mankind's death-wish coming to fruition through a final all-out thermonuclear war? Whatever the reason and result, they would be ready. Jessie was eager to show off the ingenuity of the design and execution of the more inventive aspects of the place. It had all been her late husband's pet project, as she had said before. He was Kenneth Swarthman – but of course they must have heard of him, hadn't they? The name was familiar, even to Gordon, who had led something of a cloistered life these past two years and more. Kenneth Swarthman had been rich all his life, steeped in the family wealth and business and who had married not too well – Jessi let this last bit of information slip without comment, even though she was the person referred to as Kenneth's less than best choice for a wife -- but he had seemed happy in the union and theirs had been a loving and wonderful relationship for all the time they were together. Kenneth had dropped out of sight after undergoing surgery to remove a cancerous lung. Six years later his death was announced, the obituary in the papers only listing his string of credits and holdings, saying that he had died of natural causes without any reference to the sudden relapse, the three month long series of radiation and chemotherapy that did no good and may have been at least partially responsible for the speed in which his health had deteriorated.

The press had totally lost faith in him as good copy in the six years he had spent out of the public eye since the initial, life-saving operation. Jessi and he were glad for the anonymity that had been afforded them by the press' disinterest. It allowed Kenneth the liberty of pursuing the realization of his dream of developing a self-sufficient community that would be able survive whatever nature, man or the supernatural might throw their way even as the rest of human civilization began to crumble and fall away. "Here," Jessi told them with a gesture that took in the entirety of the project that was the Blazer Motel, "is the result of all that he envisioned. Come and see."

First, they were taken to the storage and support facilities along the northern wing where Jessie let them see for themselves what was there. She gave them no encouragement for exploration on their own, however; the tour was quite specific in what was shown and allowed to be seen. "This was where he spent his last years," she said as they walked through a wide, roofless courtyard back toward the restaurant. It was a dull yard with no decoration of any sort to make it seem anything other than boringly utilitarian. The concrete flooring was battleship grey, the walls were sandy and rough to the touch and painted the same drab shade as the floor, giving the eye the illusion that there was nothing here but the dense grey of dusk over a placid colorless ocean which could not be differentiated from the deep grey of the sky. It would have been the perfect subject for an abstract study in blacks, whites, and shades, even though the sun was shining, sending chiaroscuro phantasms scattering with every passing cloud.

They walked down the north side of the court past doors set apart from one another in the grey stucco wall, each bearing a wooden plaque which identified the contents and uses of the material and machinery within each numbered room: 1 – Medical/Surgical; 2 – Foodstuffs, non-perishable; 3 – Foodstuffs, refrigerated and frozen; 4 – Library A – Reference; 5 – Library B – Fiction, Poetry, Drama and Philosophy; 6 – Entertainment; 7 – Generator A; 8 – Fuel; 9 – Heat, Air and Maintenance; 10 – Laundry; 11 – Generator B; 12 – Water and Purification; 13 – Firearms and Ammunition; 14 – Sewage and Garbage Disposal.

The north side, Jessi told them, had all been motel rooms, just like those in the south wing, but Kenneth, immediately upon purchase of the place, had them cut into smaller cubicle cells, reinforced them against radiation (lead) and heat (amphoras silica), and had tunnels dug from the more important ones--such as heat, air conditioning, medical, foodstuffs, generators, fuel, water and firearms--to the quarters of those most qualified to use or deal with those respective necessities. The rooms housing the generators, the water purification plant, and the HVAC center were not so much rooms as they were deep pits, so much of the machinery having been dug underground. Open the door to Generator A (Room 7) and you were immediately assailed with its piercing, incessant whine, and saw only the cylindrical top of its mammoth dynamo like some monster peering out at you from the depths.

"Like Helena told you, she has direct access from her room to the medical supplies," Jessi explained. "There is a tunnel from the food room directly to the restaurant, which is designed to be the main feeding center for when no one will be able to go outside, just as it is now. Mr. Girondia," she continued, and quickly, almost instantaneously appended this was a breathy *"Alonzo,"* drawing the name out into something like a melody. "Alonzo, our maintenance man and jack-of-all-trades, has a whole network of tunnels to rooms 7 through 14."

That left rooms four, five and six (Libraries and Entertainment) open to all residents via a roundabout route through all the rooms, or by a back hallway which bypassed those rooms inhabited by those persons responsible for their respective domains. A bit of poor planning on Kenneth's part, it was admitted – this back hallway was only added on by Jessi after her husband's death.

There were a writer and a musician in residence as well, filling out their little survivor family of five. There was talk of also finding an artist for the group, but that was still pending discussion and a final decision.

The living quarters had been enlarged from average overnight motel rooms into roomy apartments. Meals were communal, served in the restaurant. In the event of one of the cataclysms foreseen as imminent by Jessi's late husband, the fact that each apartment had access to the one adjacent, each following in a line like an old style railroad flat, would be a definite plus. Doctor, writer, musician, handyman and owner could come and go as he or she pleased, take their meals and socialize in the comfort of civilized company and reasonable luxury, without having to venture outside into whatever horrors man or nature might deign to witness upon the Earth.

They re-entered the restaurant by a side door and were met by a tall, slender young black woman who greeted them effusively between mouthfuls of hamburger. Actually, the odor of cooking had met them well before the summer clad young woman was encountered. She was introduced to them as Ruanda, the complex's musical prodigy.

"Violin," she told them matter-of-factly when asked about the instrument she played. "Some cello but I'm more comfortable with a smaller fingerboard. You know," she said teasingly as she stood up and did a Charleston two-step, quickly knocking knees, spreading them with palms on the knobby caps. "Don't like nothin' wooden 'tween these sweet hams o' mine." She bellowed a jocose war whoop while Jessi made some comment about Casals moving over to make room for the incomparable Miss Baker.

"Tell me, though, Sweets," the older but not elder woman interrupted the laughter. "Aren't you chilly dressed like that? Don't mean to be a Mamma Buttinsky but it's not quite summer yet, you know."

Ruanda looked down at her halter topped torso, scratched an itch in the open area between the slack waist of her flapping shorts and the fringed bottom of her top where her outy navel bugged out like a black pearl ornament from the chocolate colored skin surrounding it. She shook her friendly smiling face side to side, causing a breeze with the wave of her sheening hair, a silent negative that, with the squint of her large round eyes, said "mind your own business" as well as a solid, no nonsense "no."

The four of them talked while Ruanda finished her lunch, exchanged questions and answers like children swapping marbles or baseball cards. Jessi was open to all queries about the project – a word which Ruanda did not care for as a description of this sylvan-set, voluntary concentration camp. She was honest and lively when asked why she had involved herself in such an endeavor whose premise was based on the inevitability of a social, political or natural cataclysm. She begged them not to get the wrong idea. If they had read anything at all about Jessi's dear departed husband, then they had an idea of where the initial inspiration for the project had come from. He had been an intense anti-communist, fearful of the power and madness inherent in an ideology foisted upon the masses by an upper crust handful. It was ironic, she noted, that a man who came from a family of wealth and power, a family with mob connections, – there was no denying it – with senators, judges, aldermen, police commissioners, even the odd mayor or governor on the take, should be so paranoid of power. And paranoia it certainly was. Paranoia was what had built Blazer from a tumble-down backwoods motel that never was able to make a go of itself – nothing did up here, she said; just look at Corliss – into this. He had done the major portion of the work, was the one who got the place in working order, came up with the plan for the tunnel system, had the foresight to contract engineers and designers and developers to work up a concept and design for a viable indoor sewage treatment plant, the very first of its kind. All that was really left to do was to put a roof over the courtyard, but that had been Alonzo's idea. She pronounced the name *Alawnzo*, kicked in a sigh and a dreamy look that made Ruanda smile.

"Anyhow, it was a stipulation in his will," said Jessi. "That I keep the ball rolling after his death, make sure the place is kept supplied and peopled as I saw fit. So, now we have a writer, a doctor, a musician and a man to hold things together." Alonzo, she said with a subtle trill in her voice, the faraway look in her eyes. Alonzo used to be the chief custodian at the Balshaw Hotel in Honeysuckle. She had weaned him away with the allure of a fat salary boost and free room and board. Doctor Skelstein had come to the project straight out of residency, looking for work and experience, and complains that for all the "work" she got at Blazer she might as well be a second ship's doctor on a Caribbean cruise vessel. Cuts, bruises, abrasions, head colds, a sprained ankle or wrist once in a while, and the usual list of lady complaints...that's what her medical practice here amounted to.

Jessi gestured to Thanny, raising her thin eyebrows indicatively. "Nothing challenging, she says, but we do our best to make it easier for her to stay than to leave. If it had been up to my husband this place would be crawling with physicists, chemists, biologists, astronomers, engineers, and technicians of every description. Me? I've got a musician who stays to study and practice, a writer who needs time and seclusion to finish his magnus opus of a novel, feelers out for an artist who's sick of the city and wants the freedom here to breath, relax, live and create. I'm a romantic. I feel that these are the things that should remain if my husband's paranoid fears about the coming of World War Three or whatever should come to pass, should come true. And I only say *if.*

"I never subscribed to his opinions, though I do respect them. And now, with Kenneth gone, I see it as my duty to carry on his work, even though I don't believe in his World War Aye, or that the fluorocarbon layer in the atmosphere will be totally destroyed leaving us all victims of massive dosages of unfiltered ultraviolet solar radiation, or that we'll be visited by beings from beyond the solar system with designs on wiping out the human race. Whoa, girl! I saw that look you just gave me. Yes, you heard me right and when he came up with that one, that's when I really began to worry, not that it would happen but because he believed that it was a definite possibility. His mind was going, there was no doubt about it, but some of his worries were pretty well founded, I think. And he left me pretty well off, kind of protects me from beyond the grave. I say my prayers against all the atrocities he dreamed up, but I feel pretty well prepared and set even if even only a tiny percentage of them happen to come true."

That was the end of her contribution and, after it was done, the conversation wound down to a halt. Thanny wound it back up a bit, giving the two women, young and aging, black and white, a rundown on her and Gordon's trip through the woods, leaving out the fact that they were both, in a sense, escapees, leaving her audience with the impression that theirs was just a vacation after which they would return to whatever lives they had left behind. She spoke of Jake, their friendship with the man, his kind though partially useless gift to them. She was honest and straight forward, told them all, even down to the simple fact that Gordon's entire wardrobe, save for the outfit that Jake had provided, was what he presently was wearing. Gordon couldn't help blushing, wishing that Thanny would quit with the honesty already. She was being patronizing and he could see the commiserating looks she was drawing with her accounts. Finally, after all was said and done, she excused herself for being such a bore and nuisance.

Ruanda was the first one to pipe up and offer her help by doing any alterations that might be needed on Gordon's ill-fitting new wardrobe. With Ruanda's gracious offer out in the open, any show of authority on Jessi's part could only be viewed as something harsh and callous should it be in the negative. After all, a fellow did need a change of clothes once in a while.

Jessi remained in the restaurant to clean up while the three youngsters, as she termed them to herself, walked and chatted their way to the rear of the courtyard where the workrooms were located for wood, metal and fabric crafts, as well as the smaller rooms devoted to short wave and ham radio operations. Ruanda opened the door to a room that was fairly overflowing with professional grade sewing machines and ironing equipment, along with their variety of confusing attachments and oddments and what looked to be miles of cloth and threads of every imaginable color and hue. Ruanda's light, laughing voice echoed like a reverberating melody in the hollow between the grey walls; a surprising contrast, that sound-color disharmony. At the door to the workroom, she told them that the job would probably take a while. She was a good seamstress, she said, but dull and slow fingered when it came down to the drudgery of actually doing the work to effectuate the changes needed to be made to seams and fasteners.

Thanny left Ruanda and Gordon to their chores of the cloth. She walked the length of the north wall, trying each of the numbered and labeled doors there and found all of them to be locked. She met the doctor who was sitting comfortably on a wicker chair outside the door to her office/home, reading a paperback romance novel. She quizzed the pretty woman cordially on life in Blazer and got cordial replies of her relative satisfaction and contentment in return. Thanny mentioned that it puzzled her that Mrs. Swarthman had alluded to having made it easier for the doctor to stay than to leave. What could Blazer provide to an aspiring young doctor that she couldn't find elsewhere?

Doctor Skelstein replied that her salary here was three times what she had earned as a resident and that the rent and meals were free. Add to that, she said, that her boyfriend was living here as well.... Well, the incentives were fairly obvious and would have been fairly difficult to turn down.

She left the doctor to her pleasure-reading, and as she made her shambling way back to the eatery, she passed by an open door to an apartment two doors removed from her goal. The nameplate – the only one she had noticed next to any of the living quarter doors – said "Mr. Carpath." She looked in to see a squat, powerful figure of a man with his burly back to her as he sat studying what seemed to be a wide array of color coded three-by-five index cards spread on the table before him.

She said a tremulous "hello," wondering if his name held any relation, remote or otherwise, to the word "driveway," and was about to continue on her way when he cheerfully invited her in. He showed her his cards in lieu of an introduction – though she already knew his name from the nameplate by the door and deduced that he must be the in-house writer from the scatter of cards and the computer with its attendant monitor, mouse, keyboard and printer at the far corner of the table, along with the stack of virgin typing paper next to it. As soon as she was inside the door, he commenced to explain his system of characterization, plotting and style to her.

The blue cards, he told her, were plot notes – as all the cards were notes of one sort or another – the pink ones were individual characters, the white ones for symbolic elements which were to come into play within a single chapter only (cross referenced to the character they were intended to clarify). The green ones contained broad summaries of the action to take place in each chapter and the bright orange ones were for the equally broad descriptions of the place in which the action, the character(s), symbols and all were to take place.

"Look," he said, pulling a little file drawer that neatly corresponded to the size of the cards. "I think it's all pretty clever the way I have it all figured out. You know when you're reading a book and a chapter, no matter how engrossing, seems to go on forever and ever so that you wish the author hadn't bitten off so much to tell in that section, perhaps saved a bit for another chapter so that things wouldn't get so tediously long? Well, I think I've got the answer – even if there is no question. But look. Here I've got the main portion of the chapter, first one, let's call it A until I come up with an appropriate title. And A has ten parts to it: A1, A2, A3, etcetera and so on. Then B with ten parts and C and D, all the way to Z."

"The whole alphabet?"

"Yes."

"And each chapter – every chapter – has ten parts to it?"

"Yes, that's right."

"So that's…. That's 260 chapters," she said and whistled airily at the number.

"But only twenty six with titles. Makes things simpler for me. Each chapter will only be a page or two, so it's not as astronomical as it first might seem. The only trouble I'm having is with the brevity, in fact. It's a real chore I've stuck myself with, drawing a character fully, say, in only a page or two, establishing the personality, the quirks, the outlook, background, motivation, psyche and so on."

"When did you start all this?"

"About a year ago, when I came here. Mrs. Swarthman's been good to her promise for the peace and quiet, no interruptions. I bless her for it. A place to work without the usual worries o,f "will it sell?" and "what will the advance be?" Here, I have enough now to see me through so I can complete the project. Everything else hasbeen taken care of, so all that's left to concern me is the task at hand. And I tell you, I've sure set myself one real doozy. Tension like crazy sometimes, especially now with all this cross-referencing. It's a real pain in the old gazoong. I'm glad somebody came along to help take my mind off of it all for a little while, and I thank you for the respite, Miss."

A notion just then seemed to across his mind: a flicker of the eyelids, a puckish smile as the thought emerged. He looked at her squarely for the first time since she had come in, looked her up and down carefully with a calm curiosity. He exhibited no surprise or shock at the realization that she was actually there, that he hadn't just been talking to himself when he asked what should have been his first question to her upon her arrival: "By the way, who are you?"

She introduced herself, made her explanations and apologies, the latter of which were immediately dismissed, then ignored. It didn't matter who she was, he was just grateful for the sympathetic ear. He needed that once in a while; not often, but sometimes. She said he ought to get enough of that what with a girlfriend living only a few doors away.

"I only wish," he said wonderingly. "Ruanda and I have struck up a nice friendship since I've come here, but there's nothing boy-girl about it, no romance." He would share his latest plot twists with her, she would invite him to her room for a private recital now and then. They got along well and easily, perhaps because they were just friends and there was no relational commitment made. Thanny said that she was referring to the doctor.

"Skelstein?" he yelped, amused. "Oh no, darlin'. She's too busy doing secret lab tests with Alonzo to even look at me."

"Oh," Thanny replied, surprised, thinking of Jessi's obvious infatuation with the handyman, this Alonzo character. "Connections and attachments," she mused out loud. "This place would make for the basis of a good novel itself."

"A bit larger," said Carpath, patting one of the little metal card file cabinets with a tinny ring. "Where do you think I got the models for the original main characters of the book? And you never asked me what it was all about. Everyone does." He handed her the only portion of the book which he deemed complete, sacrosanct, and inviolate: the title page.

JUDGMENT DAY BUNKER

OR: When the Sky Falls

A Novel by

Calvin A. Carpath

Gordon was coming down the courtyard wearing his new, well-fitting clothes proudly, the overloaded aluminum frame of the backpack pressing him over into a lumbago stoop. Thanny said goodbye to the novelist as she handed him back the title sheet of his work in progress. Ruanda had followed Gordon to the writer's room, sang out her farewells and cheers to them before going right into Carpath's room, yodeling a jubilant "Hiya, Cally!" at the door that ricocheted shrilly around the courtyard.

As they passed the restaurant, Thanny looked in the wide bay window that faced out onto the road. She was about to wave, mouth her thanks and goodbyes to Jessi, but was stopped when she saw that the woman had company: a handsome Hispanic man in his late thirties, perhaps early forties, on whose lap she was sitting, pressing him into the hard wood of the ladder-back chair, a man whose glasses she was fogging up with her open mouthed breathing; her tickling of his hair; her fluttering of his generous moustache, and her gentle massaging of his muscular chest under the faded blue of his cotton work-shirt. The man was smiling, attentive, enjoying himself as he played his hands over Jessi's plump thighs under her skirt, fish mouthing kisses of his own over her shoulders and neck.

Doctor Helena Skelstein waved chummily to Thanny as she ambled down the length of the courtyard toward the restaurant on her way to lunch.

Gordon was at a loss to figure why Thanny had broken into a sudden dead run as soon as they reached the blacktop, but he was hot on her heels, the pack bouncing and rattling painfully against his back as he ran to catch up to her.

Chapter 27

After having spent two successive nights on an honest to goodness mattress, the bare grassy ground under them felt unusually harsh and hard. The fire blazing at their feet was a consolation, but with the evening meal done and the night still stretched ahead of them like a strung and pulled rubber band against which neither of them could find the solace of sleep, it was not the choicest of times they had spent together. Work in the fact that the ground beneath them was aggravating Thanny's sacrum almost to the point of paralysis (and her coccyx was tender when she rolled on her hips a little too far to the right or the left) and you have the makings of a cantankerous, insomniac night of nastily traded words.

It began innocently enough. They had left Blazer at about three-fifteen by the restaurant's still working clock and hiked along the level road away from the motel for a full five miles without incident, random chatter punctuating their progress along the way. They spoke of the "moon thing," about their respective escapes from home and hospital, conjectured that the somnambulistic attitudes so uncharacteristically taken by Thanny's family and the night staff on the ward might have been a direct result of the moonquake Thanny had read about. As they walked, the subject of their conversation rose behind them, a pale, flabby sickle against the evening's darkening blue sky. Gordon walked backwards so as to keep it in view, holding Thanny's hands to maintain his balance and direction. They crossed a bridge in this manner – Gordon back pedaling as he held onto Thanny's hands as if they were handlebars on a bicycle as she followed. Facing him, she looked down so that she wouldn't tread on his sneakered feet. Their heavy footfalls rang with deep, hollow sounding echoes on the broad, thick timbers, splintery from ages of use, but still strong enough, as the sign before the bridge attested, to allow a five ton truck to pass over them without a crack to show for wear.

"And it shook," he said, a wondering tone coming into his voice. "Shook, rattled, rumbled, made people crazy, so unlike themselves, the way they ordinarily were. It made them not care, just want to sit and stare and gawk and sleep with their eyes open, just sit there and...." And he sat, suddenly, heavily, the overburdened weight of the pack dragged him backward and down. His left heel had kicked a tree root that projected onto the road's soft, graveled shoulder and sent him plopping down onto his backside. The pack frame rattled, the sleeping bag slipped from its elastic moorings and toppled loosely onto the blacktop, then flopped and rolled a few yards away.

"Oh shit, my tailbone!" he yelled as he freed himself from the shoulder straps and let the top-heavy pack keel over onto its side. "Why didn't ya you tell me that was coming up?"

"I didn't even see it until you hit it," she said. *And now you know how I feel there,* she muttered under her breath but was not heard.

He rubbed the sore bone, squat and waddled, massaged again, then resumed his duckwalk up and down the side of the road, shimmying his behind to get the blood flowing to ease the pain. Thanny laughed hard for only a few moments before her nausea overtook her and she ran to the woods to lose her share of chef's salad. A few minutes later they were commiserating with one another, laughing at the strange ludicrousness of the situation – minor misery of the one causing the other to laugh and thereby exacerbating her own condition – each apologizing for their own singular personal reasons that the other surely wouldn't quite understand. But that didn't matter when they turned around and looked at the field across the road at what was an ideal camping spot: flat, wide, easy access to the forest, ample kindling within easy reach and running water only steps away. This was probably the same stream that ran past the Corliss Diner, by which Thanny first met Jacob Rine. It had been their guide and friend for almost the whole of their trip through the forest. They had been following it, whether it was nearby or far away; it had always been there. They had crossed and re-crossed it, bathed in it, drank from it, soaked their tired feet in its cooling rush. *Old Friend,* Thanny called it. "Nice to see you again," she said as she filled the water jar from a numbing eddy near its rocky bank.

Dinner was filling though of questionable nutritional value – franks and beans in tomato puree – and may have been the cause of the argument which followed. It began innocuously enough, but ended in a flare of complementarily acute tempers. As the talk reached its crescendo just short of the yelling that would soon come, Thanny hit a nerve – her own – when she criticized Gordon for having had designs (it was the word she used) on Ruanda, accusing him of not loving her.

In response Gordon unthinkingly said the wrong thing: "Did I ever say that I did?"

"What?!" Then, calming down to a point where the rational part of her brain could take over from the emotional, suddenly injured, outraged part, she thought about it for a moment and had to admit, "No, you didn't."

"You see," he said, ready to embark on a lengthy explanation. "To me, love is a mixture of wanting, caring and need. Also, a good-sized dollop of trust. The wanting and caring I've got up the yin-yang, and I trust you to the very limit. But the need isn't there just yet, you see? But no, wait, I take that back. It is there, just not specifically for you." He squinted, made a face, hoping that that had come out the way it was supposed to. "Understand what I'm saying?"

"I'm not sure that I do," she said, her voice rising in pitch, taking on a frosty edge.

"Well, when I met you," he said, "I needed someone. I was with Jake then, and up 'til then I thought that that was enough. I really didn't need him either, not for himself, but only because he was someone to be with, to talk to. He was enough and, for the moment, he'd do in a pinch."

"Is that what you're saying about me, then? That I was there and just convenient, that it could have been just anybody?"

"Sounds awful, doesn't it?" he said. Hearing it given back to him, defined in different words but ostensibly the same thing, made it sound horribly cold and unfeeling. "But it's growing, that need. I'd miss you terribly if you left now."

"Not too flattering," she said with the same icy tinge.

There was a quiet moment. Gordon fidgeted, got up, walked around the campfire, fed it some more wood, warmed his hands, unstrapped the sleeping bag from the pack and laid it out by the fire on the dusty ground, removed his sneakers and sat down and tucked his feet between the fold of the bag.

"Thanny?" he said, meaning to draw her attention to the bed.

"Shut up!" she snapped. "Just don't say another word!"

But he did. It wasn't much more than a syllable, a Neanderthal grunt, not even a word but she jumped on him for it with a fierce cry that made him start, frightened him.

"Jesus fucking Christ, leave me alone! What do I need you for anyway? Fucking Loony Bin Louie. Here I am, stuck ten miles from nowhere and I have to have a Nuthouse Norman for a... for a...." She couldn't think of a word that would fit, didn't want to say boyfriend or lover. The former meant commitment, the latter connoted love.

But he didn't say that, that he loved her. That was true, but there had been nothing in his manner, in the way he responded, the way he touched her so tenuously like he was afraid that he'd hurt her or break her like she was a porcelain doll, so that she had to take his hand and show him how: how much, how strong, how forceful she wanted him to be, needed him to be. And he learned quickly, was a fast study. It all felt so right. But for all that, she might as well have been a hooker on the Avenue and let him do whatever the fuck he wanted. There was no love, only lover. And what did that mean? Lover. Not much, apparently. The root word was a sham, meaningless as far as he was concerned. Not a lover but a kisser, a fingerer, a licker, a fucker. An apprentice in the art without the feeling for it, only the technique, nothing more.

Stuttering around for words that would let her anger out and not finding them, she ran away. There was fury in her step, fuming up through her hair, flaming up through her throat in a shriek as she bolted, soared, pounded the heaving ground with her feet. She reached the forest, a hundred-yard dash, and entered the sudden uneven maze of trees and spun around, confused. She slumped down at a tall maple a few yards into the sparse wood. She laughed, thinking about the last time someone had done this. *Show me yours* had set him in motion that time.

Now she had asked again, and he had nothing to show, only the long face, sorry for the misinterpretation of the warm and human gestures he had been making. Now she had been the one to run. She had found him, that last time, sitting there with his head down, his knees drawn up to his forehead like a Mexican peon at siesta time, jumped when she had said his name, just gently touched his arm. She wondered if the emotions that started the feet going, the legs to pump, were the same for both of them. Confusion, fear, the need for being alone, for self, for time to think. She first thought of love when she had come upon him like that, finding him there looking so helpless.

Before that, her word for him was friend. Now she said *love,* had said it to herself. Inside herself it was real, that he was the one, not Gerald. But he said *no, not yet.*

There was a kind of a promise there, though. *The need, that last ingredient, is growing,* he had said. He had been honest; she had jumped to conclusions, expected too much, too soon. After all, how long had they known each other? Five days. This would be their fifth night together. Two with Jake, two alone together. What basis was that for love? Even giving credit to a badly phrased aphorism she had once heard about emotions rarely being rational, though, she still could not come up with a satisfactory answer as to whether or not her feelings were real or imaginary.

She was thinking more clearly now, didn't know how long she had been sitting there. That concern was soon consumed in a dozing dream of Gerald. Gerald, standing over her, grimacing down, shouting: *Cunt! Bitch! Sleazehole! Pain in the ass! What are you to me? Squeeze my nuts and let me come!* It's just for now, only a shadow, only a sore on the lung like a swallowed nut, shell and all, pressing in on the throat from the inside, welling the thyroid, aching there, aching there. Feel the water on the cheek, a damp kiss wiping away the tears.

What are you to me? It echoed in her mind, spoke itself aloud with her own voice as she opened her eyes, looked into Gordon's concerned, frowning face, the sepia tone of his eyes gone colorless in the grey trimmed twilight that was already edging slowly to black.

"I'm your man," he said simply, answering. "Don't you know that?"

"But without..." she started to say but he shooshed her, helped her to her feet, hugged her tightly like he wanted to absorb her, make her a part of himself. He gave her his jacket, shiny at the elbows, frayed at the waist, and walked her back to the friendly warmth of the campfire.

They sat there and talked, calmly and maturely, alternating sobriety with silly animation, hugging and laughing only to regain control again, to discuss, to understand, then to hug and laugh again. This was their night, then, continuing for uncounted hours until the thick sickle moon, long gone over the western edge of the world, pulled the blue back into the sky by invisible strings, blanched the air slowly, coloring the dark underbellies of clouds with hues of orange, frosty salmon pink and sweet lavender--all the pastel colors and giddy hues of the rising dawn.

Chapter 28 - People

They each had only slept a few hours after breakfast before they broke camp and continued on their way. It was almost a forced move since it was the full light of day which had finally awakened them-- that and the shared feeling that if they dawdled too long at their present campsite, somehow too much time would be lost. Time lost to do what, though, neither of them was able to say, since theirs had so far had really been only an aimless wander rather than any sort of planned hike. Neither of them questioned the lack of reasons inherent in their wandering, footloose existence together. To use a popular phrase of the day, they were simply going with the flow. It was a friendly flow thus far, to be sure, allowing them to find a common friend in a basically decent sort of person as Jake Rine, find each other and the joys and sorrows that their union had already given them, find strangely homey consistencies in an abandoned diner, find people at a repurposed motel who could have been friends, given the chance if their new friends' karmas (another popular catchword) were not so divergent from their own. Their "flow" was special, linear and languid. Except for a few instances of pain, their ambling wander through the backroads together had been quite pleasant, sometimes ecstatic though several times downright boring but never – at least as far as physical motion was concerned – never static.

So they walked, trotted, talked – learning all the while the traits and inner ways of the other; quite honest ,with few secrets held – clasped hands, traded amenities, courtship kisses, endearments and private pats and gooses, each keeping the other going, looking forward to the coming evening which was each day's only real goal. During the evening they would prattle, leer and longingly sigh. It was a time when there would always be more to learn – spoken, heard, seen and felt – always something new, something to be recalled, ruminated over and let out in a new, homogenized form; something shown, something revealed; a fantasy performed. They spoke of things like this – verbal gooses, they called them – and time passed, the sun climbed to its noontime zenith and the day stretched and continued on.

Before it got there, however, they came upon the last of the "towns" listed on the sign at the crossroads where they had parted company with their loner friend, Mr. Rine.

Here, then, was Sunup. It was a sign itself, actually, which said SUNUP LODGE, ¾ MI. The wooden sign peeled paint and splinters, was plagued with dry rot in its upright stanchions which had been driven deep into the granite that grew out of the earth in a flat topped hump, and came whitely up to the knees like a mini Cliff of Dover. On the sheer front side of this little cliff was a black painted arrow, badly flaked and nearly eradicated by the elements so that only the barest outline of the arrow was left showing the way up a steep and rocky path accessible only by the sturdier of off-road vehicles, and the more fragile conveyance of foot power.

Curiosity, go with the flow, devil-may-care, why not? Nothing in the way of reasons are given in Thanielle's later thought-journals as to why they chose to investigate this out-of-the-way locale. She only says that no words were exchanged between her and Gordon; that they just looked at one another, nodded and started up the bumpy path. Maybe it was the second sign that they saw only a few yards up the road from the first, this one jammed securely into the softer soil, crimson paint on a whitewashed background that had made the decision likely and brought their innate curiosity to the fore. It may have been the incentive to interest, a goad to wonder, but certainly not as obvious as Thanny's notebook sketching intended it to seem. For the sign simply said:

FOR SALE, LEASE OR RENT
HANDEL & MARKUM REALTY
CONTACT MRS. HANDEL
462-5483

Gordon's usual easy, sauntering gait was no longer so easy. Even without the excess weight of the duffle tied to the pack frame anymore, he was easily hulking forty pounds in his shoulders and hips. He didn't stumble, even though the terrain was rocky enough to fell the surest footed woodsman: a minefield morass of outcroppings, securely anchored sole-tearing barbs and razor edged slates, rolling rock avalanche starters which, when stepped on, served in the manner of marbles spread out on a tile floor and ankle spraining chuckholes all along the way. He only gasped and panted, sweated and wheezed like a three pack a day smoker after an around-the-block jog. Thanny was little better, though she did not have so much to carry – maybe ten pounds to Gordon's ungainly forty – but she prided herself on the fact that, through the length of their uphill struggle, she didn't once have to sit down for a breather. It was he who had called a halt to rest, though only once, and for which she sullied his ego but good, causing him to lash out weakly: "Just as natural as your complaint was yesterday, Sister. Now be quiet or I'll just masturbate tonight."

To which she replied, "Yeah, like that's going to be any kind of a reason for anything. Okay, then so will I; it'll just be me fingering someone I love anyway; just getting and giving all in one motion, Baby."

Soon enough – an hour, to be exact – they came to Sunup, a rambling mansion that sat on the crest of a knobby peak overlooking the valley below, a vista of several mountains out in the vast, spring greening distance. For the last fifty yards or so before coming to the house, the path entrenched itself, cutting a neck-deep gulley through the forest floor, exposing roots and subterranean boulders from its sheer sides. The path was raw and even more strewn with rocky detritus than the lower portion of the trail had been. But there was a grassy field at the end where the land levelled off, all pale green and smoky greys blending together as the little meadow forced itself out of its winter hibernation back to semi-verdant life. Beyond the grass was the rear entrance to Sunup. It was huge against the bright late morning sky, green and rambling, nothing much to it but bulk, width and eight chimneys. The meadow was its backyard and it swept around the left side to the front, its right boundary being an almost impenetrable wall of briar underbrush. They followed a fresh set of tire tracks around to the front where they were met by the dual surprise of the stately grandeur of the house's front façade, and a small gaggle of people studying the house from the open doors of the vehicle that had brought them there by a strictly different route than the one that Thanny and Gordon had taken.

It was an English Tudor marvel of elegance. The house had been built of native fieldstone which made the massive structure seem almost to have grown right out of the soil. It was all shades of green and grey, from foundation to its corniced eaves. A front yard patio of multi-hued flagstones, behind which two bay windows loomed, gave the arriving couple a view of the living room and dining room which comprised the main part of the front of the house. There was a smaller, similarly styled domicile attached to the left, like the wing of a hospital or orphanage, for use by servants. The windows were compartmented, some eighty individual frames per each bay, random panes being of pastel shades of meticulously stained glass, giving the forward jut of the bellying whole a whimsical, almost fairytale quality, set as it was in the front of such a stolidly imposing piece of lovingly designed architecture. From the patio as well as from the vantage of one looking out through the color speckled windows, the view over the landscape from this windy height was truly magnificent. A cone shaped swath had been cut through the trees with the forward patio serving as the point, the whole of mountain upon mountain, range upon range, diminishing into the hazy distance as the broad, seemingly infinite base of the triangle. The effect was beautifully orchestrated by whatever landscape artist had been commissioned for the job, excellently executed to a staggeringly climactic lift of the senses. From the steep trail to trench to meadow to the mundane kitchen-end of the house, then round to the front to this. It was not quite a simple, step by step progression of logic from one thing to the next to the next until the final moment was arrived at, but once attained, however you got there, the final payoff was aesthetically enormous.

"Ngaow!" said Gordon, his voice breaking through the catch in his throat. It had begun as something of a gasp before finally coming out as a nasal cat's cry.

"It is quite splendid, isn't it?" said the man, large of body, medium of height, small of face, whose hand was a rock solid mass when Gordon shook it; all meat, the bones buried amid a thick padding of muscle and subcutaneous fat. He flourished a card that identified him as Anthony Carandino, Contractor and Builder. His wife was pleasant though distant as she greeted the hikers with a cursory nod. The realtor, Mrs. Handel, who had been in the process of showing the Carandinos the finer points of Sunup's advantages as a summer home when she was so rudely interrupted, crassly demanded to know what these young hooligans wanted. Mr. Carandino wouldn't hear of turning them away, though, was adamant in the face of the realtor's chagrin at being so unceremoniously upbraided and his wife's uncaring lethargy in the matter.

"The house," said Mrs. Carandino meekly, trying to get things moving back on track so they could be done with the damned charade and get back to town." Let's see the house for Chris'sake."

Mr. Carandino, by the fact of his wife's adamancy in the matter, plus the fact that Mrs. Handel so craved this sale and was willing to let the matter drop to please the prospective buyer, had won the round by default.

"Come along now," he said loudly and happily as they approached the front entrance of the mansion, nudging Thanielle playfully in the small of her back as they proceeded. The two hikers had been included in the little group mainly by the man's largesse, their only payment for the privilege being the answering of a few rhetorical questions through the course of the tour, most of which were directed at Thanny.

Mrs. Carandino had no questions to ask, only shifted the lovingly sculpted nest of her sedately coifed hair (silver-grey, though that was surely not an indication of her age) as she cast steamily eloquent glances in Gordon's direction as they approached the impressive house.

They entered the stately mansion through the double front doors which was situated between the two sparkling bay windows. A long, high ceilinged hallway ran through the center of the house, front to rear. They were first shown the spacious living room, sedately appointed to resemble a 19th Century men's club, replete with cushiony easy chairs, end tables supporting shaded, marble and oak based lamps that would give off a soft, congenial, almost romantic glow for an evening of friendly chats around the massive main hearth. Chairs, it seemed, were the main furnishings in the room; there wasn't a sofa or loveseat to be seen. Chairs were positioned around the room in groups of twos and threes, others isolated in the corners and along the walls under wall hangings of a small variety of weaponry such as Seventeenth Century blunderbusses, paired Dragoon revolvers, Winchester rifles and medieval shields crossed over with paired sabers .

There was nothing plastic or phony at all here, everything was authentic and fashioned of natural material, all giving off a dry odor of age and careful preservation. The severed head of a large moose overhung the fireplace and had the place of honor directly across from the living room bay window, the colors of tinted glass glinting in his deep brown eyes, giving him the look of life even now, so many years after his death throes had been humanely dealt by a crack-shot guest of the house who had come for the big game that was so plentiful in those hills and valleys that were the property for which the manse was its heralded centerpiece.

To the right and left of the head of this majestic beast were two contradictory coats-of-arms. As the viewer faced the wide eyed moose head, to the right there was an eagle, wings spread heroically, carrying a sheaf of wheat in one talon, an olive branch in the other, a U of a laurel wreath underscoring the bird and his unusual cluatch. Over this, emblazoned in the stylized flutter of a banner was the legend "IMPERIUM/SAPIENTIA/PAX/LABORIS." To the right of the disembodied head was a plaque depicting a Bacchanalian debauch in full swing around which were scattered the words VITAE, AMORIS, FELICITAS and MORTIS. Each of these words seemed to be attached to a specific area of the mutely shaded picture, meant to illuminate the happenings in the busy composition. Mortis was a beer bellied pudge laying inert under a table with a shiv buried to the hilt in his chest; Amoris was a man with his lecherous hand buried elbow deep in the bodice of a laughing wench whose own hand was investigating his bulging crotch under the table at which they sat, she in his lap, and both of them oblivious to the serenade of Felicitas, a trio of gaily singing sots, each man with his own overflowing flagon of good cheer raised in a bleary toast to Vitae-- a curtained off area from which a midwife was emerging with a newborn infant gathered carefully in her arms. She stepped gingerly over the splayed legs of Mortis as she made her way to the singing trio, one of which, presumably, was the proud papa. She was not looking at the men, however, but was directing her smiling gaze at the seamy doings of the mutually fondling pair at the table, no doubt giving them her silent blessing for their later actions which would, in time, bring her future business as a bearer of sweet tidings.

The next stop was across the wide hall into the dining room. There, a long groaning board of a table was lined on either side by a continuous redwood bench, the head and foot of each one – up to the discretion of the owner to decide which the head and which was the foot – occupied by two matching straight back armchairs, regal in size and décor though immensely uncomfortable on which to sit. The room was more sparingly appointed than the living room, though of equal size and had the same open vista through its own glittering bay window past the front patio to the immense breadth of vision beyond. Though it did have its decorative flair for the masculine – tans and browns abounding in leather and brocade, the mounted fish on the wall above the mantel, eyes of the mountain goat and cougar heads staring down at the diners as they would clean their plates of gamey stew, the stuffed and mounted owl and quail seeming about to fly and scatter from their perches in opposite corners of the room – this was seen as a place mainly for the taking of meals, said Mrs. Handel apologetically, though of course the future owners could take what liberties they liked once the sales contract was signed.

The kitchen was huge with counters and stoves lined up and arranged in restaurant fashion for maximum efficiency. Colanders, spatulas, sieves, whisks, bowls, graters, pots, pans and all the other many tools of the culinary trade hung from hooks along a rack above the freestanding preparations counter in the center of the room. The three sinks, five ovens, four stovetops, two refrigerators, several low deep freezers and a separate professional-use gas grill all might have been found in the kitchen of a five-star restaurant attached to a five-stare resort hotel. With the right chef and ingredients, a four or five course meal of gourmet quality could easily have been prepared here without taxing the available equipment any more than an eggs and toast breakfast would have taxed the efficacy of a three pilot apartment stove and a two slot toaster. The necessity of such an elaborate array of preparedness in the kitchen became apparent when the tour was shown the upstairs rooms of this three story millionaire's abode, that boasted ten master sized bedrooms each with its own in-suite bath each with its own changing alcove. The alcove in each master suite alone, Thanny said, would have been enough for her. It was – the one they were shown, for there was no time for them to be taken through all ten of the suites – big enough to fit a bed and dresser all on its own, and was only slightly smaller than the bedroom she had had in her parents' house.

"Mr. Swarthman liked to entertain his hunting parties rather lavishly," said Mr. Handel instructively, unconcerned by the sudden start that her disclosure had caused in the demeanor of the interlopers.

"Kenneth Swarthman?" Gordon asked.

"No, Edmund Swarthman," said the realtor tiredly. *Really, didn't these children know anything?* "Kenneth's father. The dear man finds that he no longer has either want or need of his country estate and has instructed my office to sell. He says that he is perfectly willing to take a loss." As soon as she had said the word loss, Mrs. Handel was immediately regretful of her unprofessional admission to a prospective buyer.

"How big a loss would Mr. Swarthman be willing to absorb?" asked Mr. Carandino as he mentally tallied up a liberal estimate of his own.

Mrs. Handel casually mentioned a figure as she opened the door to the bathroom and pointed out such features as the cushioned and heated toilet seat, the sterling silver fixtures and the necessary inclusion of a bidet to the usual collection of porcelain appliances. Thanny whistled a two-note glissando of disbelief at the mentioned price being asked for the home, drawing a chuckle and a massaging clap on the back from the prospective new owner.

"In the city a place of this size would run you four or five times that amount if you could ever find something even remotely like it," he said as he ran his hand down to her rump to give it a gentle pat. She moved away from this sudden attention and cast a glance at the man's wife, who hadn't seemed to notice. "The property there would be constricting at the best, and the only view you would have from any window would be of an office building across the street."

Mrs. Carandino lit a cigarette on her way down the back stairs and kept the rest of the group waiting while she finished it on the patio. She uncouthly blew a gust of smoke directly into Gordon's face. French custom, she told him in way of apology for the action, not bothering to explain the oblique reference. Here she took her first real appraisal of the glorious view down the megaphone shaped alley to the east. The sunrises here are truly incredible, Mrs. Handel told them, hammering her point none-too-subtly home. There was a perfect reason why the mansion was named for the dawning of each new day, she said. Even from this comparatively dull visage before them – dawn was still a long way away from this point in time, after all – they all had to agree that it was an inspiring vista.

Mrs. Handel's Jeep station wagon had a clearance high enough to take them over the most burgeoning of the boulders in the path on the trip down to Honeysuckle. Mrs. Carandino sat in the front between the realtor and Gordon with her arm draped over the back of the seat, the other, her left, placed crosswise in her lap, her hand resting gently on Gordon's thigh. With each successive bump and jostle that threw the five of them up and down in their seats Gordon was sure that he felt the grab of the woman's claw-like hand on his leg each time it slapped down. He looked back over the seat to Thanny as if to ask something while not sure if anything needed to be said. This odd sort of forwardness troubled him, coming from a woman who was probably old enough to be his mother. Not so much trouble, though, as he watched Thanny fending off the insistently clutching hands of Mr. Carandino.

At the next bump, however, he had his own worries to contend with as the woman's crony paw came down softly, not on his leg but a few inches to the right of its normal flirty position. *Proposition: This is what I am after, what I want, young fella.* Gordon was sure that she had the financial clout – if not the lure of beauty and/or personality – to attain what she was after.

Gordon, though, was not giving away what was wanted; he was frantic to keep it for himself, and as his mildly frenzied rapid-fire glances back to Thanny for help seemed to testify, she felt the same way. She was busy with her own troubles at the moment, however – but was that a giggle he heard coming from her? – and so he dealt with the offending, persistently wanton hand of Mrs. Carandino in the only way that he knew how: false surrender. He laid his hand over hers as it groped, waited for the next jounce of the car to loosen the hand's undulant hold there, and when the moment came, he hooked his thumb under her palm for leverage and pulled the hand free. He then bent down out of view of the woman's husband and kissed a white knuckle, almost cutting his lip on the ornate scrolls and curlicues of her wedding band. Looking slyly up at her from his bowed position, he winked at her and mouthed the words, "Not now. Later."

The rest of the trip back to Honeysuckle was completed in relative ease. Gordon held Mrs. Carandino's hand securely in his lap so as to offset any resumed attempt she might take in mind at continuing her seduction of the younger man. The back seat was also fairly quiet--no more giggles, if that was what he had heard, or scuffling noises, only the calmest murmur of conversational tones. Thanny and Mr. Carandino, too, seemed to have come to something of a mutual understanding of what the near future was to hold for the two of them.

Upon arrival at the storefront offices of Handel & Markum, they were dropped off, each of them given a pecking kiss, a card with an address and phone number, each receiving almost identical admonitions – *Call me, I'll make it worth your while* – before the middle aged contractor and his wife followed Mrs. Handel into the office which the realtor's husband and his partner had founded so many decades ago. She hustled them through the door quickly, so determined was she to discuss the couple's future with Sunup Lodge as its backdrop.

Chapter 29

"What did he say to you?"

They were on the corner of the main thoroughfare through town on which was located the resplendent Balshaw Hotel. Stately, square and imposing, it had once been the important social and business center of town and, even though it had lost much of its appeal since its heyday, it still continued to play host to a large and lucrative clientele of old money and young ideas. Carol Street, upon which its decorously corniced and awninged main entrance opened, had once been the main thoroughfare through Honeysuckle, as part of State Route 10-E. Things had changed since Carol was the main drag, however, with the completion of the Interstate which paralleled Agnes Street a mile to the south of the Balshaw, leaving the fast food chains, gas stations, gift shops and motels that populated that tawdry stretch of road to their sudden success, leaving the Balshaw in its own private eddy of lushness and taste out of the raucous wake of vulgate travelers.

"Nothing in so many words," she answered absently as she studied the menu posted in Balshaw's curtained restaurant window. "But I think his intentions were pretty clear."

"Mistress?"

"Something like that. Said he'd make it worth my while. He even mentioned something about an apartment in the city, though I'm not quite sure if he was offering or just making a suggestion. I was getting so angry that I guess I wasn't paying all that much attention. I just wanted to whack him where he lived. What about the lady?"

"You give her too much credit with that. Lady – yeah, right, that's what she is, a real refined lady. But she was going for pretty much the same as he was with you-- not is so many words, mostly just hands. I think she wants me for a live-in houseboy or something like that." He hunched his shoulders, feeling not too sure of the particularities which the "offer" involved. "At least for one night anyway."

They said no more about it, studied the menu in silence, and shook their heads in tandem at the prices shown in the restaurant window, debated on what to do next. The old clock that hung from the second story of the hotel above their heads said one o'clock. There was still plenty of time to find a new campsite. Some of the countryside up near Sunup Lodge looked promising. Or should they take Carol Street on out of town to seek newer fields to wander? There wasn't so much a debate between them as a listing of ideas. Neither of them wanted to search too far for a place to camp down since neither had had too much sleep the night before and both were pretty well beat, early as it still was.

They haggled tiredly for a half hour, positions having been taken – Thanielle for the turn-back to the vicinity of Sunup, Gordon for the forward rout along Carol Street and out of town – and they weren't getting anywhere near an agreement when they were pulled out of their soft spoken argument by hale and hearty greetings from a young man they had never seen before.

"Ah," he said. "But I've seen you." And he commenced to explain how he knew them – by sight at least. He eyed Thanny appreciatively before whispering, "Nice ass, I must say." From what he told them about his first sight of the sleeping couple on the floor-laid mattress in the living quarters of the Corliss Diner it was evident that his whispered encomium had been based on his actual remembered sight of Thanny's bare derriere as she slept in a coupled embrace with Gordon. "Nice everything else, too."

He was what Thanny, in high school, would have labeled as cute, maybe even foxy. His face was boyish, like Gordon's, but in his face the parts seemed to fit together more smoothly and evenly. His hair was short and neatly combed, the clothes he wore – beige cashmere casual jacket, grey corduroys, grey velour button down shirt and powder blue running shoes worn without socks – bespoke a style and taste, both of hybrid origins like his car which was parked a few blocks away. He and his college friends had fashioned it themselves – all except the plush leatherette interior – out of parts and pieces of several incompatible makes and models. They had augured out holes where bolts would not fit, stripped away chrome and rust with sandpaper, chisels and crowbars, found ways of getting parts to fit and stay by use of wires twisted and tied and welded together where more experienced body workers would have long since given up.

The final result had been a true mélange of mechanistic plastic surgery whose first impression upon any given onlooker would be a combination of distrust in one's perception and sheer wonder at what was sitting there at the corner waiting for the light to turn green. As strange and inbred a thing as it looked, the boy said, it still worked like magic at being a real chick magnet.

"Turned this young lady's head in my direction, that's for sure," he said in way of introducing his girlfriend whose name was Elizabeth.

"Call me Betty," she said as she squeezed each of their hands in turn in a quick mashing, pumping motion that pained the elbow of each of them. She was pretty, the sort of girl that, at a glance, Gordon would have called a Mamma's girl. He had dated one once during his three-year trudge through the countryside and little burgs much like this one before he had committed himself to the care of the State Hospital. He had come away from that relationship of several months standing with little to show for it but a fading hickey and the memory of scoldings from the girl's mother about how decent young men treat their dates as his waited obediently in the next room to be taken to the latest action adventure movie at the town's cinema duplex.

When the young man finished recounting the situation on how he had so easily recognized Thanny and Gordon, a gleam came across his face and radiated from his movie star eyes, warming his cheeks into a happy smile. Carey, he said was his name, short for nothing if they must know and he and Betty were just about to have a bite of lunch. Would they care to join him?

Gordon and Thanny hedged, tried to be polite but were finally goaded into confessing their current financial status.

"But I'm the one doing the inviting, aren't I?" Carey asked, a note of pain pinching his deep voice. "So, it's on me, then. On me, right?"

If he said so, they agreed as they allowed themselves to be hustled through the wide revolving doors of the hotel, through the lobby into the muted "atmosphere" of Balshaw's posh restaurant.

They chatted amiably as if they had been friends for years. Carey dominated the occasion as seemed to be his habit, with tales of life at O'Dell College, stories of professors and lecturers with academic or exotic sounding names (*Balyabantchee? San Gregoria? Deliarnay? What did they all teach?*) and tedious, boring and incredibly involved and intricate coursework on the more esoteric topics in English Literature, Physics, Comparative Political Systems and Rhetoric. The term was not over up at

O'Dell; he had come down for the week to be with his kewpie-pie – she blushed at this public use of his private pet name for her – while he waited for the grades to be posted. And what about you two?

They started to recall their first meeting several weeks ago but the mention of the last week reminded Carey of an anecdote, quite amusing, really, he assured them. Gordon gave Betty an appealing look which was answered with a shrug that seemed to intimate that that was just the way that Carey was, like it or not.

The story took some time to tell and, when Carey saw that he was not holding his audience's attention he turned to the backpack which occupied the fifth chair at the table and continued to tell the tale of the old duffer professor who brought his Saint Bernard into class and how the mammoth beast had gotten himself amorously attracted and ultimately attached to the leg of a comely co-ed in the front row. Ruined her best pair of designer jeans, he said. The professor paid the cleaning bill, it was rumored, though there was talk that the man actually did the cleaning himself, letting the pants soak in his kitchen sink while he turned his own amorous attentions to the pantless (though not pantie-less) young lady who breathlessly (panting?) awaited his academically assured administrations on his living room sofa.

After the meal (roast beef sandwiches, pie-a-la-mode and coffee all around) Carey begged their pardon and left the table. Betty giggled prettily – childishly, really, Thanny judged – said that he always had done that, like no sooner was a meal done than it was off to the little boys' room. Food must go through him like water, she supposed. A few minutes later her bladder was trying to tell her something as well and she promised to be right back.

"Lovely couple," Gordon commented after Betty had left.

"Right out of a fairy tale," answered Thanny dryly.

"Nice looking guy."

"He'd do in a pinch," she admitted but then immediately turned it around. "But so would you." A second later, she let go a shrill peep. "Gordon!"

"You said in a pinch," he reminded her impishly.

"Check, sir," said the waiter in a strict, imperious drone.

They told him that the young man with whom they had come would be taking care of the bill.

"The gentleman and young lady have already left, sir. He left instructions with management that you would be settling the bill."

"Oh. I see."

"Waiter," said Thanny. "Can this wait just a moment longer? I have to use the facilities."

"Must be an epidemic," Gordon muttered, closing his eyes to the exorbitant figure showing on the bottom line of the tab.

"Certainly, Miss. I shall return momentarily."

She returned shortly, quietly reporting to Gordon that "kewpie-pie" had indeed flown the coop with Cute Carey. No sooner was she reseated than the waiter reappeared and hung over them like a vulture from a low branch. Thanny counted out two five dollar bills, a single and a shiny new quarter.

"That ought to do it," she said cheerily.

"Nice," said Gordon dully and showed her the check. "But not quite enough."

"Forty four dollars?!" she squeaked at the sight of the figure on the bill. "For four lousy sandwiches?"

"And four pies-a-la-mode and four coffees," the waiter reminded her.

She looked over the bill in more detail and sneered. "Two and a half dollars for a stinking cup of coffee?"

"Our prices, Miss," the waiter shrugged. What could he do about it? He only worked there.

"But that's all the money we've got," she whined.

"I see," he said, sizing up the situation. "Quite all right Miss. No problem."

"No problem?" said Gordon, relieved a little bit by the man's patient tone of voice. "But.... The balance...?"

"It will be taken care of presently. If you will both just wait here."

In a few minutes the waiter was replaced by an officious looking man dressed splendidly in a snugly fitting mortician's tuxedo. He had a stern but calm face. The corners of his mouth seemed to be forcibly restrained from smiling and there were deeply cut crow's feet radiating from the outer corners of his unpleasantly piercing eyes. His forehead was high, a straight path straight to the back of his neck; the type of partial baldness that is often disparagingly referred to as "the toilet seat." He was Mr.

McLaren, the manager, he said, politic and kind as he made sure that what the waiter had told him indeed true.

"We get this thing seldom here, you understand," he told them mildly as she led them through the restaurant to a pair of swinging aluminum doors that opened into a wide-tiled room. Gordon had felt a little bit foolish hefting the back pack into the restaurant when they had first arrived, positively insane as he lugged it past scores of patrons, and into the kitchen where he was instructed to stow it behind a little used dish rack in the far corner.

"You see it in the movies," Gordon said as he was handed an apron. "Read about it in books and magazines...."

Thanny got hers, a full-length affair of coarse linen with the laundry service's stamp bleeding in ink across the hem.

"I know," she said as she looped the apron over her head and fumblingly tied a bow behind her back. "But you never thought that it really happens or that it would happen to you."

"Ah, but kiddies, it has," said McLaren sadly before he left. "And you have a pretty big tab to work off. Have Jorge show you what to do. And be nice. Lunch crowd's not too bad today but there's still dinner, as well, and being this is Friday it's bound to be a bear, I'm afraid."

They could take little solace in his well-meant sympathy, but at least it was something.

Chapter 30

The head dishwasher at the Balshaw Hotel was proud of his title and was sure to let Gordon and Thanielle know of his lofty status in no uncertain terms.

"This fellow here knows it," he said, indicating his young assistant who had thus far remained anonymous. The young fellow smiled warily when his boss gestured in his direction, sneered derisively when the spotlight was off of him so he could go back to removing dishes and silverware from the square, deep trays which had just rolled out of the steam-belching washer. His actions were quick but precise as every dish was placed on its correct stack, each cup into its own compartment in the crisscross tray, silverware wiped and each butter knife, steak knife, dinner fork, salad fork, cake fork, teaspoon, soup spoon, table spoon and jelly serving spoon tucked into its own separate plastic container. He muttered a Spanish phrase and took the silverware and coffee cups to the waiters' station.

"He knows it,'" the head dishwasher said again with little conviction as he watched the door swing closed behind the boy. "Snotty as hell, but Berto's all right. Tries my patience sometimes, but he's okay."

"Bare-toe?" said Gordon, having misheard the name so that he pronounced its syllables as they were two words rather than to be drawn together as one. "What kind of mother would name her kid Bare-toe? Does he have a brother or sister named Naked Finger?" He chuckled at the idea.

"No, no," said the dishwasher with a laugh and he repeated the boy's name, rolling the r playfully on his tongue. "Short for Al-berto. And I'm Jorge. And you two are deadbeats. So, now we all know each other, right? So let's get one thing straight, okay? No lip. I'm boss here, even if the snotty punk out there don't want to face it. Ask anybody. This ain't no kitchen here. They call it 'support' like we was a jock strap or sumpin' but wit'out us the people out there in the dinin' room would be eatin' offa filt'y plates loaded wit' germans. So we're just's important as the snobby bums on d'udder side o' the wall there who cooks the food. Clear?"

They said that it was crystal clear, but how did all the clean dishes get from here, where they were washed and sanitized to where the cooks could make use of them? Jorge smiled brightly revealing a glowing patchwork of gold, silver and natural, yellowed enamel in his wide mouth. *Smart kid*, he said and showed them both the door in the far wall at gut level that opened to the smells and sounds of meals being prepared. A conveyor comprised of numerous, hissing metal wheels led from the dishwashing station to where Berto had emptied the washer tray, then on toward the kitchen access door.

"Not much to do, really," Jorge said and told them what he expected of them: emptying the scraps off the plates when the waiters or busboys brought them in and then stacking them neatly in the washer trays was Gordon's job. All Thanny had to do was to take the dinner plates, cake plates, salad plates, soup dishes, soup cups, coffee cups and saucers, parfait glasses, water glasses, wine glasses and so on, and stack them when they came out of the washer. Berto would handle the actual operation of the machine, lugging the silverware, cups and saucers and glasses out to the waiters and give the finished stuff to the lard jockeys when they needed it.

"And what does that leave for you to do?"

"I'm the boss here," he reminded them huffily. "I supervise."

"Didn't I meet you once before beside a stream in the woods?" Thanny asked conversationally, knowing that it was probably not the thing to say. It was too obtuse, the reference, too personal to be understood by someone who hadn't been there.

"Camping? I don't go camping or for any of that kind of stuff. I get all my exercise wit' the wife and kids. Le'me tell you, they sure keep your hands full. Them and holdin' down a job like this for more'n' five years. S'nough for me, you bet."

"Five years here?" Gordon said as he scooped a handful of mashed potatoes and peas from a plate with his bare hand and plopped the mess into a plastic lined can. "Then you must know Alonzo Girondia."

"'Lonzo You know'im?"

"Only by reputation," Gordon admitted. Pressed for details he told what little he knew, amply abetted by Thanny's additional knowledge on the subject.

"And he's holding his own with two women under the same roof?" Jorge was beaming, reveling in the news of his old acquaintance's tricks. "You know, he got himself in a scrape like that here once, too, with one o' the maids. The upper head downstairs chambermaid or lady with some kind o' four word title caught them in the kissy clinches and threatened to have them both fired unless Alonzo put equal time aside for her, too. Seems that one had the hots for'im all along and just then saw her chance. It went on for 'bout a month, he told me, before he found her smooching something heavy with a busboy or something and her hand in his pants, too. He weren't so kind as she'd been and he reported the babe and got her fired. Still doing the same thing, too, sounds like to me. Wonder why he never calls or writes or anythin'."

"Too busy, I guess," Gordon said, jumping his eyebrows á la Groucho Marx. He turned to Thanny with a look that could have been interpreted as pain, but she knew what he meant and nodded wisely. Yes, that was why they had run. He smiled sweetly and turned back to Jorge who gestured vehemently at the work that was piling up.

Jorge had never been at Sunup Lodge but he had heard a lot about it and the parties that old Edmund used to have up there in the old days, the drunken hunting accidents that occurred almost every weekend, the full blown orgies that would cap each party because of, or in spite of, the injuries sustained or simply because the old man was so dead-set on hosting an all-out blaster of a sex binge that nothing, not even the death or mutilation of one or more of his guests, would stop the festivities.

And Blazer?

And Blazer, said Jorge, was a complete surprise to him. World War Three survivor camp in a reconditioned motel? Sounded kind of flaky but he supposed that he could believe something like that of Kenneth – always had been the odd bird of that family. Wealthy guy like that, marrying an accountant's assistant from one of the lesser companies the family owned when he could have had his pick of the litter of the likes of the Vanderbilts, the Rockefellers, or the Carnegies? And pissing his inheritance and holdings away on almost any Right Wing charity that came along and then being the first in his immediate family to die? Though that last wasn't his fault, of course. Cancer's a truly democratic bastard that doesn't give a shit if you're rich or saintly or what; when it's got its guns out for you, that's all there is to say.

"World War Three," he said soberly. "Flaky, just like'im, I guess, to be afraid of shadows like that. Build yourself a shelter to hide in. But in Blazer? See what I mean about him pissin' his money away? That place pro'ly cost'im a wicked price when he could've had, say, Corliss for pract'ly a song."

"Corliss' just a snatch dive," said Berto sourly, showing that he had been paying attention all along. "All's good for is takin' chicks there what wanna get laid."

"Yeah, now," Jorge agreed, a bit nonplussed by his assistant's sudden interest. "Now that it's a broke down rat bin but back fourteen, fifteen years ago when them Planepatorrys were runnin' it before they got scared out, they had it pretty nice and woulda sold it for beans just to make a profit 'steada splittin' with nuthin' but humpin' their luggage to get themselves outta there real quick to save their skins."

"You mean the Planepatorians?" said Thanny, getting into this particular phase of the conversation.

"Yeah. You one of'em?"

"No, but Gordy and me were up there not long ago. There's a big poster there, tells all about it."

"Looking to buy," said Gordon, putting in his whimsical two cents' worth. Berto snorted, muttered something that sounded like *poor boys* or *poe-brays* but it trailed off in his throat where another derisive snort was forming.

"Who were they?" Thanny asked, trying to pursue it further. "These Planepatorians?"

"Nobody really knows," Jorge said as he shoved another load of dishes through the flapping door into the kitchen.

"Know what?" asked a loud voice from the other side.

"Know that your cock needs a goddamned crane to keep it up! And I do know it, too! Your wife's been blabbin' about it all over town!" he called through the open door. "Mind your own p's and q's, willya! And cook'em up good, too! I don't wanna lose my job here 'cause you guy's're servin' up pig swill!"

"Agh!" yelled the voice from the chef's side as the door sneezed shut.

"Anyway," he continued, turning back to them. "We never really found out who or what they were all about. All we heard was this Planepatorry thing and that was it. They weren't up there too long before they were sent packin'."

"Chased out?"

"Kind of," said Berto. "But you were up there. How long do you think a bidness'd make out up there afore foldin'? Six months, maybe? That was part of it. They were just helped along to that 'clusion, that's all."

"Heathens," said Jorge with finality. "Or pagans or Jews or niggers or Japs or hippies. That's all folks up this way had to hear back then and they all went off halfcocked, lookin' for blood. Nothin' real vi'lent, now, mind you, just scare tactics. They got'em to vamoose pretty darned quick, too."

"Jews, niggers and Japs," Gordon mused, looking at the man square in the face. "Nothing against Puerto Ricans or Cubans?"

"S'long as we stay in town," Jorge answered evenly, eying the new helper suspiciously. *What kind of bigot was this?* "But even now, with things good and quiet like they are, you still ain't going to find my spic ass up in them hills after dark."

"Mine neither," vowed Berto. "But back then it wasn't so much the et'nic thing as it was them bein' heathens. Even Jews're better'n heathens around here. Least Jews believe in sumpin we can unnerstan'."

"You two felt some of that down-home type pre-jew-diss yourselves," said Jorge, turning the conversation back in a more governable direction. He knew Berto's views on the differences between religions, uninformed as the basis for those ideas largely were, but he hadn't the slightest idea what to expect of these two newcomers. He knew, too, of the vehemence which Berto could summon once he got going on the subject of heathens and Jews, his favorite pet peeve, but wouldn't at all be able to predict the attitude of these two – he hated to even consider the word but it was really the only definitive one he could think of – *outsiders.* Best not to open that particular can of worms. "Those two college kids that stiffed you for the check were just practicing a little old fashioned hippie baiting."

"Hippies?" Thanny nearly cried and then almost laughed at the idea. She also almost dropped a newly washed plate onto the tile floor. Berto applauded her successful juggling effort that kept the plate from tumbling to a shattering at the girl's feet. "There aren't any hippies anymore. That flower child thing has been history for...." She couldn't remember how long; she just know that it had come to an end long before she was even born.

The "movement," as her parents had termed the advent of flower power fervor in the nineteen sixties and early seventies, had experienced a slow and whimpering demise, reality fading away so that all that were left were the catchwords and phrases: *flower power, hippies, love children, psychedelic, acid rock, military industrial complex, love is all you need....* There had been no last stand, no final glorious show of strength that had failed. There were still vestiges left, of course, pockets of longhairs here and there, a commune or two that managed to keep running despite wholesale Judas Iscariot sell-outs to the loathed and revered *"Establishment."* There were still hippies around, devoted and incorruptible, but it was out of vogue now. No more Woodstocks or Monterey Pops. Hippies were anachronisms in the face of the profit motive and MBA's and Master's degrees in Computer Science and Business Management.

"Oh," said Jorge, a little surprised to hear that hippies were passé and no longer a force to be reckoned with. "Well, some news gets around slow up here. Anyhow, those kids that skunked you for the price of their lunches may have looked like just Jack and Jill to you, but those kids--in spite of their going to college and betterin' themselves—they's jus' rednecks through and through. Hippie baiting, nigger baiting, Jew baiting, it's all just a big ol' joke to them."

"Big joke," said Berto, getting ready to bring another clattering load of silverware to the waiters' station. "Jus' 'cause a fella's beard's gettin' a leetah bit full. Nasty suckers, them kids. Heesh!" And he backed his way through the swinging door and then did a neat about face into the restaurant dining room.

"Really?" said Gordon, delightedly as he looked around for something he could use for a mirror. "Full? My beard is that good?"

Jorge came over to him for a closer look, rubbed the raspy stubble on Gordon's chin with a slow, sawing motion of his sweaty hand. "Well, sure thing you ain't from San Juan, my friend. But you got a nice weed patch growin' there. Not bad, long's the lady don't complain."

"Hasn't bothered me so far," Thanny said with a smile.

They clattered and worked without talking for the next few hours, the only conversation among them being on subjects related to the job at hand. Gordon took Berto's place a few times, carrying out the silverware and the cups and saucers to the waiters. He even earned a pat on the back from the manager once when a particularly needed load was brought out. The man was nice, was fair, Gordon conceded in his mind as he returned to the dishwasher's section. He liked the guy.

They were allowed dinner for free, eating off of plates shoved through from the kitchen loaded with Chicken Cacciatore and Italian flat beans. They used the roller conveyor for their table. That was about an hour before the dinner trade began. Jorge had told them that that would be the last of the work that Thanny and Gordon would have to do for the day as well as it being the most hectic part of the job for all of them.

He said that it was times like this – the lull before the expected rush – that he felt like heading down to the freight yard and hopping on a northbound deadheader to just get the hell out and be free once more. *Fly the coop, go wherever, however, whyever – just up and go.*

He sighed and waved a hand like an injured wing, his elbow pressed to his side. That was so long ago, he said, he probably wouldn't know how to go about it anymore. He had been young then, unattached, full of bullshit and life. *Viva del Diablo*, his Mamma had called it, that life of a shiftless tramp, but he hadn't cared what she or anyone else thought of his life on the move. It was fun and had left him with a veritable fount of memories, train to train, bumming the country, him the only spic on the rail route, then, for sure, but it was a life – the life – and he gave it up like.... He snapped his fingers, a mushy sound amid the sharp echoes that rang off the mist covered tiles of the room like gunshots. Voices sounded louder than normal in that room, even at regular volume. His paltry finger-snap sounded flat, like the sound of a pillow being patted.

Honeysuckle Station was just a whistle stop on the old Rary-Wheelock run back then. There were regular platforms now and even a passenger line but back then the doddering old station master would have to crank up his shrill, cat-shrieking siren to alert an incoming before the engineer would give the recognition double-blast on his howling horn and slow down to find out what the need was. The current dishwasher of the Balshaw Hotel restaurant had seen the name of the town on a grimy sign as his own private boxcar slowed with the rest of the train. He liked the sound of it. It made him think of spring and summer, perfume and pretty ladies strolling to take the warm afternoon sunshine. He jumped off as the forty-car line-up crashed and clunked and rammed car into car into car behind the belching engine as it pulled itself to a dead halt, hissing like a long library shoooooosh for silence. He jumped from the boxcar in which he had been riding, sick from the stench of rotting oats that had filled the car. He had needed fresh air anyway, a drink of water, a meal. He found what he wanted and needed and more.

"A job?" asked Thanny, inviting him to continue.

"Dishwasher down at some dive along the tracks. I think it's gone now. But it was just to make enough to get along, get back on the next north or southbound loco and be out and gone once again."

"But you're still here," said Gordon. "You stayed."

Jorge nodded, stared absently at the far wall, the old dishrack there, the nylon edge of the backpack that peeked out from behind it. "What can I tell you? I liked the feeling of having a paycheck in my pocket, knowing where my next meal was coming from. That first place, the meals were half price for the 'ployees. Here, they're free. I've come up in the world and I like it. Got some self respeck, a nice family – Denita's a maid in the hotel and we got two kids in Balshaw's daycare each day 'til they'll be old enough for school – and I'm the boss in this little part of a hotel and I like where I am and what I do and, well...." He ruffled a hand through Berto's hair affectionately, causing the boy to scowl and turn away. Thanny watched the boy's face change as he turned away from Jorge's hand, from angry chagrin to glad resignation, then a gentle shudder of a facial muscles struggling to gain control of the mien that was attempting to transform his face from annoyance to content and then, once successful, back to the expression of displeasure that he wanted to convey to the world.

Thanny had been transfixed by the eloquence of the boy's face as it rattled back and forth and sideways amongst so many feelings and articulations before his countenance settled on the one silent articulation that was right for that particular moment.

Amazing, she thought as she watched the show taking place on the stage that was the boy's face; just simply amazing.

"But I still miss that footloose, fancy-free life sometimes. Just want to catch the next roaring freight out of here, leaving everything behind." He laughed nervously for a second. "If it just weren't for so many things. But I won't bore you wit' snaps of the wife and kids and tell you how happy I am and how I'm too old for that sort of thing now. It's all true but I don't have to tell ya. Take a look at the freight yard sometime and the people there, the hobos and bums and tell me if I made a bad choice. It was mine, too, you know. I didn't have my arm twisted or nuthin'. I don't regret any of it – just a bug up my ass once in a while. But there's a word for it.... It just don't seem to wanna come...."

"Reminiscence," Thanny offered.

"Nostalgia," said Gordon.

"Old fool," said Berto as nicely as he could.

"It's starting," said a busboy, coming through the door, pushing his piled cart. "Looks like a big night."

"Okay kids," said Jorge as he scraped the remains of his meal into the wide maw of the garbage bin. "Break's over."

The rest of the evening it was all the same. Work and talk, ideas and information over the clatter of automatic toil. The machine hissed, clambered clanked, shimmied and spewed forth trays of dishes to be stacked, cups and saucers to be brought out to the waiters' station, silverware to be sorted. Every time the door to the kitchen opened there was a constant demand for more dishes, faster work.

"Here it comes, slop jockies!" Jorge would yell as he pushed through another neatly stacked load for the cooks in the kitchen to put to use.

"About time, shit scrapers!" would be the call from the other side of the wall.

"I only scrape what you put on'em!" he would call back before letting the door slam shut.

It was a lively night, there was no denying that. Dinner trade ended at nine. By nine thirty they were almost through. There were still a few things to be cleared up, the machine to be broken down and cleaned, the last of the garbage to be carted out to the massive dumpster in the back of the restaurant, but Jorge told them to tell the manager that he said that they could go. He shook Gordon's hand with a firm, wet grip, kissed Thanny's cheek sloppily.

Berto waved, said, "'Bye. Take it easy," and helped Gordon with the back pack, roped the duffel onto Thanny's shoulders, brushing his hand a little too firmly against her left breast as he reached around from behind her to be sure that the ropes were secure. She kissed him near the ear and she whispered, in a warm tone, that he needed to get himself a girlfriend.

The manager, McLaren, wished them well, held a ten dollar bill out to Thanny. Over and above the amount of the check, he told them, smiling an elfin grin.

Thanny hugged him. "Thank you, you're sweet," she said.

The manager turned from Thanny and grabbed Gordon's hand with a surprising show of strength that quickly went lax so that by the time he let go of Gordon's hand the last impression Gordon had was of squeezing a mushy piece of raw meat.

The waiter that had started the whole thing directed them to the freight yards when they asked the way.

"Just look for the ashcan fires," he said as they left.

***

"So, that was Honeysuckle," Gordon said musingly as they turned off of Carol Street onto a narrow-paved lane. "We must come back to visit sometime."

"When your beard's fuller," she told him teasingly. "When the kids are grown up." She troubled herself with that last remark; as joking as she had meant it to be, she still was not exactly sure what it was all supposed to imply.

First of all, who were "the kids" she had mentioned" Who where their parents? How old were they? The answers to such questions would seem pretty facile, but then she was not so sure of anything anymore these days.

Chapter 31 – Writings

From Thanny's thought-book:

It should be enough to say that Jake Rine has returned into our lives again but, of course, it's not. It was not just a simple "hello, how have you been and here we are!" kind of friendly scenario where folks get together after not seeing each other for a while and they have lots and lots to catch up on. There was something in the air amongst the three of us. It was a kind of electricity. I'm sure that even Jake felt it; it must have prickled his skin. He seemed very nervous when I told him that Gordy and I had some important matters to discuss and that I preferred not to do so in front of his new friends.

His friends were three men, two with whom Jake had fallen in, he said, (though not in those exact words) since his arrival at the freight yard a few days earlier. The third guy, the youngest, was a frail looking fellow in tattered jeans and t-shirt who Jake had been with for nearly the entire time since Gordy and I had parted company with him over a week ago. The guy had a confused expression on his face and was someone that Gordon knew. They called each other by name as soon as they saw each other. Varnish? Was that what Gordy called him that made the guy suddenly come to life? Anyway, they chatted like two old ladies trading recipes over a backyard fence about I don't know what all, and there I was, trying to get Jake alone long enough to trade stories about where we had all been and what the three of us had been up to, but his other two friends were there, nosing in all the time, making hellacious pests of themselves.

The one man was tall and gangly, well over six feet tall. Every time I looked up at him all I saw was his sallow cheeks and the dark fuzzy lining of the insides of his nostrils. Jake and the other man called him T.R. His last name, I heard, was Arquill and he was very quiet.

"He just prefers not to talk." The third friend of Jake's told me about T.R. "But if he really needs to communicate deeply and I mean if he really, desperately needs to get something said, he writes it down and, Sweetpants, he can write like to tear the heart right out from behind those sexy boobs of yours. Be honest with me here, darlin': are those tits real or are you just smuggling softballs?"

This man's name was Phineas and his last name was Fargo. Like Wells Fargo, he told me, and then later he said that his name was like that little city in North Dakota and the nutzoid movie of the same name. He said that he thought it was Italian, though he couldn't be quite sure. I had to control myself from laughing when I first heard the name and that was when he really made me nervous. Aside from his constantly farting like some hydraulic machine gone totally out of control – real rip-roarers, some of them; I'm surprised his brakeman's overalls haven't been shredded in the seat with the force of some of those backfires of his – and aside from his blatant overtures about my physical appearance, he leers like a lovesick rapist at me every time I shift my weight, groans like he's in agony and says, "Oooh, just look at the way she moves that ass of hers; makes your mouth water just watching her." And that was right after Jake had just introduced us.

Later, while Jake and I were trying to talk, I heard Phineas say from behind me, "Just look at them scrumptious buns, T.R. Couldn't you just sink your teeth into them beauteous moons?" Then, rounding to my left side, he asked, "Couldn't you open up the next button down on your blouse there, Sweetness? Just give the world a peep at those gorgeous knockers of yours."

I'll admit that "gorgeous" flattered me despite the lascivious little moan that accompanied his use of the word. "Knockers," though, made me want to kick out his reason for being so horny. I would have, too, if Jake hadn't called him off like a dog with some rubbish about his (Phineas) having to practice for a contest. After the little perv was gone – slunk around a stack of railroad ties with T.R. following him like a walking telephone pole – Jake explained that Phineas had entered in a crepitation contest that was going to be held in the gym of some college fifty miles away. That was why he and his overgrown, silent sidekick were there: waiting to catch a northbound freight that they could be sure would stop near or at the town that was the college's support system. When I asked Jake to define the term "crepitation contest," I got my answer from behind the mountainous pile of wood where Phineas and T.R. were hidden from view: a long, windy, whistling trill of gas that sounded like the precursor to a bomb's explosion.

"A farting contest?"

Jake commended me on my intuition even though it was just a lucky guess. "The purse is fifty dollars," he said and took my hand. "Now.... You wanted to talk you said?"

I nodded and pursed my lips thoughtfully and we talked. It would take more pages to give it all here verbatim than my wrist or fingers could take to write it all down. Let's just say that he and I came to an understanding about the real reason that he had lit out on Gordy and me. He said that he had seen that Gordon and I were getting real close and that Gordy and I had more in common that either I had with him or that he had with Gordy so he decided that it would be best for him to bow out gracefully.

Graceful, he admitted, was not one of the things he naturally *was*. He had handled it badly and he was sorry. It had always been easier for him to run – or to walk really fast – than to just say goodbye and walk graciously away. Did I remember his story about the woman he had left behind in that city? Of course I did, I said, but I thought that the way that we – the three of us – had been would help us to come to a smoother break than we had, if it had to be a breakup at all. He said that he had become painfully aware that it was necessary, and that the break-up would just have been all the harder the longer we stayed together. I could understand, I told him. It was just his methods that I questioned.

That was what we talked about mostly, almost the whole conversation. It all came down to who he was, how he conducted his life, his relationship with people, with friends, the way that he alone decided when a break was to be made without consulting anyone else, whether it be with a woman with whom he had been having an affair (he hated that word as much as I loathed "knockers" to describe by breasts) or a friendship with two wayfarers he had chanced to meet along the roadside.

What would he do to that Varnish guy? I asked him that question right at the height of my crabbiness. I say height because my sour mood seemed to come and go like a tide during the course of our conversation. Would he leave the fellow stranded on some desert while he hitched a ride on the back of a motorcycle, waving toodle-loo with his free hand? I got myself pretty worked up, but we knew each other a little bit better when we were through. I am sure that the fact that I did get him so riled made him sit up and take notice, brought him to some kind of realization that maybe he actually mattered. I don't know if I changed him any – probably not – but I think I got him to take a good look at the consequences his actions have had on at least two of the people he had run out on.

"It's easier that way sometimes," he said.

"At least you admit that you do it," I said. I took his hand and squeezed it. Like a whoopee cushion, my squeezing seemed to be the cause of the sound of perforated cardboard being ripped along its holes from a hundred-ring binder. Bronx cheer, raspberries being razzed through a bullhorn, the amplified backfire of a ruptured muffler: Fartin' Phineas Fargo, rehearsing his ever broadening repertoire.

"Do me a favor," I said, making it sound like the last request of a condemned prisoner. "Keep that guy away from me."

"If you want," he agreed with a shrug. "He's harmless, though. It's just his little way of letting you know that he likes you."

"He gives me the creeps," I said, fanning at the odor of rotten eggs that was drifting from behind the stacked pillars. "And he smells like a toilet."

"Okay," Jake said. "But right now, I'm going to sic a little bit of T.R. on you."

He reached under his jacket and I thought he was going to take out the pages torn from the science fiction book he had shown Gordon and me earlier. What he gave me were several sheets of writing paper that had been pilfered from some local hotel, not the Balshaw. The writing was tight and tiny, beautifully rendered, a masterwork of the art of penmanship. "Phineas was right about this," he said, fanning the paper around. "No matter how obnoxious he made it sound, his friend T.R. has an odd, though a kind of stilted, flair for words."

The title of the piece that he gave me was "Two Characters On Paper, Conversing," by T(haddeus) R(aymond) Arquill.

When I asked Jake why T.R. had signed his first and middle initials only to follow each with the rest of the name in parentheses, he told me that Phineas had told him the T.R. believed that that was the way his name would appear in any encyclopedia or Who's Who. We were having a good laugh over that when Gordon came running up to us, telling us to come quick, that his friend was having another one of his "unrealnesses."

As we followed to the far end of the gravelly yard, Jake said that this was the second one today, that the boy seemed to lapse into these things (which I was later to find what they, these *unrealnesses*, were) when he was overly anxious or upset. Apparently the reappearance of an old friend had been the cause of some distress for him. Last time, Jake said mysteriously, he had been a raccoon.

As we followed Gordon's slim, running figure to the end of the yard as Jake and I were walking--Jake being in no real hurry to reach our destination – he asked me if I found Gordon to be sexy.

"I don't have to tell you about my physical preferences in men," I said, But when I caught Jake's eye a little later, just as we were about to enter the tarpaper shack where Gordon was hovering concernedly over his catatonic friend, I jerked my head in Gordon's direction and shook my hand in front of me in a vertical *hubba-hubba* gesture, winking salaciously as Phineas would at me so that there would be no mistaking the attraction. Jake winked back at me as he bent down to tend to the boy. Gordon, in all his sweet concern for Varnish(?) hadn't noticed our silent appraisal of his body.

Chapter 32

The shack was a flimsy structure made of plywood and tarpaper that had withstood the test of several years' standing and was used as a storage shed for the various items of the railroad brakeman's trade and dress: hats, jackets, arc lamps flashlights, wrenches of varying sizes, the largest of which had handles three feet long and weighed close to twenty pounds. Several of the latter of these tools were leaning heavily against one tarpaper covered wall of the shack, causing a noticeable tear in the black paper. The cheap lathing which was in place to support any additional walling material already had enough material to support such items as the jackets and hats and small shelves hanging from or resting on the bending nails that had been hammered into the bed of wood that formed the walls of the little building.

This was all that was meant to be here – not the slouching figure of Vardis Harblin who was leaning bleakly against a split-knot in what seemed to be a more solid section of the interior wall. Jake pulled him away from the flat surface and propped him squarely in the center of the packed earth floor. When Vardis was sitting securely upright without anything on which to prop his languid figure, Gordon went over to where several lamps were lined up against one wall like dissidents waiting for the firing squad to finish carrying out their orders. He chose one old relic rusted to red sandpaper on its bottom and ignited the wick with one of the many hoarded matches he always kept with him. He turned the petcock below the flame and filled the little room with crisp summer daylight. Two miniature suns winked on in Vardis' dilated, vacant pupils.

Jake looked into the young man's vapid eyes and waved a hand in front of his face. The action elicited no reaction. He touched the fellow on the shoulder with a hard poke and then stroked his greasy blonde hair, shook his thin, crossed legs, patted his back between the closely set shoulder blades that stuck out of his back like dual dorsal fins.

He whispered to him hoarsely, saying, "Vardis? Vard? It's me, son, Jake. You're here with me. Where are you, buddy? Wherever you are, please come back." Then, as if seized by an obsession or whim, Jake kissed his young friend on the cheek with a loud, slurpy smacking sound. An answering call came from outside across the length of the freight tyard: Phineas practicing his flatulent basso profundo scale that sounded like a mini foghorn, strangling the deep note until it glossed into a much higher register, whistling off into the still night.

Vardis came around slowly, blinking his eyes and muttering unintelligibly. He looked around himself, reacquainting himself with his surroundings, with the reality that was there. He looked absently into Jake's worried countenance for a while before smiling.

"Thank you, Unc," he said softly. "It was a sea lion this time. I was having so much fun but thank you for reminding me."

As they walked back to where Phineas was chasing T.R. from behind the piled and banded railroad ties with the intensity of his dedication to his craft, Thanny asked what Vardis meant when he said that Jake had reminded him. Reminded him of what?

"Of who he is, what he is," said Jake, wind-milling his right arm for Gordon and Vardis to catch up to them. "That he's human, that there is someone there who cares."

"It's weird," said Vardis, having overheard as he and Gordon followed. "Feeling that happen to you when you're something else – a bear, a chipmunk, a skunk or a raccoon. You're just there, doing whatever it is that you do, whatever you might be, then you feel something hot and slippery and wet on your cheek where you shouldn't even have a cheek if you're not human, and then something clicks inside of you and you remember. Then you have to come back."

"You mean you actually believe that you *are* those things?" Thanny asked as she tried to understand, to let this all sink in. "A bear, a skunk, a seal?"

"Not all at once, just one at a time," he told her. "And it's not so much just believing you're those things as actually being them when the unrealness comes on like that."

"And why'd you call Jake Unc?" Gordon said as much to change the subject as to ease his own curiosity.

His friend smiled as he looked up at the older man. "'Cause he's kind of like an uncle to me," he said honestly. "He's kin, like you could have been, Gordy, if we had stayed together. We could have been like brothers, you and me."

"If we stayed together?" Gordon was incredulous. "You ran off across the field before I even knew it. I called after you to come back but you just kept on going like something was chasing you."

Hearing this, Thanny envisioned her life as a vinyl phonograph record and a tone-arm skipping across it, always repeating the same words: *ran off, ran away, took a powder, split, vamoose, abandon. Left all on your own. Whether it was being done to her or she doing it to someone else – the names Bloris, Hyslop, Gardless and Rabandranath came freely to mind – or someone doing it to another,* she concluded, *it seemed to be the main point of a definitive pattern for her. Was this all that life was? Inexplicable fear and running feet?*

"You could have followed," said Vardis, sounding out a pain that apparently Gordon did not know existed within his friend. "I was hoping that you would."

"Then why didn't you...?" Gordon stopped that thought, knew that continuing with it would do no good. "You didn't say anything about that," he defended a moment later. What was this old scratch, this old sore still doing there, wanting to be salved again? He thought, *I thought I was done with all this a long time ago.* "Anyhow, you didn't even give me half a chance; you were already racing away into the woods before I even knew where you were going. Besides, I figured that you and I had different paths to travel. You'd already found yours, that's all."

"You could have followed!" his friend yelled with sudden anger before hurrying on ahead of them, quickly out of sight behind a low hillock that separated the yard in which they walked from the freight yard tracks.

"I'll go talk to him," promised Jake. "He's still a little disoriented from the episode. I'll talk to him."

After Jake hurried ahead of them and turned in the direction that Vardis had taken, they didn't hear voices from behind the long little hill covered with crabgrass, ditch weed, dandelions, paper scraps, rusting cans, broken bottles and cigarette butts, didn't even hear the mutest sounds of condolence, condescension or wise advice. The truth was they didn't care to. They walked away from it, went toward one of the wicker wire ashcans which dotted the dreary landscape, and which housed the dying embers of previously roaring fires. They warmed their hands in silence –even the vicinity of the stacked railroad ties where Phineas was hiding whatever constituted "practice" for his upcoming contest emitted no sounds now, sounds which would have proved embarrassing in a crowd. They watched the little nighttime city in the can wink its harlot zone lights, burst its concealed ghetto section into a momentary flame and crumble whole neighborhoods into themselves.

"Wish we could be like that," Thanny said with her gaze directed at a fire-greyed aluminum can which rose out of the incinerated center like a tilted, cylindrical skyscraper-- the downtown sector of Hades. "Like.... I guess something like a family."

"They're not family," Gordon said as he put out a single flame in the mini burg with a carefully aimed stream of saliva. "The barely know each other."

"Jake calls your friend 'son,'" she said, whether defensively or explanatorily-- it was not evident from her tone. "And he's 'Unc' to your friend."

"It's what they call each other," he said, raising his voice a bit at the end of the sentences, giving it the verbal sense of a shrug. "Doesn't mean anything."

"Well, I call you 'Lover,' " she said, knowing that she was grasping at straws – airy ones, too, at that. "Doesn't that mean something?"

"Something," he agreed, watching the little victory show in her eyes as he said it. *She needed to hear that?* "But it's because that's what we are: lovers. It's not who we are to one another, at least not everything."

"So? What are we, then?" Her tone was a demand, a goad, a question in search of an answer, a taunt, a complaint, all in one. "I have some ideas myself, but I'd like to hear what you have to say. What are we?"

"To each other? You mean you want a definition?"

"If you can."

"All right. But let's trade, okay?"

"If you like," she said unsurely. This would be a chancy thing to undertake, she could see. It could take any shape without cause: an amusing game, a charade or a painful expression of feelings and angers. She wondered if the gamble that it certainly was would be worth the risk. "You first."

"Mm-hmmm," he hummed and then remained quiet for a few moments. "Friends," he said when he came back into the conversation again. He began to stutter into something else, but then stopped.

"Friends? That's all?"

"First thing that came to mind. I was going to say lovers, but that's off-limits. So, let's see, then.... Carers?"

"Confidantes," she said, breaking the rules as they might have been understood, redefining them.

"Argurers."

"Helpers."

"Road-levelers," which he found himself forced to append with, "For each other, of course."

"Of course. My turn now. Ummm... Fighters."

"I thought 'arguers' covered that. But okay. Why not? So how about... chasers?"

"I chase you, you chase me," she said, appreciating the allusion. "Very good. Tear-driers."

"Embracers."

"Consolers."

"Same thing if you mix 'embracers,' still 'tear-driers,' kind of. But, okay. Ah-hmp! Road-levelers? No, I said that already." He shrugged, then said, "Kindred spirits"

"Talkers. And I mean real talk talkers."

"Lovers."

"Ah-ah," she warned. "Off limits. You can't define a word by using the same word."

"Not the way I mean it."

"And how do you mean it, then? Emotion?"

"I think so."

"Think so? You mean you're not sure?"

"It would be so easy to say that I was, but we can't lie to each other if we're going to stick together for anything longer than we did with Jake. So, I have to say no. I think so but I'm not a hundred percent sure, just yet."

"Love's your own definition for it," she said, her voice rising in the same shrugging inflective as his had before. "Your own feeling." She wondered if that sounded as trite to him as it did to her. Whatever his inner reaction, there was no outer indication that he had even heard her at all. He was busy watching the hellish city in the ashcan consume itself in flame. "Maybe you do but you're afraid of it," she said.

He looked at her, a little startled at the idea. "Afraid? Of love?"

"No, of loving. You put everything on the line, and you admit to someone that you love them. What if they just say, 'So what?' or say that *that's too bad but I don't love you* or, even worse, if they don't say anything at all? It's happened to me in the worst way and I know how it tears you up. You're in limbo, then. You don't know where to turn, what to do or how to act for a long time. It's horrible, that kind of rejection."

"It only has to happen once," he said, trying to sound sage, "for it to leave the worst kind of stale taste in your mouth."

"I know. You don't have to tell me. And if it happens enough times, even the idea of the good things in a relationship become frightening once you start looking ahead to the end."

"Then the very fact that you consider 'the end' to be possible maybe sows the seeds for it, even if they weren't there to begin with."

"It's possible," she said. This intrigued her. Was this the same shy, quiet Gordon Traumer she had met only two weeks ago – or was it less time than that? *Behold! The man thinks! What further surprises lay in store for her at his cunning hands?* She had a few already, that was sure. "But it doesn't have to be that way."

"Once you have it in mind that it's going to happen, it seems like a foregone conclusion. How can you head-off what you already know is going to happen?"

"Just ignore it," she said, simply. "Don't tell yourself anything but that it's a give and take thing."

Another drooling wad of clam sailed into the city, drowning some of the unsuspecting, unsinged citizenry, putting out a few night lights in the process. "Come again?" he said as he wiped his mouth.

"Platitudes," she said drolly, only now having actually listened to what she had just said. *Give and take thing. God, how mawkish that sounded. She could have come up with something a bit more original than that. But what? Tug o'war? Dance of life? Bed of roses? Bowl of cherries? Line of bullshit?*

"No," he said as she went through her list of possibilities. "Not bullshit. The dance thing, maybe. Like this...." He raised his right hand and put it on her left shoulder, jarring her with the sudden impact. "I've told you about my life and left myself wide open for you to turn me in. Just because I checked myself into the hospital didn't mean that I could just walk out whenever I pleased. There would have been papers to sign, an exit interview with my doctor, an evaluation of the progress I had made, plans to be made for my continuing treatment once I was outside, and probably a lot of other crap, too. But I did tell you, trusted my secret with you. Of course, that wouldn't have been enough if...." He took her right hand and placed it on his left shoulder. "If you hadn't trusted me as well. I've got your secrets, too, you know. A runaway, even though you're too old for Mommy and Daddy to send out the detectives to look for you. And that thing you had with Gilbert...."

"Gerald," she said dryly.

"All right, then, with Gerald and the shitty way he treated you. You trusted me with all that. You see? We do have all that from each other."

A moment of silence; hand to shoulder, hand to hand, eye to eye. Funereal, she thought as she considered the sparse physical arrangement he had made of them. She rested her left cheek on his hand and kissed his wrist with the corners of her lips. "My turn now?" she asked. "We'd look silly at a cotillion like this, trying to figure out what to do next."

"Your turn," he assented though they were both aware that permission was unnecessary.

"All right," she said and placed her free hand on his hip, moved forward to push him clear of the smoldering ashcan. "It still scares me, the way that I feel about you. I'm scared that it will be the same with you as it was with Gerald even though I know that if it is you will go about ending it much differently than he did, the shit. You'll be much kinder and more sensitive about it, but it will still end up in the same way. There will be no more *us* and I'll be just as lonely and angry as I was when Gerald went away to Europe. Only this time I'll be without you and that would be the greater loss. And...."

"And," Gordon said as he placed his left hand on her hip, completing their configuration of limbs. "And I think that for all your insecurity that you really feel that us being together is the right thing and that it will eventually all work out somehow."

"It sounds like that's the way you feel," she said, a timid smile starting to open the pensive line of her mouth. "But I'm still not so sure that you're as positive about us as you sound like you are."

"But I am," he insisted, giving way to his secret convictions, airing them with those two simple words: *I am.* He began to sway in front of her, his motion slowly becoming hypnotic like the ticking of a metronome while a serenely calming voice gently commands the listener to relax, relax.... He began to apply nudging pressure to her hip, a suggestive pull with the hand to her shoulder, making her sway with him, side to side. "You know that I am. Don't say that I'm not. It's the power of positive thinking. Just keep saying that I am sure. We are good for each other. It will work. *I am, it will, we are. I am, it will, we are. I am, it will, we are.*" With each repetition, each stressed word, he pulled, he pushed, he stepped forward, moved back and to the side. She gave into his little pressures and nudgings to move with him, backing away to the right, to the right, to the right, moving forward to the left, to the left, to the left, until they were prancing together circularly, gaining momentum to the tune he was humming that had replaced the little litany of positive thinking. My God, she thought, not knowing if the giddiness she was presently experiencing was a symptom of love or her period unaccountably returning or due to the fact that they were spinning about the freight yard at a dizzying clip. She took the lead and slowed the tempo down as she moved closer to him as much to keep from falling as to embrace him.

They pulled themselves close to one another, using their arms like drawstrings across one another's backs. Thanny was sure that, for all her voiced apprehensions and doubts, her hold would be more secure. When their bodies met and they were belly to belly, their pelvises so tightly close that she could feel the protrusion of his hip bones through the stiff material of his new jeans, she found that the arms which were wrapped around her had quickly clamped down in a locking grip that she could not, nor did she care to, break as their dance continued.

"Hey," said Phineas as he came from behind the massive stack of ties for a breath of fresher air. "T.R., look at this. They're dancin'. No music, but they're dancin'."

T.R. emerged from the shadows below the streetlight under which he had been sitting as he had watched the dancers appear then disappear like three dimensional images in a poorly crafted hologram. They moved into the dark, becoming shadowy wraiths with one step, whole and lively under the bright light with the next. T.R. sniffed the air around his friend as he approached and found it clean and crisp, that Phineas' practicing had not left any after effect as was sometimes the case when his rehearsals were finished. He smiled as he stood to watch the dancers, produced a happy chortle in his throat, clucking like a happy chicken. He drew a harmonica from his shirt pocket and began to play for them. He stretched the notes blues fashion, along the lines of a polka in tempo while Phineas kept time with an easy clapping rhythm to which the dancers adjusted their own frenetic pace. When Jake and Vardis came out from behind the earthworks hill where they had been conducting their lengthy private conference, the audience was complete. Jake immediately broke into a wild yell which Vardis took up and the two of them hooked arms to spin each other for their own little hoedown. T.R. added his own little shuffle footed two-step as he played something on his mouth organ reminiscent of "Turkey in the Straw" while Phineas clapped and tooted his sphincter horn in gleeful, though equally restrained, accompaniment in the tenor range.

"No offense to T.R.'s playing," said Jake loudly as he jumped high and turned a full 180 in mid-air. He stopped the square dance while Vardis regained his balance which had been boggled by Jake's leap. "But we need some real music. Thanny, darlin', you still got that transistor I saw you packing away last time we broke camp?"

"In the duffle," she told him, craning for a look at what he and Vardis had been doing. Light on their feet, both of them, she thought. "And whatever you get, make it something nice and slow, Jake. And keep playing like you're doin', T.R.? You play real pretty. I like it a lot."

T.R. nodded at the compliment and hit a series of sour notes which he managed to work into the emerging structure of impromptu phrasings, the changeable refrain which he was currently building up into a series of lilting crescendos. *If I knew how to write music,* he considered as he played, *this is what I'd want to put on paper.* He shook his head at the thought, causing a burble of saliva to froth behind the harmonica, which changed the chord to a sharp instead of flattening it out as he had meant to do. *So much raw talent and no training,* he thought. *My Lord, what a waste.*

"What's this thing?" Jake asked as he rummaged through the duffle. He held up the blue plastic diaphragm case. "A compact or something?"

"Personal stuff, nosy," Thanielle yelled so she could be heard over the controlled chaos of mouth organ and clapping. The fact that she had to yell to be heard served to camouflage the anger in her voice. "Just keep looking. It's in there somewhere."

Jake found Thanny's trusty transistor and switched it on and diddled the tuner until he hit upon what seemed to be the only music station that was broadcasting or else the only one which the little pocket radio could pull in. All the rest was rushing static or news reports, at this late hour. The song that was on was already partially through, caught in the middle of a wah-wah'd guitar solo that was quickly and smoothly supplanted by what sounded like a raucous children's chorus.

Where are you going now, my love?
Where will you be tomorrow?
Will you bring me happiness?
Will you bring me sorrow?
Ahhh! The questions of a thousand dreams,
What you do and what you see.
Lover, can you talk....
To me-e?

The guitar wah-wah'd into where it had previously been while Thanny's hand slid from its position near Gordon's should blades to below his belt and grabbed a healthy handful of gluteus flesh. "Gotcha!" she whispered into his ear as he flinched, then said, "Please don't let go."

"*Oh, when I was on my own,*" the castrato choir came in again. "*Chasing you, girl! What was it made you run? Tryin' your best just to get a-round?*"

"Lookit, Jake!" said Phineas excitedly. "She just goes and grabs his ass like that's what she wants and so she just goes and gets it. And there! He's got hers now. She-yit! I wisht I was him. She's got the kinda ass I'd love to be playin' games with. Just wanna dive right in there and set up housekeepin' between them scrumptious buns o' hers, then come 'round to stick my face up front to lickety me a cunt juice breakfast each mornin' and then busy my balls a-fuckin' 'til I'm dry and so I'll have to go and get m'self reloaded for lunch. Oh yes and my, my yes!"

"Phineas," said Jake disapprovingly. "Don't you have any respect at all? Just look at them, the way they look at each other. Don't you have even the shadiest clue of what it is you're looking at?"

"Yeah, I know," he answered disgustedly. He looked over at T.R. who was also watching, smiling as the dancers danced. They seemed oblivious to the fact that the song was over, the disc jockey was signing off, even that an advertisement for a shampoo had begun. T.R.'s eyes were soft, his face tender as he sat on the ground and tucked his long legs under him and simply appreciated the peaceful scene. Phineas rested a hand on the tall man's shoulder who, now being seated on the ground, was at a height where the smaller man could reach it. "Yeah," he said again. "But that kind of thing don't last."

T.R. pulled a little pad of notepaper from a pocket and jotted something down. When communication was necessary, this was his means of being heard. He tugged at Jake's pant leg and gave him the scrap of paper he had just torn out of the little bound book.

"Another gift?" Jake asked.

T.R. shrugged and motioned broadly for the man to read aloud.

" *'That which lasts does so because of perseverance,'* " Jake intoned, squinting at the tiny handwriting. He turned and angled the piece of paper to catch more of the meager light from the street lamp. " *'The glory of attainment is arrived at by the attempt which makes the gained thing even more desirable for having thus been striven for.'* "

"Pretty," said Phineas appreciatively. Then, catching himself in what he expected was most likely an exhibition of vulnerability, he let out a derisive yuck. "Big words, T.R. Tell me, then, what the fuck is all that supposed to mean?"

"It means," Jake said as he folded the slip of paper into a fat little cube and tucked it in an inside jacket pocket along with the similarly wadded and dog-eared pages that he had collected over the past months, perhaps years of wandering. "That at least they're trying. They're making the attempt." He turned to watch Phineas fidget, jam his hands into his baggy trouser pockets in an attempt to hide the erection which his watching the dancers had helped to produce. *Pocket pool?* Jake thought. It would seem likely, very much in keeping with the character he had observed in this crude young individual. "Have you?"

Phineas huffed, not wanting to offer an answer since he had none to give. He grumbled as he stalked away, driving his hands deeper into the holey pockets as he went back to his hiding place behind the stacked ties. He elbowed past Gordon as he and Thanielle were leaving the floor of their open-air ballroom. Phineas kept walking, leaving a sulfur-pungent stink of decaying garbage in his wake, the force of whose constant production fluttered the loose seat of his baggy overalls.

Chapter 33

There was no authority to say what could or should be done about the sleeping arrangements in the freight yard but all four of the "hosts" – Jake, Phineas, T.R. and Vardis – magnanimously voted to allow the new coming couple to have the storage shed for the night. Some compromise that would be mutually agreeable to all involved could be resolved in the morning – presuming that there would be enough nights for them in their collective future together to make such arrangements viable. No one heard Phineas' muttered remarks that he hoped that he would have his turn with her soon. A vociferous debate ensued among the other three of them, leaving half of the football field sized yard littered with T.R.'s angry appraisals and retorts, Phineas with a case of constipated inability to practice his craft, Jake with a headache the size and color of a blood smeared cudgel behind his eyes that he couldn't shake until the following morning and which left him helpless to aid Vardis who had sunk into still another attack of "unrealness," the third one in the past thirty six hours.

They were oblivious to all that was transpiring some fifty yards away from them on the other side of the licorice colored walls of the little shack. They could not sleep even though they had been awake, walking, working, talking and dancing since ten a.m. (now one a.m.) on only two or three hours of sleep. Overtired, said Thanny. The brain working overtime, holding sway over the body which craved rest. The body says NOW, let's sleep but, since it was the brain that actually slept, no sleep was forthcoming. *What should we do?* asks the mind. *My eyes are wide open.*

They could not make love – what if someone should come in? It was too risky, much as they both wanted it. And neither of them was of the type whose excitement was heightened by the danger factor, got their jollies doing it in the doorway or an open alley for the thrill of the possibility of being discovered naked and in flagrante. They tried massage and their bodies responded with almost automatic numbness of limbs, but the eyes remained open, both sets, and the minds were both still keen and curious.

Thanny suggested reading and pulled out several sheets of hotel stationery out of a side pocket of the backpack where she had placed it after receiving it from Jake. She unfolded the little packet carefully several times to reveal a minute script which, when tilted, dipped and slanted in a luxuriant, lovingly ballpoint penned, almost feminine cursive hand. It was a dialogue, she said.

Gordon dug a diamond tip match from another of the side pockets and scratched its sulphurous life into flame on one of the rough slatboards that gave shape to the inner sanctum of the shack. The brakeman's lantern took him a few minutes to figure out but soon there was an approximation of daylight in the square room and Thanny began to read aloud from the pages in her hand. She soon realized that it was not going to work. She was putting Gordon to sleep with the rhythms of her reading and the dialogue while alternately maintaining and suppressing her own wakefulness. It was a dialogue, she said and that meant two people. We should each take a part, she offered; we should do it together.

Gordon agreed, cuddled close to her for a better view of the page. It might be seen as a mistake since reading and the discussion which accompanied it – arguments about how certain passages should be read for full dramatic effect, the personalities of the characters they each took on at random, the questions raised by the tenor, temper and subject matter of the dialogue – kept them from getting any real rest for more than an hour before they actually began the reading. It might also be seen as just what was needed, for when it was finally done, they both fell almost immediately into a deep and sound sleep. Gordon only rose once in the night to relieve his bladder, met Thanny at the thong-hinged doorway to the shack when he returned, as she was preparing to exit the shed for the same purpose. He directed her to a secluded spot, told her to be careful of the puddle he had left. When she returned, they necked drowsily and went back to sleep, a sleep which lasted motionlessly and restfully until close to noon of the same day.

Thanielle's thought-journal contains T.R.'s dialogue just as he had written it in his rather stiff sounding prose in as verbatim a copy of the original as she could manage without too many grammatical changes. It was the one section of her continuing work-in-progress to which she returned to read over, again and again. Every time she did she found herself wondering whatever had happened to that silent, lanky man and his flatulent and obnoxious little friend.

***

CHARACTERS ON PAPER, CONVERSING
A Story in Dialogue
by T(haddeus) R(aymond) Arquill

—   Come in, my friend, come in. Don't stand out there on the porch in the cold. You know you're always welcome here. Come in, take a seat. Tell me what troubles you.

—   Troubles me? Is it so evident in my expression that I come to you for counsel and not just a friendly, idle chat?

—   Not so dreadfully evident, no. It just seems that we only seem find time to talk, you and I, when there is something bothering one of us. Since I have nothing more pressing or vexatious on my mind than my shoelace breaking in my hand this morning when I was in something of a rush to be dressed, then I assume that it's you who has some tale of woe or pique to share at this time.

[SHORT PAUSE]

—   Pique. I like that word. What I have to talk about is certainly is not a case of woe by any means. No one has died or in any way has stolen out of my life that I would have bidden to stay. And not even "pique' as you so eloquently define it. No; just a nagging sense of some undefined anxiety which I feel would be best dealt with in conversation, Just to help me clear my mind, you understand. Even to talk around the subject – anxiety about what, I'm really not sure – would be of great help to me.

—   And you have no idea where it comes from, this sudden attack of... what? Nervousness?

—   Marvelous! How did you ever know? That seems to classify it to a T. Nervousness. [SHORT PAUSE] Perhaps it comes from thinking too much. Too much thought about who you are seems to change the character of the person you always thought yourself to be, thereby making you a bit apprehensive. Who am I? The answer to that is a slippery thing, always seeming to sliding right out of your grasp as soon as you think you have a hold on it. It happens like that time and again, over and over. Frustrating enough to give you gas pains.

[A LARGE BASSO ERUCTATION FOR EFFECT]

—   Gesundheit! [Mild laughter from both friends]. You know I had always understood that action defines the person whereas thinking simply stagnates him, makes the thinker – at least the one who thinks exclusively on the matters of self and "selfness" – makes less of who he or she is by the simple fact of delving so much. Maybe that's your problem: not the thinking in itself but what it is you you're thinking about.

—   Perhaps. But if I'm in a pensive state of mind, what do I think about if not myself?

—   Oh, the past or the future, I imagine. What has been achieved and what there is still to be done. You don't have to be a scientist to dwell on the subjects of mankind's role in the world, his responsibilities to the world and what he or she makes of it.

—   Past or future, I still will be put in the position of thinking of things in terms of myself, sooner or later. Then that will almost inevitably lead back to square one: Who am I? Who was I? Who will I be? [SHORT PAUSE]. Like a strange variety of snare or trap. Damned if you do; caught if you don't.

—   Only if you think of it in that way. [Contemplative pause lasting only a moment or two]. The best course I could suggest, then, would be poetry. Pensive yet focused on something or someone other than yourself.

—   [Excited]. Oh that does sound good. You mean something like this?
[LONG PAUSE FOR CREATIVE REFLECTION AND COMPOSITION]

—   *If I ever see her again,*
I know that I will cry.

Her face casts a new light
On old memories, always memories
Easily at hand, like books
On the shelf, tucked away in far recesses.
Like her face, blushing, filled with warm antagonism.
Her limbs, akimbo, uncaring, slack.
The tensed muscles of her thighs, framing
My fractioning loins for their fervent, loving thrusts.
Memories of mousy squeaks
And low moans when I know she has reached a new peak
And yes, she had, but not I; but knowing that she was there
Was enough, more than enough.
Past, past, only a brain cell glimmer
Somewhere in the dusty far reaches of cranial storage.
Still, she can make me cry,
Just by my envisioning her calm,
Viciously lovely, an oh-so human face.
And she would love to know that she still affects me so, even in abstentia.

[PAUSE]

___ Better? [SHORT PAUSE; a silent answer received]. Whatever happened to that woman of yours? Years ago, wasn't it? And she still affects you that deeply? Look, you are crying.

___ Yes. [Sobs, regains composure]. I don't know what happened to her and I don't care. It was so long ago.... But the thought of it – the memory, all so clear, as if it happened only one day or one week ago even though it's really been these many years – it still affects me. You know, if I met her on the street tomorrow and somehow could talk to her without remembering, without feeling that something had been unaccountably, unfairly denied me by her, I'm sure that it would start all over again. [SHORT PAUSE]. And maybe this time it would last forever.

—   But you know that you can't forget and neither can she. The break-up was a blow to both of you, just short of coming to real violence. I was only a spectator but I was aware of what was going on. You two argued horribly, and not over anything puny or paltry but about the kinds of things that we had just been talking about a few minutes ago. Who am I? Who are you? What is it that we're holding onto in this relationship? Who are we that we should remain inextricably tied to one another? [SHORT PAUSE, to catch his breath]. You argued, the two of you, attacked each other's most sacredly held values but you gained nothing that I could see, then, either of you, but the hurting of someone you each professed to love and care for. [SHORT PAUSE]. But it's over now, a long time past.

—   Yes, a long time. I still think about her a great deal, though.

—   And about yourself. [Another silent gesture of agreement is given and acknowledged]. Have you learned anything since then? About yourself? No, not about her. You can only learn about another person from that person herself. Thinking about her doesn't give you any more clues than you already had when you started ruminating. But about yourself? This soul-searching thing you've been wrestling with must have gained you some insights.

—   Some. [PAUSE, a stammered start as answers begin to formulate, thoughts begin to transmute into words]. That, maybe, I still do love her, or else just that I enjoy the memory of love and of being loved by her back then. I don't know, really. [A shrug]. In love with the idea of being in love, maybe?

—   Maudlin. Now you're getting all mushy and trivial about the whole thing.

—   [Sighing]. Sounds that way, doesn't it? [Nervous PAUSE]. Maybe that's the reason for the anxiety, the soul-searching as you call it.

—   You lost me there. Can you rephrase that?

—   No, but I'll try. [PAUSE]. It was the most influential period of my life then and she was the most important person to me at the time. She still is now, in a sense. Back then I was developing mind, body, sexuality and outlook at the time, and she helped me in all those aspects of "selfness." I must say I do like your choice of words so far. All of them so apt. Soul-searching, selfness, nervousness, trivial. Yes, trivial, too. That's what I've been doing all along, you know, for all my penny philosophizing: trivializing that whole important period of my life until I can't even recognize it anymore. It's all become just the memory of sex and outrageous arguments with her. I've degraded her in my mind, you see. That's what's got me so... nervous, anxious, frustrated. Pick a word, it'll fit somehow. I've forgotten her. Oh, don't misunderstand me. I can see her face in my mind as if I've just been looking at a photograph of her: clear as a bell. I can conjure up the way she looked as she undressed – or as I undressed her – and can see the tone and texture of her naked skin; place every fold, dimple, mole, body hair, curve, crack and cranny in all the right places. I'd be able to draw you a picture of her, clothed or naked, from memory, if I were gifted that way. I can hear her voice right now as if she were standing next to me, whispering sweet secrets in my ear like she used to, telling me her favorite positions, her fantasies of how she wanted our life together to pan out.... It's all there, I have everything in my memory about her but, you see, I've forgotten.... Her.

[PAUSE]

—   Her? You mean you've forgotten the things that made her the person who she was, the subtleties that made her.... Her?

—   Exactly! [SHORT PAUSE]. At least I think so. I....

[Anxious PAUSE as if waiting for the thought to be completed].

—   Yes? Something else?

—   No. [SHORT PAUSE, then, angrily]   I don't know!

205

Apologies from the author, T.R. Arquill, for the sudden ending of this dialogue, but the limitations of space demand that it ends here. Plus, the author himself "doesn't know." He hopes that you, the reader, understand.

***

"I don't understand," Gordon complained wearily. "He only used one side of each sheet of paper. He had room enough to continue it."

"He didn't know how," said Thanielle, yawning, snuggling down into the warmth of the sleeping bag. She didn't much care what T.R.'s reasons were for not going on with his ho-hum dialogue. It was a curious diversion, a nice soporific, and that was all. They said their good nights and that they would discuss it further in the morning, if that was what they wanted to do. Gordon turned the lantern down until the flame went out, taking the only reason for their wakefulness with it.

Chapter 34 - Endings

A chicken-wire grid had been laid over the open top of one of the fiery ashcans with Jake Rine's blackened saucepan filled with water settled on top. They shared what they had for breakfast, the six of them, calling it breakfast though it was actually lunch for Jake and Vardis. When the water came to a boil, Jake threw in about a quarter of a jar of cheap instant coffee, passed out some Styrofoam cups that he and Vardis had pilfered from a diner not far away. Maybe it was the same one in which Jorge had started his career as a dishwasher, Gordon speculated as the water started to bubble on the fire. The counterman never knew what happened, Vardis told them proudly.

The coffee drunk, empty mini cereal boxes and granola bar wrappers added to the blaze in the can, Jake excused himself for a piss. The sound of water being hosed onto the far wall of the little shack brought a flicker of mirth to all their faces, some of them close to laughter. Jake came back rubbing at a fresh streak of moisture in the left leg of his grimy trousers. Double stream, he explained as he pawed briskly at the spot and then, giving up the effort, he hunched his shoulders that brought a silent pause with it that cast the small group into a mutual feeling that they were all gathered among strangers. *Something sad here*, Thanny thought as they all smiled nervously at one another, *all discomfort and watchful eyes. We all know each other here, she thought; it's not as if we've just met. And yet look at us – what do we have to say to one another?*

"I was a skunk once," Vardis said, seeming to answer Thanny's silent question. This was a true ice breaker; the silence had begun to annoy him. "I loved it. No one would come near me. Not foxes or bears or mountain lions or wolves. I was my own boss and I was lonely there."

"Did Jake kiss you awake?" Gordon asked innocently.

"I hadn't met Jake by then. I stayed a skunk then for more than half a day. Somewhere in the a.m. until nighttime. I came to in the dark. I got so scared that I sank back, this time as a snake. You remember the snake, Gordy? With my cousin.... When I tried to put my hand...."

"Yes, I remember," said Gordon. "But you said that it was an accident, a misunderstanding. You didn't actually try...."

"Oh yes, I did."

"You did? But you told me...."

"White lie," said Vardis, cutting in. "I'd come out of that one, being a snake, only a few minutes before and so kept up the act of it a while longer so I could sneak my hand up her skirt." He turned to Thanielle and told her to have Gordon explain the whole thing to her later on.

"But why? She was your cousin."

"I was horny," he said, adopting the shrugging *What else could I do?* tone of a child caught poring over his father's hidden collection of pornography. Of course, that was not sufficient an explanation, he could tell by the inquisitive, expectant looks he was getting from his audience. "My doctors at the hospital seemed to think that the animals I turned into reflected my dominant emotions at any given time. So, a skunk equates with loneliness; a hawk with freedom; a bear – anger; a raccoon – the need to be appreciated, maybe even mothered; a wolf – when I know that I'm right but don't show it or assert myself; and a snake with sexual tension or desire."

"And a seal?" Thanny asked. "Like you were last night?"

"Happiness,'" said Vardis as if it were the most obvious association to be made.

"I'm glad to hear that," said Gordon, genuinely pleased. "And what do you attribute it to? The happiness, I mean. Certainly not to us."

"Why not?" said Vardis, a little shocked that his friend had missed even that blatant a connection. "Old friends, you and I, together again, sharing and traveling and living together again. Why shouldn't you be the cause?"

"Good enough reason, I guess," said Gordon, glancing uncomfortably at Thanielle, *Did they really want this? He made an impetuous decision and acted upon it.* "But Thanny and I were planning – I think – to be moving out on our own pretty soon."

"You didn't say anything about this before," said Jake. "But I suppose that I kind of expected it." He took Gordon roughly aside and had barely begun to berate his young friend for the way in which he had so insensitively handled the situation when he felt Vardis yanking at the tail of his jacket.

"'Sall right, Jake," he said. "I understand. I'd jumped to conclusions before asking. I don't blame Gordy. I'm the dumb one here. Let's us have some more coffee." Thanny was secretly relieved that that had been so easily resolved. She was a bit disappointed that Gordon hadn't consulted her before making their proclamation of freedom, but she was glad, nonetheless. If they had talked about it, they would have reached the same conclusion between them. She would have agreed that this parting would be in the best interests of all concerned. Agreed – but for her own reasons. A simple one would have been of petty revenge: Jake had hightailed it out on Gordon and her and so now it was their turn to do the same to him. The only sticking point now was that this time there was another party involved – Vardis who seemed to wish them to stay, despite his brave show of understanding regarding their reasons for going their own way. His motives for wanting them there, to make up a distinct part of their impromptu "family" seemed to be directly mainly at Gordon, an old and respected friend.

But what if one of his "unrealnesses" had him be a snake again, harbinger of sexual desire, this time the target of his horny hand being herself? And Jake, for all his kind, fatherly ways and advice of the sage, was just as prone to human desire and weakness as any man. What if, someday he should find her naked again at a stream, bathing? He had looked away once (so he claimed), but if the time came when he decided to put away the role of advisor and supervisor and strip himself naked and join her in the water, maybe even forcibly join himself to her in a prodding embrace from behind, forcing her by dint of surprise and his superior strength to bend over, allow him his animal pleasures to be performed on her?

And why did she trust Gordon so implicitly? Given such a scenario might not he, out of fear or arousal, simply join in the rape or else do nothing at all to stop it? If Gordon hadn't propitiously slid his arm around her waist at that moment and pulled her tightly to him to ask her why she was looking so thoughtful, she might have continued her line of pondering to a deeply depressive conclusion. As it was, she kissed him on the cheek, said that she had just been thinking that he was right. They had best be going as soon as they could. That is what she was thinking, she told herself. *It is best – or else I wouldn't know who to trust, other than myself.*

With the second cups of coffee in their hands, Jake told them what had gone on in the yard that morning while the two of them slept through "the best part of the day." The four of them – Jake, Vardis, T.R. and Phineas – had made a reconnaissance trip to the yard master's office beyond the brakemen's tarpapered storage shed. While the fellow was away from his office inspecting or supervising something or other along the tracks, Vardis had hoisted himself through an open window and gotten the scoop on that day's arrivals, departures and run-throughs. Phineas and T.R. had found the very northbound for which Thanny and Gordon had been searching. Phineas, the talker, the "brains" of the duo, would never have thought to check the schedules, would have been just as content to sit and wait, listen to the shouting of engineers and loading men in an effort to learn the destination of any given train. The two of them were then hiding out near the sidling a little south of the yard from where the last ten cars would be attached to the main body of the northbound train. It was to be a fairly short line-up of cars so that the whole thing – arrival, couplings, departure – should only take about an hour, start to finish, and was scheduled to pull out of the yard at about three-thirty, but might be closer to four or even later before the piggy-back diesels began towing the thirty car line-up onto the north-bound mainline.

"There's only one other train stopping in Honeysuckle today according to the yard master's sheets and that one's going south, full out to the big town from here. It'll be coming in from Rarey, drop two cars, pick up five and then head on out. It isn't even going to stop in Wheelock, just whistle on through."

"To the city?" Gordon said it while Thanny was thinking the same thing. They turned their heads in unison – Gordon to the left, Thanielle to the right – until their eyes met in an unspoken query. The city: what will be there for us in a place like that?

In fact, what *was* a place like that?

"Only one way to find out about it," said Jake. It was as if he had planned it all along and was eager to be rid of them. This was understandable in a way; they – through Gordon – had voiced their intent to leave so it would be best to get it over with as quickly and as painlessly as possible. All right. But why the pre-planned package?

Listen: he had even said that this was a one-time shot. Sure, there would be other trains heading south or north for one city or another, each with their infamous guard laden hearts of incoming goods, stores, foodstuffs, energy sources, hobos, tramps, hick brakemen and boozer engineers, but then the next express run going through any specifically desired direction probably wouldn't be for another two weeks or more. Expresses, yes, but they would all be passing by Honeysuckle like a priest passes a whore's crafty come-on with a sneer.

"Cover all bases," he said, being reasonable. "Chances were always good that you two would want your ...hhmm... freedom. Just thought I'd give you the opportunity as long as it wouldn't cause any undue trouble."

"That's our Jake," Gordon warned Vardis quietly. "He'll give you anything as long as it doesn't inconvenience himself."

"I wouldn't take bets on that," his friend answered tersely and then walked away while Jake gave the outbound couple their instructions. He took them to the crown of the earthworks that separated the barren freight yard from the tracks nestled in a gulley, three sets abreast. He pointed out their train resting on the far track and gave them pointers as to the best means of getting on without being detected, the best spot on the train to board, the best kind of car to choose and the most likely departure time.

Then he told them that he had another present for them as he led them away from the knoll on which they had been standing and back to the ashcan in the yard, where his fire blackened saucepan was gaining some more color in its enameled bottom simmering over the heat. He threw the little pot onto the ground, bent over and picked up a brown paper grocery bag and handed it to Thanielle.

"We were going to use this for kindling," Vardis said, rolling the top of the bag down, closing it securely. "We had something of an argument last night about who would get to use the shack next and with whom. Phineas wanted it for last night – a moot point now, of course – and I'll let you guess who he had in mind for a bunkmate to shack up with."

Thannielle's expression changed from mute interest as she accepted the bag to the silent-comedy rage of a slow burn. "If you ever become a weasel in one of your 'unrealnesses,'" she said, seething. "Just watch out because that will mean that you're going to go into pervy competition with that shitty smelling bastard Phineas."

"Anyhow," Vardis continued, enjoying Thanielle's show of anger and sympathizing with it fully, "This was T.R.'s part of it, not Phineas'. These things he's written will probably read like fortune cookie bits, all taken out of context – they are all jumbled together, let me warn you – but they'll give you an idea about what you missed by not staying out here and being with us last night." Then, thinking about it, he shrugged and sucked a piece of cereal from between two rear teeth. "Nothing else but that, really."

Silences seemed to blossom like springtime buds when there is waiting to be done. They spread out and change colors in the mind, grow unusual associations on the tongue. One that took them all by mild surprise came up and added to each of them a look of wonder.

It was Gordon's query about the science fiction novel from which Jake had gleaned the jagged-edged pages he carried with him in an inside jacket pocket. For Gordon, this question was only a time passer, idle talk, a momentary curiosity. Jake patted his chest – left side, over the heart, that was where the pages were kept. To Gordon it looked like a gesture of pride, as if the man were patting some invisible badge of distinction on his droopy lapel, as if he were about to disclose the fact that he was wearing a bullet proof vest. *Standard gear for a G-man,* he would say. *Here's my badge and ID. Undercover. All very hush-hush.* But those associations and fantasies all were of Gordon's making. The look in Jake's face was pride, however – in the stealing or in the having, he wouldn't say, wasn't asked.

Authorship. He mulled that one over for a second. The book was by a Charles Lotwidge, he said and yes, he knew the man.... In a manner of speaking. Lotwidge had been an old flame of a woman he had once lived with, the copy of the book being Lotwidge's prized gift to her, inscribed with bubbling, amateur verse, X's and O's for kisses and hugs lined along the flyleaf like football players on a coach's play diagram. Jake's petty theft, then, had served a twofold purpose (though he disagreed with the suggestion when it was made: surely it wasn't all that petty): defacing a prized possession of the woman he was leaving as well as garnering a reminder of her.

What, thought Thanielle suspiciously, *will he take from Gordy and me?*

He gave, though, and took nothing in return. He transferred as much of his and Vardis' provisions as he could from the burlap carry-all to the backpack and duffel, said that he and Vardis could get more anytime that they needed.

Vardis was a real sport, almost a chip off the old block, Jake said. Maybe they were related in some remote way, he considered idly. It would be so nice to find that one of his last love makings with a woman had produced a son and he turned out to be Vardis. He chuckled at the idea, muttered, "Soap opera shit." He shook his head as if to clear it of dust and said that even if he did had a hypothetical son the kid would only be maybe five years old at best. He studied Vardis for a second before quietly admitting, "We are quite a lot alike, though, he and I."

"Not now," said Gordon and pointed to where Vardis had propped himself against the outer wall of the brakemen's shed, deep into another "unrealness." "What do you suppose he is now?"

"A bear," Jake answered without any hesitation, as if he knew for sure.

"Anger?"

The man shrugged, his favorite gesture. "Had to come out sooner or later. It's only natural. It's his way of dealing with shit, not that I care for it as a coping mechanism a whole hell of a lot."

"Doctors at the hospital didn't seem to help much," said Gordon. "The medications he took there made them fewer, he told me, but they still came."

"You ever see him have one?"

"Not until last night. And I saw him every day we were in the hospital. We roomed there together."

"Well, since I've been with him, he's had at least one a day. Yesterday he had three, the third one after you two went back to the passion bin."

"We read," said Thanny, angered by the inference that she and Gordon couldn't keep their lust for one another bottled up, despite the fact that she had practically confessed as much to Jake the night before. "And we slept."

"Looks like you've got someone who needs you, Jake," said Gordon. "And I mean really needs you. Think you can take that?"

"Do you hear me, Jake?" Thanny nearly shouted. "I said that we slept, that's all...." She stopped, hearing the desperation in her own voice, that need to be heard, given credence, believed.

"Yes," he said to both their questions. "I guess I can handle it, maybe even grow to like it. It's possible. You say you read? You mean T.R.'s thing?"

"Yes," said Thanny. "And I better give it back to you before we go. It's in my duffle."

"It's a gift," he said, waving off the offer. "Another one. T.R. gave it to me, I give it to you. Write me an essay on the two characters. Five hundred words should do it. Send it to me care of the yard master's office and I'll give you your grade in the mail. As human beings I give you both a B-plus. Not perfect by a long sneeze, but not much more work that really needs to be done."

Gordon had to excuse himself to evacuate his bowels from the accumulation of dinner and breakfast. He took a roll of toilet paper which he and Thanny had been carrying with them since their stay at the Corliss Diner. When he was out of sight, Thanny give Jake his grade. She approached him amiably and thanked him for all that he had given them. The hug nearly knocked the wind out of him. The kiss – he had turned his head for a peck on the cheek, closed his eyes when their lips met, when her tongue slid alongside his own in his mouth and fluttered there for a moment – was, needless to say, a complete surprise. "You're not my father, after all," she explained badly, seeing the questioning look in his face.

"No, nor am I your bother, uncle or cousin. Neither is Phineas, but you wouldn't even want to get near enough to him for a kiss like that, let alone to actually do it. Why, then? A promise of things to come? A silly flirtation?"

"Parting," she said and then, after a moment's pause: "Does it bother you, having a friend flirt with you?"

"As long as I know that that's all that it is," he said. "And that's who we are to one another. Friends." He raised his eyebrows lasciviously, then fluttered his tongue at his lips as if licking at a part of her anatomy for a last taste before turning away, aiming his trajectory toward Vardis, his new responsibility.

Chapter 35

"When such an act is even contemplated it should first arise as a chord of fervency, not an overheated fantasy of the lascivious imagination. It begins in the heart, not in the loins."

"Someone of your beleaguered mentality would deign to think of such an orifice as fit for your carnal intentions. So tell me: what other sodomist designs lie dormant, seething in your seamy little mind tonight?"

"You don't have to be contumelious about it. I was only trying to be helpful by pointing out the ethical, moral and logical delinquencies in your contumescent craving for a woman who obviously doesn't care a whit for you. I am only thinking of your feelings in the matter, my friend. Please believe me."

So read three of T.R.'s minor contemplations which Vardis had defined as fortune cookie bits taken out of context. T.R.'s handwriting seemed to have deteriorated immensely from what Gordon and Thanielle had previously seen of the earlier quality and legibility of his script, which was tight and controlled, while the letters and words in these scribblings were all in a broad and looping scrawl with but a single thought covering a single page. The size of the page, it seemed, governed the length of his observations or an answer to some undefined question.

Thanny let yet another scrap slip from her fingers to join the litter on the humpy hill on which she and Gordon sat as she looked up at the commotion going on down on the tracks.

"Hey!" Gordon groused, grasping at the floating bit of paper. "I didn't see that one yet."

"Doesn't matter, really; just more of the same old shit," Thanny said absently as she watched a brakeman coupling up a third boxcar. The men on the tracks shouted to one another about hitches and pinnings while they worked the couplings together. A thin cheer went up as the cars pulled together for the last few inches as if by magnetism, joining themselves with a ringing peal of struck iron.

"That's the third," she said as Gordon caught the cast-off scrap of hotel notepaper. Another car came down the tracks, following the preset course from siding to switch track to siding to main line. A brakeman rode the roof of the car like a stagecoach driver, his gloved hands taut on the brake wheel. The car jostled past switch points, swayed the rider side to side with a clattering gait, squealed its wheels like a well-stocked and burning pigsty once as it reached the main track and then creaked and drummed along another ten feet and gave off a second, shorter squeal of terrified pork on the hoof before slamming itself into the back of the newly connected boxcar. The brakeman called his apologies to the men on the ground as he scuttled down the ladder to help with the hitching pins.

"And that one's the caboose," Thanny said with a satisfied finality. "Almost time, Gordy."

"What does 'contumelious' mean?" he asked, only now having deciphered T.R.'s chicken-scratch word.

"Do I look like Mr. Webster to you? You a need a dictionary handy when you read some of his stuff. Come on. We'll have to make a run for it soon. We can read some more when we're on the train if we really feel like it."

The diesel sounded its breathy, nasal air horn down in in the wide gulley and the brakemen and their accompanying ground crew departed. The coast was clear for the run and they made it with time to spare. Jake would have told them that it was foolish to hop a freight in the loading area in broad daylight. Anyone can see your feet between the wheels from the other side of the car and blow the whistle on you. The guards that patrolled the tracks were not known for their leniency and would call in the police and press vagrancy charges, perhaps even trespassing, which could land the careless or inexperienced person in the poky for at least a few nights. But Jake was surely also aware of the often quoted but seldom believed truism that it is the fool who usually gets by the easiest as if some benevolent hand were guiding his or her actions to coincide with the least dangerous route of consequence to follow.

The car they chose was not one of the three new ones which had just been added to the line-up. They were abiding by Jake's warning to be as far away from both the hooting, gurgling engine and the busy, tending caboose as possible. They threw the back pack, the duffle and the paper bag through the door of the boxcar that seemed to be all splintering brown wood on the outside, bearing the name of its leasing company and green letters and numbers so large that they seemed meant to be read from the air or from across an open, expansive prairie. Its interior was warm and smelled stale. Hay bales lined one far, narrow wall near the forward end and that was the extent of the cargo. There was a pungency rife in the air-- urine, manure, sweat and horseflesh. It was a glue factory Black Mariah, this car, with the living contents having most likely having been taken off in Rarey, which was known for its congestion of husbandry related industries: glue, pet food, fertilizer, bone meal, leather.

Gordon built a confinement of hay bales, forming a cubicle within the rectangle of the moving car and he fell forward onto a matting of rank yellow stalks as the train pulled slowly away from the press of hillocks and earthworks that walled in the three main tracks like riverbanks. At what seemed to be a safe distance by feel, Thanny opened one of the sliding doors to watch the landscape go by. It was still a confusing profusion of tracks that slid into and under the wheels of the train from many angles like threads, strings, ropes being dragged across the floor to lure a kitten. A landscape of slowly passing boxcars, refers, tankers, flatbeds, coal cars, trellis sided auto carriers, all in a line, a phalanx that continued in procession as the engine hulked and roared, its horn blasting its greetings to another man of the same union local while the air outside mixed its choking scent of diesel exhaust with that of the sulfurous stench of rotting corpses. The train slowed and stopped with a crashing of car into car into car to its end while the two men up front traded amenities and small talk, leaving Thanny directly across from another boxcar, an open door, a familiar face for Thanny to place in her mind's eye.

The train on which Phineas Fargo and T.R. Arquill had flagged their ride had been held up for some administrative reason and there he was, smiling, calling soundlessly across the short distance between them, his voice blunted and stolen by the chuff and sigh of the two halted engines. She turned away, not wanting to look at him, the very sight of him making her angry. But she had seen him; a man wanting, desiring, silently pleading in his own pathetic way for the human pleasures which were denied him except for those that had been paid for in advance. He was pathetic, really, she thought as she looked over her shoulder at him, then turned squarely around, saw him smiling and waving idiotically. He deserved something, she thought. She moved to her side and hid behind the door to the boxcar in which she rode. When Phineas saw her again she had her back to him, was bending over with her pants and underwear about her ankles. If he were closer, she thought, disgusting herself with the notion, I'd fart right in his smiling face. Then an even more repulsive idea crossed her mind: that if it were possible and she had done so, he would probably just lick his thick, chapped lips, inhale deeply and, like Oliver Twist begging at the orphanage owner's table, ask for more, *sir, please I want some more.*

He was yelling, shouting, telling her that it was just as he had imagined it, a truly beautiful work of natural art. If he had a camera, he shouted, he would have taken a snap that would remain ever close to his heart. She redid her pants behind the door again, glanced out as the train began moving again as if this had been its sole purpose for stopping. She saw Phineas preparing to reciprocate her hasty disclosure, fumbling with the shoulder buckle of his overalls. She was glad that he was out of sight before the gesture could be completed, though she clearly heard his keynote song of despair above the din of the engine, fizzling and shifting with Doppler efficiency from B-flat to B-sharp like the happy, lilting boom of a tuba.

She hauled on the door to the boxcar in which she and Gordon rode and then turned toward the house of hay which Gordon had erected and in which he had laid out the sleeping bag. He had seen nothing of her silent correspondence with Phineas, only stood before her naked, bandy legged as a young rooster, long and lean. He came to her with open arms which she kissed from his wrists to shoulders before kicking off her sneakers and, stepping back, did a slow and silent striptease.

She watched with fascination as his flaccid penis stiffened and stood, hardened and drooled in time to her dance, dancing itself until it and he were quite ready for anything that would be asked of him even before she flirtatiously unzipped and zipped her fly a few times, slid the pants to the floor with the swing and sway of her hips, the undulations of her tanned belly, and kicked them away near where her shirt had floated into a gossamer heap on the floor. She led him, still in dance rhythm, to the alcove of hay bales, weaved slowly side to side before him as she took his hand and slid it into the waistband of her panties where its middle finger instinctively cleaved her hairy outer labia and found her clitoris to begin its own dance of recognition, stimulation and slow, slithering vaginal penetration.

The dancing had acted on her as an aphrodisiac, especially in conjunction with the stimulation of seeing the effect of her motions and the revealing of her naked body was having on Gordon and his almost simultaneous erection. Now, there was his hand

and, as they lay down together on their bed of fiberfill nylon and hay, she was having an orgasm that she wanted to share with him, him who had been its cause and initial excitement, the very need. She bit his tongue as they kissed, as their hands fondled and she groaned for it to continue, for him to *do that, do that, to not stop, not stop*.... But, too soon, it was all over. The danger, if they wanted to call it that, had passed; the need was no longer there. There had been no time for the application of the cream to and the insertion of the diaphragm and now, it was no longer needed at all. She sighed, looked at him, felt guilty for her orgasm, her relief. She kissed him, loved his mouth with hers, played his still hard, blood engorged cock in her hand as it patiently waited. She kissed it as she had done once before but then only as a prelude to intercourse.

Now her mouth was the love instrument and she actually used that phrase in her mind – *love instrument* – as she slurped and gobbled his shaft noisily in and out of her mouth until in mere moments she felt the stiffening of him against her glottis until she had to swallow with quick gulps or be in danger of drowning in the drench of semen coming in sudden waves into her mouth. *One, two, three, hard and fast* and she felt the guilt that her earlier orgasm had caused her be quickly assuaged. She swallowed hard one last time, held her breath to fight the sudden wave of nausea until it passed. *Salty,* she reflected, tasting the slimy residue, then kissing his belly, his chest, his mouth. A first, she thought, adding a new carnal talent to her repertoire. I must really love him to have done this.

The train gained appreciable speed, the boxcar rocked gently. Their ears popped as they lay together, stroking one another's bodies, exploring. Thanny got up and went to the duffle, cast aside the bag of T.R.'s wordy philosophizing to zip open the handled blue case. Gordon lay on his side, head propped in hand as he studied her intently as she opened the plastic box, removed and opened a tube of white cream and squeezed out a worm of what looked like loose toothpaste or acne medicine and proceeded to smear it on the convex, then the concave side of the hat shaped diaphragm. She closed the tube, tucked it neatly into its blue plastic case which she then snapped shut and dropped into the open maw of the duffle. She squatted before him with her knees spread wide as if her purpose in doing this were the exhibition of her open vagina which was directly at the level of his eyes. She placed the index and ring fingers of her left hand to either side of her vagina, spread the labia and massaged the ovoid opening with her middle finger. She placed the diaphragm at the opening, folded it in half and slid it inside first with one, then with two fingers each to the second knuckle. She worked the fingers inside herself until they were all the way in and she took a deep breath. She held her fingers there for a few extra moments to be sure, by feel, that the contraceptive was securely and properly in place over her cervix before removing her fingers. Gordon had not taken his eyes from that maneuvering hand for the whole of the performance. She smiled, maybe blushed, for the notion crossed her mind that, like her dancing, that was exactly what all this was: a performance.

She lay down on her side facing him, matching her pose to his – head in hand, elbow propped on the padding afforded by the sleeping bag – and, looking calmly and severely into his sweet brown eyes, ran her hand up and down his side, raising goosebumps, causing him to flinch each time her tickling reached a point just above his jutting pelvis. He giggled, he chortled and laughed, snorted and whined and begged her to stop. When it was apparent that she couldn't, he started a bit of his own shenanigans, touched his free hand lightly, delicately, maddeningly against her midriff, drew circles with his finger around her navel, slid the hand up to her ribs and dug in as she did the same to him.

They rolled, they wrestled, whooped and squealed delightedly until the match ended in a draw, an embrace, a friction of genitals, a conjoining of mouths. Perspiration formed a lubricant between them. They slid and held tightly to one another with arms and legs. She laid her thigh over his for support as she felt herself sliding down along the nylon outer layer of the sleeping bag and then felt his erection touching her other, securing leg as his encircling free hand came over and around from behind her to guide himself into her. His finger, accidentally brushing past her anus, made her gasp. He heard that and reacted to it by repeating the motion, more slowly this time and pressed the finger there and began to stimulate that most private of openings in time to his coital thrusts, pressing himself close to her slippery, seal-like body, the hairs of his chest tickling and exciting the nipples on her breasts to a largeness she could not see but which they both felt, now larger, more tender and excited than they had ever been.

Electricity was flowing through her, waves that warmed her, frightened her with their intensity, rocked and moved her in counterpoint to the even, clattering cadence of the train. She moaned in his ear, stroked his back down to the tight haunches that flexed and loosened with his neat, hard strokes. She worked an index finger into the cleave of his ass and drew it down like a surgeon's scalpel, following the deeply curved line. She wanted to reciprocate all that he was doing, that he continued to with his own finger down there, back there, as if there were a motor attached to it, wishing that she could show him what it was like, how it felt, him loving her there like that at the basest of levels like that and he did say *love*, whispered it, groaned it, barked the word in her ear just as she felt the heat of him fill her like a viscous flush of life that would die at the rubber wall he had so intently watched her insert deep inside of herself so carefully, watched her implant it there in the well of her as a deliberate hindrance.

A few moments later, the heat expanded and brooked outward like a wave from some indefinite point behind her navel and she sang the word back to him for that was what it certainly felt like: aching, growing, spreading, accentuating, glowing *LOVE* so she said, so she died right there in his arms. His penetrative embrace and came alive again kissing him, telling him no lies.

Love, she said; *wonderful*, she said; *you are the only; you are the best; you are mine.*

Then there was the denouement, the tender necking, the feeling of beauty and love dissipating, the wondering what to do next. She lay there placidly on the bag, not caring to get up while Gordon went to the large, barnlike door and slid it open. She began to read the bits and pieces of the scatter of T.R.'s displaced answers to unheard questions. She read quickly over the scrawled notes, made little sense of them but for one, the only one in this whole batch that had been penned in that neat, bitsy, feminine hand of his. On the reverse side was a note in the careless scrawl: "Jacob – here is an idea I had for a short story. What do you think? Turn over, please."

Gordon breathed deeply at the open door, watched his urine turn into rain in the wind that blew alongside the train and back to the very end, to the caboose. He sat cross legged there for a while, watched the spring green scenery of the plains and farms below the mountains pass swiftly by. He unhooked his legs from under himself and swung his bare feet over the side to let his legs cool, feel the rush of air on his sweaty skin.

She turned the crumpled little sheet of paper over and read T.R.'s story idea. It made her shudder.

"There are two individual spirits – or call them entities – inhabiting a body. One wants to live, to continue to experience of life and living, to explore all possibilities. The other has no use for living and wants to die, is insanely bent on suicide. So far, the one which wants to live has been the stronger of the two, the more dominant and has succeeded in staying the killing hand of the other. One thing, though, is certain: one of these spirits will die first. If it is the one bent on suicide, then life will go on. If, however, the one who hankers after life succumbs to death first (by natural means, of course), the body which plays host to both of these entities will not have long to continue. The one bent on suicide, freed from the dominance of the Life Force (let's call it that) shall have its way. Only the means, then, will need to be determined."

There was more to it, only a few more laxly written lines, but her attention was drawn by Gordon's call from the open doorway. She responded slowly. He wanted to show her the passing landscape, she assumed – farmland, meadows, open pastures dotted with distant, lowing livestock – show her the road that followed the railroad embankment along which their express freight traveled its tracks to the city, still a good number of hours away.

She stood beside him, looked down at him tenderly as he wrapped his arm about her leg, kissed her on the knee. She ruffled his hair, watched as a Cadillac gained on them. It was a convertible with the top down. The train was doing over 50 miles per hour by her estimation and still the car pulled quickly alongside the open doorway to their boxcar. Two faces looked up at them from the open vehicle which then slowed to remain parallel with the open boxcar door that framed the naked couple.

Mrs. Carandino waved and blew a kiss; her husband, driving, only nodded as he focused to keep his vehicle safely on the road. The distance between them was not so great that expressions could not be discerned. First there was surprise on both their windblown faces at seeing this couple so brazenly, shamelessly exposed, then recognition (the wave, the blown kiss, the nod), then something inscrutable crept into the faces of the middle aged man and his wife. *Sadness? Disappointment? Ardor? Resignation?* Gordon got his legs inside the car as Thanny slid the heavy door shut with a thundering rumble. Shameless? No, nor were they ashamed, neither of their naked bodies nor of what they had been doing and perhaps which the Carandinos had extrapolated from the very fact of their nudity in the open doorway. No; only embarrassment for having been so easily spotted for what they were: lovers – in all senses of that simple word.

Chapter 36

"It's not the dreams themselves that cause us to lose ourselves in wonder," she said, voicing a stray thought aloud to herself. It was a partially developed idea streaming unhindered on the soft wave of her own voice amid the more mundane observations and disclosures that had preceded it, and which would follow. "It is the thing – or are the things – that make us dream that hold our most avid attention."

It was all an elaborate non-sequitur, to be sure, but to the two people there in the familiar room with her took the expounded idea as the maddened mutterings of a woman being fraught with the excitements inherent in returning home after having been away for such a long time. How many years had it been since they had seen her? Was it ten? Nine? Maybe it had only been eight? Surely more than seven. However long the time the prodigal daughter and her handsome husband had both been warmly welcomed with tight and deeply affectionate embraces by both of her parents.

And a belated congratulations on your wedding. Sorry you missed Wilbur. He was here only yesterday with his lovely wife and their three beautiful children: Constance, Bonnibel and Ronald. That's right, married and doing well in his own business now, an expert in surveillance techniques don't you know. All the latest equipment for listening and snooping, getting the goods on whatever errant wife, husband or business partner the opposing party had hired him to check up on. And the children? Darlings, every single one of them, good as lambs, sweet as sugar, though your father and I might have chosen less conspicuous names for them, were they our own. Constance, Bonnibel and Ronald. Now, really, they should have realized what the nicknames would be. Constance, being the first, made no difference but I had to control myself when he told me what the second kid was going to be named and then little Ronnie came along and, well, they're really such dear, sweet little buttons – three, four and five years of age – that you have to hold yourself back pretty strongly from laughing when they introduce themselves. Strange that not one of them bears any real resemblance to your brother. The woman he'd married had a past, we heard, a real scorcher of a reputation both in high school and college. Every man, Dick and Harry had had his way with her to hear it told but your brother Wilbur caught, tamed and kept her, he did. Even though the fact that Connie has raven hair when Wilbur, as you know, is blonde and Gloria, his wife, has mousy brown hair and Ronnie is a carrot topped little Irishman to look at him....

But we love' em all. And you, dear? When are you going to make me a grandmother? Gordon? I certainly hope that you two aren't practicing celibacy in your marriage. There will be an offspring soon enough, I trust. Assure an old woman of that much, won't you dears? Even if it's only to lie and make your mother happy and have something to look forward to.

Hm? Your father? Hadn't you heard? A stroke felled him last year. Put him in the hospital for a month and a half before he could even come back home. He called it apoplexy, the old-fashioned fool and thought nothing of it. Just something that happens to folks, he said. Home not more than two weeks when the second one hit as he was shouting something at a bill collector – telephone, heating oil, electricity, mortgage; I don't recall what that partic'lar one was all about anymore. So, back to the hospital he went. Slid into a coma and from there into the hands of the Lord. Perhaps now he's free of that vile temper of his. Maybe he's found a cure for those boiling rages he used to work himself into so easily. You're one to know about all that, eh, Thanielle? Anyway, now we can only hope and pray it's all been for the best.

***

"So, which will be the dominant one, then?" said Thanielle after quoting the last gracefully written scenario by her and Gordon's taciturn friend who only communicated through the smudging tip of a ballpoint pen which, when he was careful and wrote slowly, could charm the eye with the fluid grace of the shapes of the constituent letters of a word as well as the sound and logic of the sentence of which each word was an integral part. She read the final few sentences of the scenario T.R. had given. "Will it be the one who desires life in all its guises who will be the last to die, to live on or will it be the one who wants it all to end who, if he gets his way and is the last of the two, will find a means to end the rest of it with a horrid finality? Therein shall lay the tension, the very impetus of this story."

Gordon put his jeans back on while Thanny remained naked as she scanned the elegantly minute handwriting on the open sheet of paper.

"That man is a deep thinker," he said and shook his head. It was just another statement that seemed to bear some relation to an unspoken thought; he had no idea whether what she was reading had anything of depth to it or not, had only spoken in order to proclaim his presence, to be heard, to speak. He bent down behind where she sat among the scatter of the contents of the brown paper bag and kissed her shoulder, lifted her tawny hair from her neck and slurped at the nape, causing her to shiver.

Thanny pulled on her shirt, fingered the buttons through the holes, let her attention stray here and there within the cubicle formation of hay bales Gordon had made. Backpack, duffle, emptied brown bag bearing the blue stamp of the market from which it had originally come, the sleeping bag with its fresh streaks of secretions – love juices, both hers and Gordon's – and sweat stains where their sides and legs had met the nylon matting while they had made love.

That, Thanny thought, did not seem to be the proper phrase for what they had done. They had made nothing that was not already there to begin with, had only expressed an emotion, and emotions are not so much made, like a doily or a cocktail is made or a joke is made, but more to the effect of the phrase she had used as a child and she had been asked what she was going to do in the bathroom. "Make a poo," she would answer, for she knew what was to be done, how to do it so that it was made even though she was unsure of the mechanics, the biologics behind the actual "making."

There was something right about that sort of thing, the exercising of the bowels to evacuate the unneeded, the unnecessary, the vile refuse of the body. Food when in one end and was magically converted into something gross and stinky that floated like dead brown eels in the bowl before being flushed away by some other magic means which a child would be at a loss to comprehend. How it was converted from last night's roast beef, potatoes, string beans, gravy and chocolate pudding into today's excrement was any child's guess. Tasty, even delicious food (she had always loved roast beef) turned into shit.

Love seemed to be a product of a similar conversion, though the process seemed to be a reverse of the biological one. Just as the body stole whatever nutrients that were needed from ingested food as it passed through the digestive tract, so the raw ingredients of emotion, adversely, are added to as they are ruminated through whatever system of psychic canals and repositories they pass to be transformed into the "positive" feelings of happiness, joy, pleasure, rapture, humor, love.

The components were rather vile and sickening in themselves upon closer inspection: the mawkish look on Gordon's face as he watched Thanny's mouth as she spoke, the intimacy of being allowed to watch him clean his toes of lint and road grit. The stories he spouted about his travels before he committed himself to a life of contemplative, therapeutic repose in the State Hospital, the animal sighs and belches after a filling meal, the dopily awkward way in which he tripped along as he walked as if he weren't quite sure of the relationship of his feet to the ground, his spontaneous cries of pleasure at the sight of a robin only to cast a stone to chase it off and watch its frenzied flight. Endearments. Not as disgusting as the product of the colon and anus, but taken all together, all the little personal traits and pieces might indeed seem a bit disconcerting.

They would, at least, if all were not internalized, personalized, metabolized to a sufficient degree to make the component little exigencies of the observed personality of another a part of one's own (to use the word of one of T.R.'s dialogue characters) "selfness." The person became an extension of you and you of that other person, forming an emotion that would not have been possible without the other's many personal habits, put-offish as they might individually be. Nothing had been made, only shown, expressed without words. Even the inherently disgusting act of fingering your lover's sphincter, then, became not a perversion, but a sign of trust and intimacy.

They sat together, side by side in the unzipped sleeping bag, she covered from shoulder to waist, he from waist to ankles. They spoke of the sadness they thought they had intuited in the faces of Mr. and Mrs. Carandino and wondered aloud if they had let an opportunity slip through their fingers. The couple was very well off, it seemed, and had considered – if they had not already done so – buying a palatial mansion up in the mountains. Might the concessions that they, Thanny and Gordon, would have had to make to the sexual preferences of the middle aged couple have palled in the face of what they might have received in the way of continuing favors? They talked of apartments in the city, jobs with prestigious firms with high salaries, healthy bank accounts, jewelry, clothes, luxury cars, vacations in Tahiti, Hawaii, Bermuda, the Riviera, Vegas, Hong

Kong, Acapulco. All for the occasional (all right, maybe frequent) performances of loveless sex with a paunchy man, a dowdy woman.

They laughed, threw off the temptation of further speculation and contented themselves with the writings of a friend, for so they considered T.R. to be. They had only known him for a few days but already he was a common factor to them because of his oddball writing, what they held in their hands and shared of him with each other.

But the most interesting piece they had found and read had not been scratched out in either of T.R.'s ends-of-the-spectrum qualities of penmanship--neither the quick scrawl sloppy nor the careful minute and easily legible as might be found in a facsimile edition of some 19th Century gentleman's or lady's handwritten diary or memoir. The writing wasn't even T.R.'s. This was a different sort and style of writing altogether. It was stiff and angular, almost mechanical in its lack of any style whatsoever, as if no human hand had anything to do with its creation. Unlike T.R.'s small oeuvre of short-short takes and missives this belabored composition covered both sides of one sheet of Balshaw Hotel stationery and much of the front side of a second sheet. The pen was the same one that T.R. had used for his writings – a smudgy pointed Bic. The author this time, however, was someone quite different.

"*Children,*" it began, a short salutation. "*We will probably not see each other again for quite a long time and we have known each other only for a short, interrupted span of days. I feel, as I think that you feel as well, that I had once deserted you when you might have needed me the most. Now, you have done much the same to me, though you have at least left me with someone for whom I care and who I cannot, with any amount of integrity or poor justification, leave. I hoped that you two would have stayed to aid me, abet me in caring for my new young charge but I do not blame you for deciding that your own lives and consequences should now take precedence and be of your own design and choice. Do I make sense? I am saying that I forgive you as you have forgiven me. Sounds like I am saying some sort of 'grace,' doesn't it? A kind of a prayer.*

"*But there is something of which you cannot know for which I also need forgiveness. I had lied to you and it was a lie of omission. I had led you to believe that I have nothing but the clothes that I wear and whatever stolen articles I carry with me in my sack. This is not so. I am not rich by any means, but I am financially comfortable.*

"My vagabond life is of my own choosing, not of necessity. The articles I have 'stolen' to feed myself and my friends, such as you, have been bought – in Taragon, in Honeysuckle or wherever. The money I use is retrieved from a sizeable, open account in my name in a bank in the city toward which you are presently headed or, if you find this missive later than I think that you will it will be in the city in which you presently find yourselves. Funds are arranged for over the phone through a lawyer and then received by me via bank check at whatever Post Office I happen to be near at the time. I made my last call here in Honeysuckle the morning when you two slept late. That is why I have chosen to remain here: I am awaiting the arrival of my next imbursement.

"But now, for the expiation of my sins, for the desertion of friends in need and for that white lie of omission…. With that last call I gave the lawyer (whose same, firm, address and phone number I will include at the end of this rather lengthy note) both of your names. I have advised him to expect either your call or your visit. He will arrange accommodations to be made for you there in the city, funds as you need them drawn from my account in reasonable increments until you can get yourselves settled. He has also been good in locating work for friends and friends of friends of mine in the past through the use of his many connections. Nothing too fancy or demanding but just honest work. Don't want you pimping or prostituting just to afford a meal and a place to stay now, do we? Anyway, whatever type of work you would be comfortable with and feel is best for you I have no doubt he will be able to find and arrange for both of you. And that should be enough, I should think."

And that was all. Seemingly out of words, bereft of the main points he had wanted to make, all that was left was a post script saying that he would try in some hazily described future to come into the city to visit with them. Then there was the promised lawyer's name for them to get in touch with and the firm of which he was a founding partner, its address and ten-digit phone number and the initials *J.R.* in lieu of a signature. Thanny turned the letter over as if she expected it to reveal more than was there, perhaps to contain something more than its meager explanation for such generosity.

"Happy ending," said Gordon as he stroked the smooth skin of Thanny's bare thigh near her pubis, feeling himself becoming excited again under the stiff cloth of his jeans. He kissed her lightly on the cheek and rose to scavenge up the rest of their clothes, came back to hand her her pants and a clean pair of panties from the backpack. As he put on his shirt, he offered a question in monotone: "If this were a story you were reading in a magazine – us and all that's happened with us so far – would you put aside what you know of reality long enough to buy this as an ending?"

"You mean 'suspend disbelief'?" she asked, supplying the college English Lit phrase. He was at the door of the car again, had pulled back the heavy panel on the breezy dusk, the purple sky burnished orange at its western edge.

"If that's what you call it," he said, studying the crisp brilliance of the horizon. "Would you believe this as an ending to a story?" He gestured to the disappearing day, the coming night. "Us riding off into the sunset."

"I've read worse endings," she said. "And maybe this one's already been written by…. Well…." She stopped, not caring to continue with that particular line of thought.

"Written by God, you mean?" he asked. "Are we talking philosophy here? Theology?"

"Just talking," she said, motioning for him to come away from the open door. He closed it and came back to her, sat down in front of her, studied her face, her mouth as she spoke. "Just letting my thoughts have free reign."

"Sounds like me you're talking about," he said.

"Mishmálaca," she said then, apropos of nothing,

"What about it?"

"Isn't that where we're going?"

"Maybe." *Where on Earth did that come back from?* he wondered. *Where had the idea been hiding all this time?*

"Castles and paradise-towns and cities of rainbow colors and feelings in the clouds, riding the thermal waves. That's you, when you want to be, Gordy, my lover," she said, feeling his hands resting in hers, the pressure of his fingertips against her palms. "Let's take each other there. Mishmálaca. Make our dreams come real."

"You're talking crazy," he said and was gladdened by it, this shift, this change in her tone and the feeling he was feeling rolling off her in gentle waves. *I could become a bird of a million brilliant colors if I were allowed to take refuge in those glorious eyes of hers.*

"I'm making my own reality,"' she told him, squeezing the hands that held hers. *What does he see inside of me with that sweet, tender, boyish gaze of his that just makes me shiver with delight? It's as if he were studying the very center of me, scanning my soul-core and knowing all the "what, who, how and why" of me with a single laser leer.*

"I'm in love." She said this softly though quite audibly. She gazed tenderly into the creamy brown hues of his irises, felt the weight and pressure of his strong hands in hers. Readily, she allowed him to ingrain himself in her eyes. They were both at home, then, in and with each other. Each was a part of the other's lunar heat at the very bottom depth of their shared and singular soul.

END